THE GIRL IN THE BOX

SEVEN SEAS SERIES: THE NORTH ATLANTIC

GAY COURTER

Published in electronic form by Egret E-Book Editions,
Crystal River, Florida
For information contact www.gaycourter.com
ebooks@gaycourter.com
Jacket design: Rachel Chevat
Library of Congress Cataloging-in-Publication Data
Courter, Gay. Girl in the Box/Gay Courter—electronic
edition E-book ASIN B07XY2M91W

PUBLISHER'S NOTE

This is a work of fiction. Names, characters, places, and
incidents either are the product of the author's imagination
or are used fictitiously, and any resemblance to actual
persons, living or dead, events, or locales is entirely
coincidental. There is, however, an East European
contortionist whose act includes folding herself into a 50-
cm box.

Created   with   Vellum

Also by GAY COURTER

Fiction:

The Midwife

The Midwife's Advice

Flowers in the Blood

Healing Paradise

Code Ezra

River of Dreams

Non-Fiction:

I Speak For This Child: True Stories of a Child Advocate

The Beansprout Book

How to Survive Your Husband's Midlife Crisis (withPat Gaudette)

The Seven Seas Series

At last Gay Courter is launching a series!

A bestselling novelist for decades, Gay Courter's debut psychological thriller will forever change the way you experience cruise ships from the passenger's point of view. Crossing from the fantasy world of the plush carpeting and impeccable service to the stained linoleum and crammed crew area, you'll be fascinated by the exhausting life of officers and staff—where passions reign and secrets are kept.

Like a story ripped from the headlines aboutwhen someone disappears on a cruise, people go missing on ships, bodies "fall" overboard, and the best laid plans go awry, and the whole lavishness of the artificial world comes crashing down.

The Girl in the Box marries the sumptuousness of a dream vacation with the horrors that lurk around the bend. Courter's attention to detail has the reader rocking along with the waves and smelling the pungent salt air as Dale Lane—her fictional bestselling writer turns sleuth to find who murdered Tatiana—the young and vulnerable contortionist. This smart, taut thriller has everything: a lovable heroine with a tragic past, a searing view of unbridled lust, a complicated woman whose life has been manipulated since birth, perplexing forensic clues, and an urgency to find the killer before the ship reaches land.

As Courter weaves together the true and the imagined, we share the breathtaking anxieties of a potential killer on the loose.

CONTENTS

Prologue...1
Chapter 1...3
Chapter 2..76
Chapter 3...148
Chapter 4...216
Chapter 5...255
Epilogue...323
Acknowledgments 339

For Philip,

Thanks for cruising through life with me

You get tragedy where the tree, instead of bending, breaks.
—Ludwig Wittgenstein

Prologue

We may have all come on different ships, but we're in the same boat now.
—Dr. Martin Luther King, Jr.

"**W**hat's worse?" I once asked David. Living in South Florida, we were often on hurricane watches—and he experienced the Category 5 Hurricane Andrew first-hand. "The aftermath was worse than when it happened. The pool cage crumbled as if a giant had grabbed it in his fist. I watched a neighbor's roof peel off like scab." He'd sighed and said, "Fire destroys everything. At least with a hurricane or flood you see what you've lost."

"That's a consolation, I guess," I said with a sardonic laugh. "Ever since *The Wizard of Oz* I've had nightmares about being caught up in a tornado."

"There's plenty of warning with a hurricane," he said. "Earthquakes catch you by surprise."

"Sometimes it's better not to have all that anxiety about whether or not to evacuate."

We didn't dwell on disastrous thoughts. They were theoretical conundrums, intimate banter, and perhaps an incantation to ward off evil spirts. If you spoke your fears aloud, they would never come true, right? With whom would you want to be stranded on a desert island? If you could take only three things with you when fleeing a fire, what would they be? If you could only save one person in the family, who would you choose? I knew that these suppositions were inoculations against free-floating anxiety, probably a healthy way of vocalizing fears. Until the questions stopped.

Because by then I knew that the worst thing of all is a death so sudden, so unexpected, so senseless that every belief, every hope, is obliterated as swiftly as breath annihilates a flame.

One

It is better to risk saving a guilty man than to condemn an innocent one.
—Voltaire

Friday, November 20
At Sea: Position: 264 Nautical Miles Southwest of
Ponta Delgada, Azores

I never sleep as well as I do on a ship in a rolling sea, mimicking the womb, soothing all aches, muffling every sound. The phone jangled jarringly—my brain vaguely remembering the requested wake-up call—but the rest of me was not ready to be reborn into the harsh world, even one as comfy as a luxury ocean liner. I lifted the receiver, set it down, and tried to recapture my reverie to no avail. Have to get up…promised… I propped the extra pillow behind my back. I'd left the curtains open purposefully. Not even one sliver of dawn dappled the lapping sea although reflected lights from the ship winked back at me. I closed my eyes, feeling the motion's seductive lure. I forced myself to stand and slid the veranda door open a few inches and inhaled the sharp salty air as if it had medicinal properties. Slightly invigorated, I stepped in practiced rhythm with the slipping and sliding of my cozy compartment and hurried to get ready.

"Thanks again for agreeing to interview so early," Callista Standish, Cruise Director on the *Empress of*

Seven Seas, said as she followed me into the elevator before dawn.

Callista and I had become friendly on another ship more than a year earlier, and we continued to enjoy each other in the odd moments when either was free. "You know I'd do anything—well almost anything—for you." I yawned, wondering again why I had agreed to her request. "Your new format for Rise-and-Shine is a terrific idea."

"But you sleep too late to watch it."

"I see one of the reruns at bedtime. Helps put me to sleep!"

Callista laughed. "That way you find out everything you missed by being a recluse."

The cruise director knew that this voyage was hardly a vacation. I regularly book six-week trips to sequester myself while writing a novel. "At least you didn't force me to clean up my cabin." My floating office, littered with piles of books and printouts, was not ready for primetime. "Where are we heading?"

"Ellwood has a few ideas," she said, referring to Ellwood (don't-you-dare-call-me 'Woody') Hawthorne, the assistant cruise director and sometime videographer. "We're meeting him on I-95."

"I hope that's not where the meat locker is!"

"That was his *worst* set-up ever!" She wrapped her arms over her chest and rubbed her shoulders. "My teeth actually chattered on camera! These early morning productions are tough enough without causing actual pain."

The first chore of the cruise director's never-ending day was taping the Rise-and-Shine show, which played on closed-circuit television throughout

4

the ship at seven in the morning and was rebroadcast every hour. Originally it had been a series of dry announcements with some photos of the next port interspersed with a scroll of the day's schedule: Bingo at 3 in the Pirate Cove, Cooking Demo at 4 in the Treasure Chest dining room, Tango Classes at 11 in Hernando's Hideaway, Line Dancing with Lindy on the Lido, and so on. On this cruise the production was more like a television talk show, although the underlying purpose was to boost the bottom line. Callista hawked spa specials, martini tastings (for a small fee), and a celebrity look-alike contest with prizes (company logo key chains). The head bartender blended the cocktail-of-the-day, topped it with a paper umbrella, and offered it to Callista to taste. She trilled, "*So* refreshing!" and winked into the lens.

I stifled another yawn. "Anyway, moving out of the studio was a brilliant move," I said.

"Coming up with a different location for three weeks is easier said than done." The elevator opened on the Pacific Deck—the lowest one open to passengers.

"That's a relief," I said. "I was worried you were taking me to the engine room."

"Gotta have something for the guys now and then," she said, referring to one of last week's shows, "but I hope you will appeal to the higher sensibilities."

"It would be hard to top yesterday's locale."

"Don't remind me!" she said, looking around for her assistant.

The day before we had arrived at our last European port: Ponta Delgada in the Azores, and now we were heading for Florida. All summer the *Seven Seas* had been doing weekly jaunts between Venice and Barcelona and was on the home stretch of the ship's bi-annual repositioning transit. During the winter, it alternated cruises to the east and west Caribbean from Ft. Lauderdale before heading back to the Mediterranean in the spring. With the last of continental Europe in our wake, Ellwood had filmed from the crew deck—the most forward point on the ship—which was out-of-bounds to passengers—recreating the iconic scene from *Titanic*. Callista had unpinned her hair so it could undulate in the wind as she mimed "My Heart Will Go On."

"Where is he?" Callista asked impatiently.

I looked around. The only time I came down to this deck was to visit the medical center, when this area was used for debarkation onto low-lying quays, or to use a tender in ports that could not accommodate the *Seven Seas* at a pier.

Ellwood beckoned us to where vertical overlapping leathery strips curtained the crew area from the elevator lobby. "Sorry mate, I was just checking out the lost luggage room. Thought people might be curious, even though it's noisy with the baggage shifting in the swell," Ellwood said in an exaggerated Aussie drawl.

"Our novelist suggested the climbing wall," Callista kidded in her best Kiwi retort. Their down-under sparring was a staple of the morning show. At the end of each cruise, Callista would burst out with a Maori war chant supposedly besting him. Funny thing about cruise directors, they have to have a British Empire accent—anything from Cape Town to

Auckland, Sydney to Oxford—to create the requisite jolly mood. While Empire Shipping began as a British company, an international conglomerate now owned it. Still, the illusion was kept. Empire frowned on staleness and rewarded innovation. Ellwood's first "on-location" show on the bridge with Captain Luigi Giambalvo was so well received that it was edited into a "special" and shown several times on each voyage.

Callista noted my impatience and elbowed him. "It's a bit too early to sort out your sarcasm."

"No worries, mate." Ellwood tapped his shaved head with his forefinger. "First, we're going to give Ms. Bestseller—and likewise the viewers—a tour of what goes down on I-95, then we'll pause somewhere scenic for the interview portion."

"No climbing then?" Callista pretended to be disappointed. "At least Ellwood's Go-Pro phase has passed. I'm still trying to live down the wardrobe malfunction in my swimmers on the tube slide."

"Just walk along naturally," he directed us, "and Cal, point out the sights." He held his hand up for us to wait as he positioned himself in front of us. As he started walking backward, he gestured for us to come toward him.

"We're on the Pacific Deck—the first deck above the waterline—but in crew lingo we use numbers so we call it Zero Deck, though it's actually Deck Four, counting from the keel."

"That's confusing," Ellwood said.

"Shall I go back?"

"No just continue."

"Anyway, this wide lane is nicknamed 'I-95' because it's the ship's main artery," Callista continued. "It goes twenty-four-seven pumping services to…" She strained to keep the metaphor going. "Ah…keep the…creature alive." She made a cut sign across her neck. "That was awful, can we start again?"

"No, no, it's spot on," Ellwood said.

"What about an 'Upstairs/Downstairs' approach?" I suggested.

"Just keep it up, we're running out of time," he insisted.

Callista took a deep breath. "It's fairly quiet now, although on turnaround days, forklifts maneuver towering stacks of luggage off the ship first thing in the morning and by noon are doing the same for the incoming crowd. For me, the most amazing part is the provisioning. From the moment we dock, they begin loading pallets containing crates of poultry, steaks, and burgers, tons of fresh produce, bottles of booze, wine, and beer, and oceans of soft drinks."

I only had to nod and look impressed. Ellwood made a circular motion with his finger for her to keep talking.

"Last week when Chef Donatello was on the show, he said we stocked 9000 dozen eggs, 350 pounds of crab, 2000 pounds of lobster, and 10,000 pounds of chicken for the transatlantic segment alone."

She pointed to a sign depicting a man screaming in a tight spot between two doors that read: WATERTIGHT DOOR CAN KILL OR MAIM YOU! Another noted: 256 DAYS SINCE EQUIPMENT

ACCIDENT. She indicated one more, "CALL 4444 TO REPORT DRUGS."

"Cut," Ellwood said. "The point isn't to scare the cones."

Callista shot him a look of disapproval, as if I hadn't heard that disparaging slang before.

"That's enough for now," he said. "Why don't you two review some questions while I scout a good background?"

As he strolled further down the long, wide corridor, Callista turned to me. "Okay, so how long have you been on this ship?" she asked, "And please don't say 'too long!'"

"For six weeks...blah blah...which is the only way I can concentrate and finish a book." I held up my hand. "What *is* the deal with that four-four-four-four drug sign?"

"It's an internal matter—nothing for our guests to worry about."

"Illegal drugs? Are they a big problem on the ship?"

Callista sighed. "We have the same problems as any small city. Alcoholism is much more common than drugs, but sometimes a crew member takes stupid chances, especially in the Caribbean where it's easy to score ganja. We have zero-tolerance for drugs. There are peer counselors to help with the stress that the crew experiences on contracts from six to nine months away from family and friends." She lifted her hands as if to ask: Are you satisfied? I nodded.

"Anyway," she continued rehearsing the interview questions, "I know your readers are impatient for new books."

"Not as anxious as my publisher."

"And you publish how many each year?"

"They want four, even though I can only produce two."

"How does being onboard help inspire you?"

"I don't have to prepare a single meal, clean, do laundry—but best of all, I am almost impossible to reach. At home, I not only have the usual chores, I'm expected to be available for publicity. Not to mention needing time for family— Actually, I'd prefer not to get into all that."

"Okay, I'll just ask about the book that's coming out in a few weeks."

"Good. That way I can tax deduct the whole trip."

"I thought you did that anyway," she chuckled.

"Now I can double it."

Callista arched her eyebrows. "We can't do that in New Zealand."

"You haven't had your cuppa have you?" Ellwood said as he approached. "Like, she's kidding!" He scratched his scalp. "Ready, ladies?"

"Where do you want us?"

"I found some pallets of beer that haven't been moved yet."

Callista sniffed. "Hardly suitable for a literary event. I knew we should have used the library."

"Bor-ring. We could hoist her on a forklift."

"Safety would have our hides!"

"We can't stand beside a forklift, can we?" Ellwood snapped. "Gotta get this show on the road," he said. Ellwood marched forward and stopped just before the corridor curved toward the bow. Several disabled forklifts were parked beside a battery charging station. "Bugger! That ruins the shot." He indicated a yellow-canvas laundry cart pushed against the wall.

"What's that doing down here?" Callista mumbled.

"Wild!" Ellwood pointed to the lifeless leg of a broken mannequin poking out from some sheets.

"Must be from the shops," Callista said to me. "They use the carts to carry merchandise from the storeroom to the atrium stores. Just move it out of the way."

"Wait," Ellwood said, "it could be an artsy shot." With his eye pressed to the camera's viewfinder, he maneuvered himself to capture the odd angle of the leg almost touching the wall.

"What the hell?" Callista screeched. Ellwood was focused so close that he didn't see her reaching to shove the camera down.

He threw his arms up in protest just as Callista whipped the sheet off the cart. "What? Oh my god!" She lifted a waist-length golden braid, then dropped it as if she had been scorched. "It's Tania!"

"She's…dead," I stated before I crumpled like a deflated rubber raft.

□ □ □

Although I'm a passenger, I'm not what the crew calls a "cone"—which isn't as disparaging as it sounds. It's far worse to be labeled a "banana"— someone who never tips. A cone, short for "conehead," is derived from the *Saturday Night Live* skit. Although they were obviously weird, when a

11

human would ask a conehead where it was from, the response would be "France." No matter that every crew member is wearing a name tag identifying his country of origin, he has to answer a similarly dumb question about his origins.

For most of the crew it's too enervating to befriend passengers who are aboard for so short a time. They are most wary of a certain species of traveler who dons an invisible Velcro vest when they leave the confines of Cleveland or Chattanooga and glom onto a member of the staff either because they are socially awkward with their peers or want to be able to brag that they became "insiders." A sociologist might explain this bonding phenomenon as a way to form a temporary tribe as a defense against travel stress. Other guests select more appropriate fellow passengers as their "besties" and stick with them at meals and excursions. Many plan their next cruise to be on the same ship with people who they might never include on land. Fortunately, I have enough work-avoidance tactics without adding senseless socializing.

I hit upon this solution to write at sea when I was more than halfway through a multi-book contract and only had three chapters of the first book finished. When my agent reminded me of the looming deadline, I panicked. I thought about going to a writer's colony where some meals are delivered to your cottage in wicker baskets by tiptoeing sycophants, and then you join the other cooped up artists for dinner and whatever amusements they can contrive in their bucolic salt mine. Still, one needs to apply, get references, and be deemed worthy. My light romances, while commercial, would not pass the literary gatekeepers' sniff test.

The eureka moment came as I showered in my second bathroom, which I was using because the master was being renovated. I'd had enough therapy to understand that redecorating is my way of fixing the unfixable, to order my chaotic emotions one room, one color scheme at a time. I noticed that a houseguest had left an aquamarine bottle with a gold Empire crown logo in the shower caddy. Friends cruising in and out of Ft. Lauderdale often stayed with me for a night or two, another disruption, yet one I enjoyed. As I lathered my short crop, I envisioned getting away from all landside distractions until I had finished my delayed novel—by sailing away and returning with a finished manuscript, not that I could leave my son.

Then, a week later David's mother Peggy arrived "to give me a break"—but then she wanted me to visit her relatives, go with her to the orchid show, and kept interrupting me to chat. There were also the little tensions when she told Bodhi, my six-year-old son, he could do something that I had already said was out of bounds.

"This isn't working," Peggy announced before I could figure out a tactful approach. "I walk on eggshells because you need to work or I might say something to Bodhi that goes against your grain."

She was right, although I still resented her intrusion even though I wanted her to spend as much time with her grandson as she desired. Peggy had lost her husband while I was pregnant and then her son a few years after that. Still, I felt as if I were pedaling backward.

"You need to get out of the house—not just to an office, but far, far away from all the distractions…obligations."

"I can't just leave Bodhi—"

"He's fine with me. What difference does it make if he wears a jacket or eats his peas?"

I nodded. Everything David and I worried about seemed obscenely ridiculous when all that mattered was being alive.

She pointed to our view of the Intercoastal Waterway. "Have you ever thought of jumping on one of those cruise ships?" She gave me a penetrating glance. "You aren't protesting." Her steel-gray eyes—yes, David's eyes—glanced across the Intracoastal Waterway. There was no point hiding my thoughts because she could read me almost as well as David could. "The ships…they come, they go…you just go for a long ride for a few weeks. No cooking, no shopping: they even do your laundry."

I laughed. "I admit the idea is tempting."

By the end of the day, I was booked on a month-long cruise that departed the following week. I returned both refreshed and with the finished book. While still onboard, I was offered a discount for booking the next cruise, and thus my course was set.

When I'm aboard, I'm "off the grid" for anything but communicating with Bodhi—who's now eight. While there is Internet service, ship-to-shore phones, and sometimes-mobile service, all are intermittent, slow, and expensive. I download my email daily, my landside assistant handles fan mail, and pays bills and

I email Bodhi at least once daily and Skype with him from an internet café with a better connection when I'm in port. I know that Peggy buys him candy bars, artificially colored popsicles, white "cotton" bread, and they bake cookies every Sunday. He has way too much screen time and they only go to the library every two weeks. And he only has to put away his toys once every two weeks, the day before the housekeeper comes. He's happy; Peggy's happy—and I know he is safe, loved, and knows a great deal when he has one.

▢ ▢ ▢

My name is—well, which one do you want? I was born Donna Allison Schmidt, but by the time I was 12, I insisted on being called Dale, a name my mother abhorred. It wasn't because of Dale Evans, wife of Roy Rogers—that was more my mother's era—and certainly, not NASCAR driver Dale Earnhardt, Jr. My best friend in sixth grade was Gail and we thought that Dale and Gail would be a fine name for a musical duo, although our friendship was more harmonious than our singing. I entered Swarthmore with a clean slate as Dale and jettisoned the stuffed-nose sound of Schmidt when I married David Lanier. My post-911 travel identity is Dale Allison Lanier, although most people know me as Dale Lane—the nom de plume on my bestselling novels—five if you go by the New York Times list. My book jacket designer sets "Dale Lane" in typography that has turned into my visual brand:

DALE
LANE

On this ship, I live in a mini-suite midship on the starboard side, the most stable location. The beds are set up as twins and the spare one is blanketed with my research materials. There's also a convertible sofa, a combo desk/vanity, mini-fridge, two televisions, and a bathroom with a Jacuzzi tub. There's ample storage under the beds and in the closet, which also contains a safe, where I keep a jump drive with copies of my writing saved daily. When there is a strong enough Internet connection, I send my agent my most recent revision. If the ship goes down, at least my book will be saved for the benefit of Bodhi. However, this will never, never happen because I promised him I will always come back.

Many envy my shipboard lifestyle. It's no wonder Coco Chanel lived in Paris's Ritz Hotel, albeit with the same view every day. Mine is ever-changing. I not only avoid time-sucking chores, I can't procrastinate by scrubbing the tub or making over-the-hill bananas into mini-loaves for my neighbors. There's no grocery shopping, meal prep, or clean up. All my meals are included, even free room service. Currently, my cabin steward is Dante, a Filipino who pampers me far beyond what his job description requires.

With all these comforts and few distractions, I have the final draft ready to send my editor at Utopia after six weeks at sea. I may not be a brilliant writer—but this way I churn out the pages fast. I started my first novel when I was on bedrest for the last few months of my pregnancy due to some unexplained bleeding. I gobbled up books—at least one a day—until I tossed one across the room shouting, "I could write one better than that!"

"Great idea!" David said. "Just take a sad song and make it better."

"What are you talking about?"

"Think of all the troubled people we come across in our work," he began.

We'd met while I was working as a paralegal. He was an investigator for the Broward County Sheriff's Children's Protection division, who interviewed one of our clients. Every case was a story with twists and turns that were crazier than fiction. So, I based my first novel on a deaf child with a blind mother who David had helped and sent it to a cousin who worked for a literary agent in New York. *How My Light is Spent* almost earned enough money for me to quit my job and stay home with Bodhi, but not quite. In my "spare time" I was supposed to crank out another book in six months—a deadline that might have seemed possible before his birth, although I had miscalculated how much time it took to care for one tiny life.

"You'll never create a brand that way," Miriam Jansky, my cousin's boss—and by then my literary agent—said. "You can do babies the hard way—or get help like I did," she continued in her raspy voice. "The toilet doesn't care who cleans it. Turn over the scut work to someone who needs a job and figure out the rest."

David did his part by coming up with a schedule when I would be "off-duty" and free to write without guilt. I paid him back, if not with equal time off, by making sure he had season tickets for the Dolphins at-home games and time to fish with his brother. By the time I received the final advance payment on my contract, I could quit my job.

My next book, *Leave it to the Planets,* bought him a fishing boat and a pool for our backyard. Half the advance for *Catch a Falling Star* went into Bodhi's college fund. Best of all, there was a steady flow of royalties from the other books. David and I talked about him becoming a licensed therapist and quitting his high-pressure job if the book took off.

Even after everything that happened, most people consider me lucky and blessed. They envy my notoriety, my independence, my beautiful child. They should fantasize about one of my protagonists instead. At least their stories have a beginning, middle, and satisfying ending that ties up loose ends. It's gratifying to engineer chaos, impose structure, and play god. My fiction offers meaning, redemption, and second chances. In reality, every life is like a train chugging down a track until it tunnels toward oblivion. We all hope for the best and suppress thoughts of disaster until the worst happens. And then—

You go on.

□ □ □

"You okay?" Callista asked perfunctorily, a military persona replacing her usual jovial overlay. "Did you lose consciousness? Does anything hurt?"

18

Although she looked slightly blurry, I said, "I'm not sure." The peculiar angle of Tatiana's rigid leg had triggered an old-fashioned swoon, or in medical parlance, a vasovagal syncope.

The cruise director is a ship's officer who reports directly to the captain. Without another word to me, she marched off to notify the bridge, security, and the ship's doctor.

Ellwood gave me a hand up and steered me back to the elevator lobby, which was quickly filling with crew. Someone found me a chair and another handed me a bottle of water.

"It's the Russian girl, right?" I asked for confirmation.

"Yes, it seems so," Ellwood whispered. "Did you know her?"

"I've translated for her a few times." Tatiana Zlatogrivova was one of the ship's headline entertainers.

Callista returned. "Nobody can leave this area until released by security."

What happened next was a whirl of the brisk efficiency that soldiers, law enforcement—and sailors—default to in crisis. The port side of I-95 leading to the bow was blocked by a forklift and was under guard by two security officers. The elevator opened and out marched Captain Luigi Giambalvo with Officer Mae Ocampo, head of security, who wore a camera around her neck. The captain paused by the vertical curtains that looked like floor-to-ceiling flypaper, then went to the scene. In less than a minute he returned leaving behind a wake of strobe flashes.

As Captain Giambalvo approached me, Callista and Ellwood flanked him. "We must contain this information," the captain said, his tone changing from maître d' suave to martial Mussolini. "Officer Standish, you are to turn up the volume on the entertainment," he said to Callista. "Complimentary Bellinis in the dining room and whatever else will make it seem like a—regular, how-do-you-say-it?—a festive day."

"Certainly, Captain," she said as she placed her hand on the small of my back, propelling me toward the elevators. "I'll meet you in your cabin as soon as I get a break," she said, waving me through the door that opened on cue.

Ellwood steadied me forward before blurting, "He should have offered White Russians."

"Who?"

"The captain," he said, mopping his forehead. "Sorry. Sick humor in a crisis."

I steadied myself by grasping the elevator's brass railing. The door opened onto my deck. "Apologies," he said as I lurched toward my stateroom, unsure whether I was wobbly or the seas had become more turbulent.

I dipped my room key in the slot and stumbled toward the balcony door, pulled it open, staggered to the rail, and gulped long salty breaths.

Tatiana! I began to shiver violently and went inside, leaving the door open enough to keep the air circulating. Papers on the extra bed took flight. I lay back on the sofa and closed my eyes as they fluttered like a flock of frightened gulls.

That lovely girl! Thrown away like a heap of trash—naked, stuffed, twisted, upside-down. The gymnast was famous for being able to fold herself inside an impossibly small acrylic box with one leg curled behind her neck and the other folded in front of her. The posters promoted "Tatiana: The Bendiest Girl Alive!" She had either died in that distorted pose or had been forced into it by her murderer. As rigor mortis set in, one leg had straightened—like a signal for belated help. Tatiana—Tania to her friends—had been an astonishing contortionist who could manipulate her limbs into distorted shapes, then let them spring back like an angry cobra. Some of her most spectacular poses so defied the natural laws of human movement they made me queasy. Her newer routines featured a more choreographed story. The latest, where she opened like a blooming rose, was more suited to the sensibilities of this cruising audience than her more erotic nightclub act.

"When I played at the Cirque du Soleil, I was a center-stage star," she told me when we first met. "I had to get in that damn *korobka* every single performance—sometimes twice a day. Now, so much easier. I only do the box when I want."

She complained about the long hours her father, who was her coach and cabinmate, made her spend in the crew gym doing conditioning and stretching exercises before she rehearsed with her partner, Oleksander Lopatkino. "Our routines have to be one seamless movement."

"You make it look easy."

"I must never reveal the torment from turning myself inside out. 'The more it hurts, the more you smile'—that's my Papa's rule," she said, demonstrating her practiced rictus.

Since Tatiana joined Sea-Cirque her routines were simpler because the show had to go on no matter the oceanic conditions. She did not perform her box routine on every voyage, so when she did, it was a rare treat like a whale or celebrity sighting. Passengers bragged if it was performed on their leg of the cruise.

The Girl in the Box was heralded by an edgy version of "Lara's Theme" from Dr. Zhivago. Kitschy, although it sent the right frisson through the audience. The 22-inch wide acrylic box was placed on a pedestal that rose from the stage and revolved to reveal that all the sides were translucent and that there were no tricks, no mirrors. Scrim over the eerie blue and green lights masked some of her less graceful maneuvers. In less than a minute, Tatiana pretzeled herself into the impossibly small chamber. The act was always the finale—often on the last night of a cruise's segment—and when the curtain fell, it never failed to leave the audience gasping.

And now all that training—which had begun at infancy—was for naught.

□ □ □

My cabin's doorbell chimed "ping-a-pong!" When I first heard it, I imagined all the research-and-development dollars that went into determining the least irritable sound to alert the multi-national clientele. This time, though, my heart, which had just begun to normalize from the shock, lurched.

"I'm so very sorry, Cal," I said as the cruise director fell into my arms for a mutual condolence hug.

"Anything can happen…" she sputtered.

"Anytime…to anyone!" I answered.

"But Tania! Who would wish her any harm?"

Something had clicked between Callista and me when I first met her two cruises earlier. Although the ship's rules required professional distance between guests and crew, friendships could not be legislated and with the exception of sexual liaisons—which were a dismissal infraction—were tolerated. We first connected in Venice in the hiatus after most of the passengers from one leg departed and the new onslaught had not yet boarded. I had just completed a first draft and was taking a stroll around the promenade to clear my head when I actually almost bumped into Callista when turning a blind corner.

"Don't continue forward," she warned, "they're painting and the fumes are sick-making."

"Thanks," I said, "I was just going to find myself a cup of tea."

"Mind if I join you?"

Flattered by the officer's attention, I followed her to the closed dining room. We took a seat near the entry and one of the waiters who was reorganizing tables for the next sailing rushed up, seeming thrilled to serve us.

"Hi Baxter," she said.

"Your special tea?" he asked.

"You're the best!" she said to him, then to me, "Have you ever had a proper Kiwi tea?" I visualized something infused with the green-and-black fruit.

"Zealong, it's a bit of a religion. It's organically grown in our mineral-rich soil and only the top three leaves are handpicked."

"By virgins in moonlight?"

She laughed. "Something like that."

Two steeping pots arrived. She lifted off her lid and passed the brew under my nose. "There are floral notes, but it—no, you try it first." She poured my cup.

I hesitantly sipped from the steaming cup. "Nice."

"Do you taste it? Green, yet it shimmers like pale gold."

"Good," I mumbled, because it was.

"Like an orchid cupcake!"

I took a second swallow. "Maybe. Also…a bit buttery."

"Yes!" She grinned. "That's because of the ewe butter."

"Really?"

"No! I'm kidding." She paused to try her own cup. "Hey, do you know how a Kiwi finds a sheep in the long grass?" She waited a few beats before delivering the punchline, "Adorable." It took me a second too long to laugh. "Never been down under?"

"Once." I had a mental picture of the child-welfare conference in Auckland. David had been sent to investigate their family-mediation system and I had tagged along. "Even have the T-shirt: Three million people, sixty million sheep."

"How do you like writing onboard?" Up until then I had thought nobody knew who I was or what I was doing; still the question didn't surprise me.

"Of course, it helps to be free from routine chores, yet there's something indefinable that boosts my creativity."

"Delta waves," she replied.

"I know about alpha and beta, but what's delta?"

"About a year ago we had a research psychologist—maybe you've heard of Phyllis Goldberg?—lecturing on board about relaxation, meditation, and health. She said that one reason people become addicted to cruising is because of how the ship's motion affects brainwaves. Delta waves are the slowest, yet loudest, brainwaves. They rumble in low frequency and penetrate like the beat of a drum."

"As in chanting 'Om'?"

"That is precisely what she claimed. Since then, I've noticed that some combo of engine vibration and rocking motion quiets the "noise"—both what surrounds us and also the chatter in our heads—so we relax and restore almost automatically."

We bantered about several other subjects, and for the first time, I felt I had a friend onboard—one who would not be insulted if I said I needed to work.

In fact, I had picked the *Seven Seas* because she had been transferred to it. Six weeks earlier, we celebrated our reunion by going ashore in Venice for a snack at a café near the port. During our catch-up conversation, she described a recent incident. "It turned out that this guest from Brazil had had both his wife and mistress on the ship. In separate staterooms. And then someone in the spa introduced them—because they both spoke Portuguese."

"You're kidding?"

"No! The two women became friends without knowing what—or should I say who—they had in common."

"Did they ever figure it out?"

"That's the funny part—we don't think so. But the guy saw them together and the only place he felt safe was in his cabin. It became theater for the crew to report if they had seen the ladies dining or playing cards together. Apparently, they both had sick 'spouses' in common!"

"That's too crazy for anything except a Neil Simon comedy."

She had said, "My is motto is: 'Anything can happen…anytime… and to anyone.'"

"When I was younger, I would have found that the height of pessimism; now it's a refreshing dose of realism." I sighed as I thought about David.

"I've told you about my ex—as in boyfriend—but you're divorced, right?"

"No, a widow," I said, miffed that she had forgotten—or maybe I had just said that I didn't want to talk about it.

"Oh! Sorry. How could I—"

"No, it's okay." A familiar weight rose from my toes to my chest. The reason I avoided telling the story is the look in the other person's eyes: shock, disbelief—and worst of all—immense pity. They never understood my underlying emotion was an intense anger that had never, ever diminished.

After that, we rarely mentioned our shore lives. She knew about Bodhi, although I didn't like talking about him because I felt I had to explain how the interlude was good for him and even better for

Peggy—which sounded like I should have felt guiltier than I did. People never judged a man for being away from his child; a mother was assumed to be neglectful. I had heard how fond Callista was of nieces in Wellington and grateful they kept her parents from hassling her to settle down. Like old college roomies, we could start again mid-sentence, mid-ocean without missing a beat with the subject veering from the personal to ship life to books we were reading, the latest crew gossip or passenger tantrum.

When our hug melted, we stood with our bodies lightly touching.

"I needed to see you, alone," Callista said. "It's a nightmare out there…"

"I'm still…overwhelmed. I just can't believe it."

"I know," Callista said. "I keep seeing her legs…" She gestured with her hands askew.

I closed my eyes to try to blot the same image. "Can you take some time off?"

"Impossible. I'll have to muddle through."

Her legs wobbled and I steered her to my desk chair. "I liked Tania very much," I said. "No—more than that. I had a sisterly feeling for her."

"You spoke the same language," Callista said without sarcasm.

Tatiana was Russian, which was the second language of my childhood. My maternal grandmother lived with us and she never became fluent in English. My father spoke no Russian and my mother refused to translate, feeling her mother should make some effort. So, I was the family's official translator and my grandmother and I had a special bond.

Callista had introduced me to the entertainer early in this cruise because Tatiana needed an interpreter at the medical center. "You're the only woman on board that I know speaks Russian."

"Who usually translates for her?"

"Her acrobatic partner, but she said it was a girl thing. I suspect she might have a yeast infection."

When I met Tatiana, I'd asked her, "Who else speaks Russian on board?"

"There's a guy on the bridge who does something with computers, two engineers from Belarus, and Jerzy, the gym guy. He's Polish and supposedly speaks ten languages." She threw up her expressive hands. "*Vse oni muzhchiny!*" she said in a tone reserved for cursing. "Yes, they are all men!" She gave me a woman-to-woman glance. "If I had my way, I'd only have women in my audience."

I understood her pique. Early in the voyage— somewhere in the Adriatic Sea—I'd overheard two men talking while balls, ribbon banners, and hoops aided Tatiana's rubbery maneuvers. One of the guys, who wore a white silk shirt and several gold-by-the-inch necklaces, loudly whispered, "She sure knows what to do with balls."

The other, who had a rattlesnake tattoo wrapped around his bare arm, had sniggered lewdly, "It's all about her snatch. Nobody's looking at any damn ball."

"Yeah," the other added, "you can't help but imagine doing her in all those positions."

That fleeting memory caused my heart to clench painfully. Callista touched my shoulder. I took a deep breath. "Just...so...unbelievable!" I took a seat on my

28

sofa. "I was just remembering some crude remarks I overheard about her. At the time, I thought they were just creepy and gross, now I wonder whether some bastard acted on his sick fantasy."

"What about suicide?"

"You saw the way her body was found. How could she do that to herself?"

"I know, yet lately she's been…"

Tatiana had entrusted me with a secret and it still wasn't mine to reveal.

"Do you really think someone was threatening her?" Callista asked.

"Anything is possible," I said, which is what David would have responded. Just when he thought he'd seen the most bizarre case, another would give him yet another version of the evil people inflict on each other.

"You need to tell the soco anyone who might be suspicious."

"Soco?"

"Crew slang for security officer."

"That woman—Mae or Fay or—"

"Mae Ocampo. No, the corporate soco who's been onboard since the bomb scare in Istanbul."

"Oh, the German with the cleft chin right out of central casting?"

"Rolf's Austrian, actually." She gave me a knowing smile. "Hard to miss, right?"

"He registered on my radar—although I doubt I made a blip on his."

"Officer Brandt wears professional blinders, otherwise—" She shifted uncomfortably. "Anyway, he's taking over this investigation because Officer Ocampo has never handled a murder on board." "

"And he has?"

"I've never heard of another one, although it makes sense since he's from fleet security."

Murder. It's a part of our language, on the news daily, and a staple in fiction, yet most people go through life without ever knowing someone who has been murdered. So why had I known so many? Not only my husband, but far too many children in abuse cases. What might be plausible for a plot seems impossible if you know the person, especially one as sweet, talented, hardworking, and beautiful as Tatiana. From the moment we met, I had felt protective of the bird-boned performer who was so thin she appeared serpentine in her skintight costumes.

"There's something else." Callista's voice had changed from distraught to confused. "I don't think you looked at her as closely as I did. I can't get her face out of my mind."

"I'm glad I didn't see it."

"No, it's not what you think. She looked really happy. Whatever light she followed into the tunnel, I think she found what she wanted on the other side."

□ □ □

Callista's pager lit up. "May I?" She pointed to the phone. I nodded and she dialed the extension. "Yes, I'm just about to ask."

She stood and smoothed her uniform's skirt. "That was Rolf Brandt." She pushed her forefinger to her chin as a reminder of his cleft. "He's taken charge of security and is reporting directly to the Fort."

I knew "the Fort" was what they called Empire US headquarters in Ft. Lauderdale, while "the Castle" referred to the international offices in London.

"What does he want from me?"

Callista waited several beats before blurting, "The Fort would like you to write a statement with any and all information Tania shared with you."

"I promised her confidentiality."

Callista bristled. "She's dead, Dale. There's nothing worse that can happen. They need to have as much information as possible by the time we reach Florida."

I stood up and went to close the balcony door because the wind was thrashing the curtains like whips. The sky was steely and the metallic reflection in the ocean was lathered with silvery foam. I turned back to Callista, whose face had blanched the white of her officer's uniform. The vast gulf between her role as obedient servant to a captain and corporation and mine as a paying passenger loomed between us. I chose my words carefully. "Cal, I cannot give you what you want." I was about to say that she should have known why, but then I had never explained. It wasn't a secret in Florida—not after the headlines and lawsuit. Anyone could Google it and figure it out. I just couldn't explain it because the gap between sense and insanity was too wide.

"I don't understand why you of all people wouldn't want to help."

"I won't. Please don't ask me again."

"I'm sorry, Dale, I was ordered to ask you. On a ship, we don't have free will. I am doing my duty."

"And I have no responsibilities other than to myself and my conscience," I said as I opened the door and ushered her out.

☐ ☐ ☐

How I wished I could talk to David! By all statistical averages, he was supposed to be here. Wasn't that what to "have and to hold" meant? I was supposed to have him and hold him—and to have him hold me—right now when I so desperately needed him. Screw the "till death do us part" part. I shouldn't have agreed to that bit. My yearning wasn't depressing—it was infuriating.

Sometimes, though, I hear his voice. I'd be staring at the computer screen stymied, and I'd almost feel his touch on my back, his whisper in my ear. "Might I suggest…" was how he put it with a fake British lilt, knowing I was more likely to take a hint than a criticism or command. When the words wouldn't flow, I'd wait with fingers fluttering over the keyboard, for one of his "suggestions" and in that way, he still helped me over a hump the way he had guided me when he was my boss.

When I covered my eyes to ask for his guidance about Tatiana, I thought I heard his answer: *Stay clear of this. It involves a corporation that will do what's necessary to protect its rep and will throw you or anyone else who threatens them under the bus.*

I muttered: "Wrong analogy, hon."

Someone knocked softly at the door. I hoped it wasn't Callista coming back to plead her case and was relieved it was my room steward.

"So sorry, Miss Dale Lane"—Dante always used both parts of my pen name—the only one on the ship to do so, probably because I gave him several paperbacks when I first boarded in Rome. "It's about—" His hand partially covered his mouth as a sign he didn't wish to speak in the corridor.

I stepped back so he could enter and the door closed automatically behind him. "The doctor, he needs you to speak to someone—you know, in their language."

"Where?"

"In the medical clinic. They need you there."

▢ ▢ ▢

This was my second trip in one day to the Pacific Deck, which is where the geographic names stopped. Everything below was reserved for the crew and had only numbers. The ship's uppermost deck—number ten on the elevator—was called the Arctic Deck—probably due to being buffeted by chilly winds in high seas. The next deck down—number nine—is Atlantic, which featured several swimming pools, suites on the bow, and The Terraces buffet restaurant midship. Deck Eight is the Baltic and keeping with the alphabetical order Deck Seven is the Caribbean. New passengers became confused because logically the subsequent deck should have begun with a "D"—but following the "Seven Seas" theme Deck 6 is the

Gulf, for the Gulf of Mexico; followed by Deck Five or the Mediterranean; and finally, the Pacific on four.

"Anything below the waterline is a Stygian hell" or so Callista once claimed when I asked for an unofficial tour. "Besides, that's the one rule I dare not break."

My cabin, M-511, was on the Mediterranean Deck. Lower numbers like M-202 were forward, M-511 was smack dab in the calmest middle of the ship, while M-780 was aft facing. Even numbers are the port; odd numbers starboard. It's so confusing that most neophytes are lost for the first week.

The elevator doors opened with a bump. I turned away from the swaying partition curtain, avoiding any glimpse of I-95, yet I couldn't ignore a sound that was more animal than human.

"Ai! Argh!" came something between a frightened wail and painful spasm.

I tried the clinic door, which was locked, then rang the bell. No pleasant chimes here, just a raucous buzz that could wake sleeping personnel. Security Officer Mae Ocampo opened the door. She had helped recover my computer when it disappeared from my stateroom several years earlier on a different Empire ship so our nods to each other were those of special recognition.

"*Moyego rebenka, moyu shizn!*" I sucked in my breath as I silently translated: I have lost everything— my heart, my baby, my life!

Joy Barbarosa, a Canadian nurse with a heart-shaped face and blonde hair tinted pink, waved me back to one of the treatment rooms.

Tatiana's performing partner, Oleksander Lopatkino, leaned against the wall in the corridor, his hooded eyes closed, his fists clenched. I had never been introduced to the self-proclaimed "Sun God"—dubbed that because his most famous Cirque role had been based on an Incan dance in a costume that made him look as if he had been chiseled from gold and encrusted in jewels. I'd heard about his fall from the silks swinging over the audience. His disastrous plummet had been captured on numerous mobile phone cameras and went viral on the internet. His broken shoulder never healed to the point that the Cirque underwriters would allow him to perform as a headliner again. An unsympathetic entertainment reporter had commented "The Sun God immolated himself with his outrageous demands."

I brushed past him and entered a small exam room, made more claustrophobic by the presence of a Soco, Dr. Marius Kotze, the ship's chief medical officer, and the odor of sweat and vomit swiped hastily with mint disinfectant.

"*Ya tak sozhaleyu o vashey potere*," I said to Mr. Zlatogrivov. "So sorry for your loss." I suddenly recalled how Tatiana had introduced me to him saying, "I want you to meet *Papa Medved*, which means Papa Bear." Later, in private, she had referred to him as her "*knut*" or whip because he was a cruel taskmaster.

As I knelt beside his chair, I touched his arm and whispered "Papa Medved, do you want me to explain anything for you?" He covered his face with his hands and shook his head.

Dr. Kotze gestured for me to follow him. Olek waylaid him in the corridor. "You have *her* now, so I go to rest. Okay?"

The doctor patted his shoulder. "Sure, yes. Call me if you feel ill again or need anything."

The doctor waited until the door slammed and said, "I apologize for asking your help after what you've been through today."

"I can't believe that only last week Tania asked me to translate for her in this clinic. And now—" He nodded sadly in agreement. "Do you think it had anything to do with her...condition?"

He rubbed his shoulder. "Can't say, and I mean that two ways. I haven't yet examined her thoroughly and I am required to follow the Fort's protocol. We've had people die in accidents or fights, although in these instances I've always known the cause or the assailant."

We heard a crash, then a thump. The doctor rushed back into the exam room. Tatiana's father was slumped over the dressing cart. Dr. Kotze lifted the floppy wrist. "Pulse is fine." He lightly slapped the man's hands and then upper arm. "Mr. Zlatogrivov!"

"*Gde moya devochka?*" he mumbled.

"Where's my little girl?" I translated automatically.

The doctor held the father's large mitt-like hands in his refined ones to soothe his quivering.

"Did you know he was on the Russian Olympic gymnastics team?" I said to bridge the silence.

"He still has a remarkable physique."

The nurse filled the doorway. The doctor acknowledged her with a nod. "They've found another cabin for him," she said. "You know Jerzy Skala, the personal trainer? He speaks also Russian and said he would share his."

"Good, it wouldn't be wise to leave him alone," the doctor replied. "Anyway, it's only for a few days." He and the nurse exchanged shrewd glances.

"That will cramp his style," she said under her breath.

Even I knew that Jerzy was rumored to breach the no-contact rule with many a willing passenger and received outlandish tips.

"Do you think the father knew?" The nurse was still present, but she also had been there at the last clinic visit.

Dr. Kotze exhaled loudly. "Doubt it."

☐ ☐ ☐

I didn't want to be alone in my stateroom. The ship was designed to have many public spaces where you could have a sense of privacy if only because you were a face in the crowd. Most staterooms were cramped, the worst being the inside cabins without natural light. Their inhabitants staked out the best nooks and crannies, using pool towels, knitting totes, books, magazines, and other paraphernalia as place-keepers. The comfy armchairs in the library were the first to go and the adjoining room buzzed with mahjong and card players. The Internet café had uncomfortable chairs to discourage hogging the terminals. One island of tranquility was the adults-only Solarium with attentive service and floor-to-ceiling views of the aft wake. The exterior portion was carpeted with a real creeping red fescue lawn and had gazebos to protect you from the sun. Considering how much I paid for six weeks on board, I bristled at shelling out the daily fee for its use although I knew someone who worked there. I decided to see if Maccabee was on-duty. The last time I was on the *Seven Seas*, his six-year-old twins were traveling with his wife and his mother. I knew he was Bahamian, but his mother told me that they were from the most remote island—Mayaguana.

"I've been there!" I said.

She seemed surprised because there was no public transportation other than the mail boat. "Friends kept a sailboat in the Turks and Caicos and we sailed to your island." I didn't mention it was our honeymoon.

She had been delighted, especially when I mentioned one of her cousins, a cook who grilled fish for visiting mariners. I'd had my editor send a box of children's books to the family that Christmas and Maccabee welcomed me with open arms whenever we'd run into each other on this voyage. "Come see me at the Solarium," he'd said with a wink, which I had interpreted as a free pass.

Needing to burn off some nervous energy, I skipped the elevator and hurried three flights up to Baltic Deck. The Solarium was not as popular during this repositioning crossing from Europe to the United States in November as it was for Caribbean cruises when passengers wanted to escape the blaring music and children's squeals on the pool deck. I entered the glass portico and was relieved to see Maccabee refilling glass jugs with sliced lemons and bottled water.

He gave me a welcoming grin. "Finally, you come to visit me!"

"How could I not?"

"Can you stay awhile—as my guest?" He made a wide gesture to show the area was almost deserted. "I've saved you the best spot on the ship." He directed me to an over-stuffed lounge chair facing the churning wake, which reminded me that Europe was a distant memory; North America a promise.

I glanced around. I saw a few others but nobody was talking; the only sound was the continual hush-hush of a crosswind. "Perfect," I said. "Just what I needed."

Usually the ship offered me anonymity. My prolonged cruise began with several Mediterranean segments with most people staying on for only one week. More prosperous travelers were "back-to-backers" who combined trips to visit more ports. I had added the "Adriatic Explorer," which included Turkey and Greece, to "Elegant Europe" that stopped at Rome, Florence, Monaco, Toulon, Le Havre, and Barcelona—then continued on the "Magic of the Transatlantic," which visited Lisbon and the Azores before the long crossing home. The revolving manifest of newcomers kept busy with shore excursions, trivia tournaments, dance contests, and wine tastings, and they tended to clump with old or newfound friends and only approached me with a pleasantry in an elevator or off-hand remark about the weather on deck.

When I first started writing onboard, my travel agent arranged a discount for giving a few writing lectures although the few dollars saved cost me my privacy. Many passengers invited me to join them for dinner, which was hardly a gift since everyone's meals are included in the fare. I came to resent that people thought they could buy my precious time with a few glasses of wine. Most wanted advice on getting published or had an opus in a drawer they wanted me to read. Many of these people were kind—even somewhat interesting—still, dinner in the dining room is a leisurely affair that takes at least two hours. In order to complete a book at sea, I need to put in four solid hours in the morning—that's when I write my fresh material. I can usually knock out 5000 words, a bit less with a difficult section—10,000 when I'm on a roll. One writerly trick I use is that I never take a break at the end of a chapter—or even a paragraph or sentence. I end my creative flow in the middle of a thought, before I've typed even a period. I call it "writus interruptus." Supposedly the idea originated with—or was promoted by—Hemingway as a cure for writer's block. He said, "Always stop while you are going good and don't worry about it until you start to write the next day. That way your subconscious will work on it all the time. But if you think about it consciously, you will kill it and your brain will be tired before you start." Initially, I couldn't bear to leave something dangling, although it's a habit I now recommend.

By noon I need a break from sitting hunched over my computer. If we're at sea, I try to walk a mile around the promenade deck. If it's a port day, I may go ashore and explore the area around the pier. Several times on this trip I managed to visit friends on shore. A Swarthmore roommate, who lives in Rome, drove to Civitavecchia and squired me to the Etruscan village of Tarquinia for lunch. A former editor, who retired to Provence, met me in Toulon and took me to the perched village of Gordes. Getting from Southampton to see friends in London isn't practical if we're only in port for one day, although I have coordinated with people visiting Venice and recently met a friend who was on holiday in Mykonos.

Mostly, I keep to a tight work schedule. In order to finish a book in six weeks, I begin writing at 7:00 AM when my brain is partially in dreamland from whence my plots ebb and flow. After 90 minutes, that creative burst is over and I usually breakfast in my cabin—on my balcony if weather permits, followed by a brisk twenty-minute walk—indoors or out—then shower with an aggressive shampooing, which I hope will help recalcitrant ideas surface. By 10:00 AM, I buckle down and put in three hours, whether I am in the mood or not. Truth is that I am *never* in the mood any more than a taxi driver, longshoreman, or manicurist might be. I slog away creating, revising, imagining, manipulating—whatever it takes to get the words on the page. Lunch is usually at the buffet—or if I need to keep up the flow, I'll order room service again, which is always delivered promptly and graciously.

When mid-afternoon rolls around—literally on a ship—I am relieved to quit for the day. When the word faucet is flowing, I have to force myself to stop because the inevitable exhaustion results in mediocrity. Rejuvenation comes with reading. About 4:00 P.M., I order a carafe of milky oolong tea and read literary fiction to marvel at masters of the craft.

On the rare days when Callista can take a break, she'll stop by my cabin around 5:30 P.M., when the first-seating passengers are dining and the second are having cocktails. We rarely indulge in anything more potent than a San Pellegrino—a slice of orange in mine, a lime in hers. Her job is far too pressured for her to miss a cue. We avoid meeting in a public space because she's a flame to chatty passengers who either want to bask in her glow or bitch about a minor glitch in perfection. Hardly anyone else ever visits me in my cabin. If I need to "unstifle" myself, I eavesdrop on conversations, what I think of as absorbing the "hum of the ship." I also make mental notes on interesting characters to include in my descriptions. I couldn't invent the woman in the pirate's bandana with a stuffed parrot on her shoulder or the ninety-year-old twins in matching purple sweat suits.

The most efficient place for me to dine is The Terraces—an indoor and outdoor seating connected to a lavish serpentine of buffet stations. The first days of a cruise, the recent arrivals are so dazzled by the myriad choices that they pile their platters with tacos, fried rice, lasagna, with sides of fried okra, hummus, and quiche. It all looks so luscious and everyone wants just a taste—and besides, it's free! Eventually they realize there is no penalty for a second round and their platters look more palatable. By the end of their vacation, most people have dealt with rebellion in their digestive systems and I see more bowls of soup and simple salads.

With my sedentary profession, I've had to tame any tendency to gluttony. For dinner, I select the simplest protein: a slice of the carving board roast, grilled or baked seafood, the vegetarian main dish on offer. I add a salad topped with olives, green peppers, and sunflower seeds or pine nuts and dress it with fresh lemon juice and olive oil. I'll include a sautéed vegetable like broccoli or green beans and finish with fruit. There is an endless stock of exotic fruits like mango, cactus, or my favorite: papaya, even mid-ocean. I peruse the bakery bar, if only to admire the pastry chef's mastery, but only allow myself one serving after I've written 100 fresh pages, which comes to approximately once a week, When I'm revising, my rule is: No sweets until it's polished. Only then is the most decadent item on the menu mine!

I rested back in my lounge chair and fixed my gaze on the smudge where the sea lapped the horizon and tried to lasso my zinging thoughts. Only a few hours ago—even before my first cup of tea—I was hurrying to the interview with Callista. Now, not that many hours later, my head throbbed, my eyes were sore and red, my limbs heavy, and my heart was skipping beats. My computer, only a few floors downstairs on my desk, could have been on the other side of the ocean because reaching for it, opening the lid, and trying to write a single word felt as unlikely as swimming to Florida. I was too exhausted to even worry about making my self-imposed deadline. My head fell back and my eyelids closed. Images of Tatiana swirled off like a departing cyclone. Gone. Like David. No warning. Here one moment and then vanishing into nothingness. Her enchanting spirit, her prodigious talent, her golden future— What *had* happened? Had she suffered? Supposedly, David hadn't, not that the coroner's assurance that "he would never know what hit him" had given me a moment's peace. He *should* have been aware, he *should* have been able to think a final thought, to say a few words. That was yet another existential moment when I am forced to consider where we come from, where do we go—and why. I remember when I first saw my son lifted from my body, pulsating umbilical cord still attached, and thought: this is a *real* baby—like what else had I expected? A new life had come from somewhere beyond my rational mind. Likewise, the end. How could someone as transcendent as David—or Tatiana—be here one moment and not the next? I focused on the roiling sea swirling like a web with the interstices enlarging and melding into different cellular patterns like our wondrous, brief lives intersecting before undulating apart...

□ □ □

"Hello there!" I startled and looked to my left. "Other side" came the mellifluous voice, followed by a chuckle. Three chaises down a body lifted up so I could see a Van Gogh-beard peeking out from under a hood that deflected the sun and provided a modicum of privacy. He waved. "Vance Sharkey." We had met several times, but as the ship's art auctioneer he was a professional Mr. Congeniality who knew it was a kindness to not make me riffle through my mental Rolodex for a name.

I nodded and turned away from him to indicate my desire to be alone. He missed the message because he transferred to the seat before mine, engulfing me in a cloud of pricey French cologne. "We both wanted to be alone," he said, without realizing the incongruity of his intrusion.

Macabee broke into our impasse. "Soy hot chai." He placed a mug on Vance's side table. "Just the way you like it."

Vance took a long whiff. "Perfect!" he said to the server, then to me: "Did you know they have lactose-free alternatives?"

"Mrs. Lanier?" Macabee asked. "What might I bring you?"

The gingery aroma seemed just the right combo to ease the ache in my contracted gut. "I'd like one too."

Vance grinned like the Cheshire cat. "Takes away the chill—both of them, if you get my meaning."

"Didn't realize you could get specialty teas or coffees up here."

"They don't advertise it, but they will deliver anything you want," Vance said. They'll even bring you the bottle of wine you didn't finish at dinner last night or a pizza from Florentina's." Vance's perky sales voice changed to a stage whisper. "What do you know?"

I was reprieved by Macabee serving my chai on a tray, which was indented for a mug and was surrounded by several flavors of mini quiche, a spray of red seedless grapes, and freshly-baked shortbread cookies stamped with the Empire logo.

"Whoa, how do you rate?"

"I'm a paying passenger and you're staff."

"Technically, I'm a hybrid. My cabin's comped, although we kick back a sizeable chunk to the Castle."

Something about his easygoing manner softened my shell. "You're American, right?"

"New York born and bred."

"Sometimes you sound like an Eton man, and other times—"

"Guttersnipe?"

"That's not what I meant!"

"Is this better?" He modulated his accent to that of a mid-Atlantic auctioneer.

"Very continental." I picked up the cup and inhaled the spicy steam.

Vance was a likeable guy who wielded considerable status. It was rumored that when commissions were figured in, the art auctioneer earned even more than the captain. He worked for Beaux Arts Galleries International, headquartered in Geneva. A few weeks earlier he'd asked me to decipher the Russian labels on some Dasansky serigraphs for a potential customer. He had sent three bottles of Prosecco—Callista must have informed him that it was my favorite—to thank me. His note had a PS: Let's have dinner some time? Thankfully, he had never followed up. Romance was the farthest thing from my mind on board, although my landside friends suspected I was more hedonistic so far from home. David may have been gone for almost five years, even though I felt as though he might walk through the door at any moment, ending this awful pause in our lives.

I passed my platter to Vance. He popped a tiny quiche in his mouth and steadied his gaze. "I heard you've been helping her father."

"That didn't take long to get around."

"I can't imagine what he's going through. She was his life." The only answer was the wind screeching like a wounded animal. "He kept her on such a tight leash to protect her—and then this—the worst thing imaginable happens." Vance's voice choked.

I knew almost nothing about Vance other than gossip. Because he wasn't an Empire employee, he could fraternize with both passengers and crew. I'd seen him flirting with some of the show dancers, several of the shop girls, and many a passenger. He went for long-legged, pencil-thin blondes—just like Tatiana. "What's your connection to her?"

He turned slightly toward the receding horizon. "We were very circumspect, we had to be," he mumbled.

"For how long?" This was more of an essential question than he could have suspected.

"We've been friendly for a while on board, but we got to know each other better when I invited her to the Art Biennale in Venice. I knew that she never went anywhere without her father, so I asked him along." He sat up straighter. "Did you know that he insists that she sleep in his cabin?"

"Very old school."

"Not even this century." He lay back on his chaise again. "Anyway, he had bronchitis when we were in Italy. He told her she couldn't go unless *Olek* went along." He uttered the partner's name like a curse word.

"That bad?"

"So arrogant! He had something nasty to say about every work of art."

"You know his story?"

"Just that he was a big Cirque star, the guy who flies on the silks out over the crowd. When the rigging failed, he was seriously injured."

"I heard that one of his rivals sabotaged the equipment."

"Those Russians don't mess around," Vance muttered. "Not long ago a male soloist at the Bolshoi arranged for an acid attack on the ballet's director, because he was slighted for a lead part."

"Artistic rivalries can be—"

"Deadly?"

"I was going to say 'passionate.' Why would Olek harm Tania? She made him look good—and she adored him. She told me, 'He saves my life every night.'"

Vance clenched his fists. "Yet she was always quarreling with him—in Russian, and while it was gibberish to me, they behaved like siblings rehashing old business that never got resolved."

His warm brown eyes were filled with tears. "Did she ever mention me?" I shook my head. "Her father—I don't think he knew, although Olek might have suspected."

I reached for the chai and sipped. The knot in my gut began to unclench.

"I can't believe it. I *won't* believe it." His cheeks dappled with an instant rash. "How?" He choked. "Why?"

"All I know is that they don't suspect suicide."

"Most people don't understand the abyss of pain."

Something in Vance's melancholy tone indicated he was well acquainted with depression. After David died, everything was so hard. I'd felt dragged by heavy chains while I tried to find a path through a dismal fog. "Suicide was impossible—" I stammered. "I was there…she was contorted—almost like she had been in the box—"

He covered his face with his hands as if to shutter the image. "What kind of a monster…?"

"I've helped prosecute many of the most twisted perverts—the ones who prey on children. Oddly enough, I usually end up having some compassion for them."

"How is that possible?

"My husband once said, 'You can never hate someone once you know their story.'" It was a noble thought even though I would never, never forgive the man who killed David, no matter the circumstances.

"All that suffering…all her life…for nothing!" Vance shouted more to the wind than to me. "You know who I blame? Her father! She was just a tool in his grand scheme. He began massaging and stretching Tania's muscles from the day she was born."

"She also told me that."

"Did she also tell you that it was never her choice? She never learned how to walk or stand like a normal girl. She said, 'I make it look easy—that's the secret—but I'm always, always in pain!'"

"So are ballerinas and most professional athletes," I said. "I know she took a lot of meds."

"Did you know that her father gave her injections?"

"For what?"

"Some vitamin combo for energy, and steroid shots for muscle spasms. She was terrified when she had one in the middle of a performance." He shook his head. "Whatever he gave her didn't help. Maybe her smile fooled the audience, but I could tell when she was in agony."

"She once told me that if she missed two performances in a row, they deducted a week's pay. Isn't that illegal?"

"This ship is registered in Bermuda, where they have very lax labor laws," Vance responded.

"I used to work in the field of child protection," I began tentatively, "and I've reviewed many x-rays of broken bones, most from supposed accidental falls. More than ten percent had multiple fractures in various stages of healing, indicating a long history before the abuse was suspected."

"Do you think someone has been hurting her over a period of time?" he asked.

"Sometimes it's difficult to distinguish between an athletic injury and abuse."

"Even her father wouldn't harm his cash cow."

"Anyway, they'll x-ray her during the autopsy," I said.

"I almost feel guilty," Vance muttered. I let him fill in the silence. "I admit that I was just as captivated with Tania's flexibility as anyone. It was so—well, erotic. Especially in the box. Seeing her folded and trapped seemingly nude in that flesh-colored bikini—" He took a quick breath. "I'm sure I'm not the only guy to have those fantasies." Sweat pearled on his forehead. He blotted his face with the napkin on the table, stood abruptly and walked to the marble counter. He poured himself a glass of lemon-infused water from a jug with a brass spigot, took a few noisy gulps, then filled the glass to the brim. "I did try to help her. She complained of being hyped up after a performance almost like she was on speed, so I gave her some of my sleep aids." He looked in the distance. "Just a few, not enough to—"

"Like Tylenol PM?"

Vance looked sideways. "Trazodone—a form of Xanax. I told her to take half because she didn't weigh much."

"Did they help her?"

"She said her father complained she was snoring." He laughed slightly. "Did you know that a contortionist's flexibility is due mainly to genetics? Given that both her parents had much of the same abilities, it's no wonder she exhibited the right stuff so early."

"How did you two manage to communicate so well?"

"We used the voice translator in my phone. Sometimes the results were funny, but we learned to simplify our sentences and—well, we began to understand each other." I nodded to encourage him to keep talking. "The other factor is pure strength," Vance continued. "She started lifting weights before she could walk. Did you know her father attended classes at a medical college as part of his training to be a gymnastic coach?"

"And that supposedly qualified him to prescribe for his daughter?"

He shrugged.

I switched gears. "When did you take her to the Bienalle? We moored in Venice several times this summer. I spent a day there on the final leg."

"You were wise to wait. We went in June and it was hot as hell, so we didn't stay very long."

Long enough…was my first thought. I wanted to probe further, yet knew it was best to let him chatter on without being challenged.

"Tania believed that the human body is only limited by the structures of the skeleton, and these have far more range of motion than most people think…" Vance's voice tone changed from despondent to wistful. His desolation seemed genuine, yet something was missing. The ship's rocking movement had increased. As the wake churned like molten metal in the misty air, a thought formed wordlessly: Where was his anger?

☐ ☐ ☐

I returned to my cabin drained by my encounter with Vance. My forehead pounded with the ominous prodrome of a migraine. I pulled a San Pellegrino from my mini-fridge and took several quick gulps from the bottle. I'd left my laptop open, so I punched the space key and tried to read the last paragraph I had been editing. The words buckled and blurred. I blinked and shut my eyes. I pressed the cool bottle to my forehead. Any further productive work was absurd.

I clicked on my spreadsheet program where I keep my writing schedule projected on the forty-seven-day itinerary. I had been on track to finish the final polish the day before reaching Ft. Lauderdale—but just. I'd hit a plot snag after drafting the first third of the novel and it had taken almost a week to backpedal and then recuperate. Writing on board is expensive—a motivating factor, which prevents pretending I'm on holiday. The hardest part, yet also the most absorbing, is coming up with fresh material every day.

"I write to find out what happens next" is what I say in interviews, which always evokes a chuckle. I don't try to parse the mysteries of creation. All I know is the story percolates in my subconscious; my job is to enable a pathway between airy ether and digital page. If I waited to be in the mood or feel inspired, I'd spend my day lounging by the pool. Most of the time, I plop myself in front of my computer, place my hand on the keys, re-read my most recent output, then let it flow. I assume every stroke a great writer types comes from a well of brilliant syntax and fits into a meticulously engineered structure. My sentences are sloppy, too wordy, and often out of order. I know every page will be edited several times by me, again by my editor, and lastly, the copyeditor will detect anything we've overlooked. It takes less energy for me to fill a blank page than it does to correct myself—one leaves me joyful, the other exhausted.

For top performance, I require an absence of duties as well as a barrier against distractions. On board it's expensive for anyone to call me; I receive no social invitations; I don't have to prepare a cup of tea or a three-course dinner. Nobody needs me—except for the tugging guilt that Bodhi is missing me. He has a calendar with a quarter taped to every day I'm away and the first day back we count up his stash and go shopping. The longer I'm gone, the more money he makes. Okay, maybe I am instilling the wrong values, but it works. I think I long for him, more than he does me—at least that's what I tell myself.

Even with a few days ashore and some breaks to see Callista or socialize at dinner, I was on schedule to finish on time. I always build some leeway into the calendar in case of illness or a writing glitch. Still I was down to the wire because I had lost yardage when a character did something brilliant—yet unexpected—which forced me to rewrite some earlier bits. With only five days until we arrived in Florida, I was on the homestretch, although I had underestimated how many spots required scrutiny to be certain the revised plot unraveled seamlessly.

I chugged the soda water to quell a nausea that had nothing to do with seasickness. I pushed my chair back and headed for my balcony. The sliding door needed an extra push to override the pressure billowing back from the wind across the bow. Usually a mild breeze slips alongside the ship's flanks, so I hadn't anticipated the harsh lashing that pressed me back. I reached for the railing to steady myself. Damn my sacred schedule! My contractual deadline wasn't in jeopardy. The publisher also had plenty of leeway in its rollout. Fretting about my timetable was absurd when compared with the brutal end of Tatiana's life.

My grip on the railing tightened. I leaned out and scanned toward the bow. About a month earlier, I learned that multiple cameras were angled alongside the ship's flanks. Ellwood, Callista, and I were having pizza not far from the dock in Civitavecchia, the gateway to Rome. Ellwood had relaxed like a rag doll, saying "I really needed this! I was ready to jump ship—one way or another."

Callista had lifted one of his floppy hands and dropped it. "Don't even joke about it. You need to stop signing up for transitions."

"Keeps me from spending a fortune on purses, dah-ling."

Callista laughed and explained, "I did some damage at the San Lorenzo market in Florence last week." She patted Ellwood's wrist. "When *was* the last time you were ashore?"

"Almost a month. I admit that I've been feeling a bit claustrophobic but hardly suicidal. Not that this is helping much, I'm feeling a bit landsick."

"Is that what's it's called? I really feel it in enclosed spaces, like a restroom stall."

The two cruise directors had nodded in agreement. "Me too," Callista admitted.

"Right now, everything's tilting," I added. "Seriously, how often does someone jump?"

"It's rare, but—" Callista stopped herself. "We're not supposed to discuss it."

Ellwood didn't feel the same compunction. "You read about drunk passengers doing stupid things, even so it's usually crew."

"Are they ever saved?"

"More often than you think, especially if someone spots them. These days nobody goes over the rail without the plunge being captured on camera."

"Are those mostly suicides?"

"There's a website that keeps a global man-overboard list," Ellwood said. "Check it out. They give known or suspected reasons."

"A whole website! How frequently does it happen?"

"There's one somewhere in the world every few months," Callista answered.

"With passengers, though, it's usually due to booze or drugs, but sometimes we'll find a note or other indication of suicide," Ellwood added.

"It's generally guys and they are more likely to go over on the last night of the cruise. Most are drunk or doing stupid stunts like climbing on the railing or crawling between cabin balconies."

"Pain in the butt," Ellwood groused. "Always sets us back a day."

"That may be true although there are a good number of rescues. Last year they found a guy alive after eighteen hours in the water."

"So mostly drunks or suicides," I summed up. "Any accidents?"

"I've heard of some," Ellwood said to me, then to his boss, "Of course, they *could* be murders." He had a playful glint in his eye.

Callista looked annoyed. "Don't start any rumors. Anyway, you know that the ship's flanks are well-monitored so we can see exactly who went over and when."

"Not every single inch," Ellwood countered. "No cameras at the waterline, for obvious reasons."

At the time, I had made a mental note to see if I could find a case of someone who was found guilty of a murder that first appeared to be a suicide because novelists are always plot-hunting. Now my eyes flooded as I recalled my ghoulish curiosity.

Tatiana was good and truly dead and she did not go overboard. If she had wanted to die—and I knew she had one possible reason—leaping into the ocean made sense. If someone else wanted to dispose of her body, tossing her overboard would have eliminated the evidence or so someone who didn't know about the cameras might have believed.

The sea—endless, timeless, soulless—churned by. Even the waves were out of sync. Some swelled from the center and headed in various directions before overcoming a lesser one, sucking up its energy. The little ones had been absorbed; they would never reach a distant shore. I raised my arms in a tai-chi pose in order to gather waves of healing energy. David's mother had taken me under her wing after David's murder. She coped with Bodhi's hyperactivity; I wanted to curl up in a dark room and rot. He had turned into the most terrible of twos and it took both of us to manage him. For a break, we went to the Y—Bodhi loved the children's room—and getting away from our hovering. I tried cycling, Zumba, aqua yoga, although the only one that stuck was tai chi. Instead of distracting me from my angst, it focused it, which doesn't sound as helpful as it is. I sent the little energy I'd gathered out to sea.

"David—" His name strangled in my throat. I closed my eyes and whispered "Tania" as softly as a prayer.

▢ ▢ ▢

Chilled and shivering, I stepped back inside but left the drapes open as well as a crack of the door.

The whining was white noise that helped quell my racing brain. So why hadn't Tatiana's body been chucked overboard? Any crewmember would not only have known that the act would appear on a security camera, but precisely where those cameras were. A passenger, though, wouldn't have that information, which possibly eliminated a guest, assuming the perp was thinking logically. Most likely the killer was crazed, desperate…or— What if his plans were foiled and the body was stashed in the basket until a more propitious time? Tatiana certainly had her admirers. What if she had spurned one of them…or had been cajoled into one of their cabins or…? Still, a passenger wouldn't have had easy access to an empty laundry cart and wouldn't have known how to access the crew and freight elevators that led to that section of I-95.

I felt lightheaded and needed more air, so I pushed the door open again. The sky had darkened like a curtain pulled around a hospital bed. Needle pricks of rain battered the ship. I lifted my face to the sky to accept the punishment. The curtains blew inward toward the bed, which I didn't want to get soaked. I forced the door closed, although not in time to prevent all the loose paperwork from swirling to the floor.

I heard the captain's six P.M.—1800 by ship's time—message and flipped on the television's bridge cam channel to hear it better. Captain Giambalvo stated the vessel's mid-Atlantic position and warned that there would be "a fair number of bumps and lumps" through the night. He suggested using caution when on deck and to remember the handrails. In his cheeriest voice, he promoted a photo opportunity with the maître d' at the champagne fountain in the atrium within the next hour. No mention of Tatiana, not that I had expected one.

My fingers quivered as I gulped the last of my San Pellegrino, a sign that I was both hungry and exhausted. I was reluctant to get a quick meal at The Terraces. Even though I usually took comfort in the anonymous mob, I didn't want to run into anyone like Vance who also want to talk about it. Besides, the idea of the long, rolling corridor and being squished in a packed elevator was repellent in my moody state. Complimentary, unlimited, and punctual room service was my favorite cruise perk—a one button option on the bedside phone.

"Good evening, Mrs. Lanier."

After five weeks on board, I recognized my room-service waiter Cozmin's Romanian lilt.

"Oh hello, Coz. I'm dining in tonight."

"Of course. I hope you are feeling well."

"Just tired."

"What would you like?"

"Any special soups?" The room service menu always featured chicken noodle for ailing guests, even though there were others bubbling in various stockpots.

"The main dining room is offering cream of asparagus, double consommé with rye croutons, and gazpacho as the vegetable-tarian option."

I smiled at his pleasantly fractured English. "Anything else on the buffet?"

"I think they continued the one-ton and beanie-weenie from this afternoon."

"I'd like the wonton," I said. "And could you do one of your grilled cheese with Gouda, tomato, and prosciutto?"

"And a pot of tea—Early Grey or Minty Mint?"

I couldn't help laughing at his joke about my usual choices. "Too late for the early one! Mint would be lovely."

"I'm sending some cookies, okay?"

"Sure," I said, knowing this meant an entire platter of mini-pastries left over from high tea.

I avoided desserts on board, although one or two petit fours might perk me up. I thought of what Yoko Ono said after John Lennon was murdered about eating all the right foods to keep them healthy but what did it matter in the end? After that, she let her son eat anything he wanted. It was especially curious for Tatiana, whose diet had been regulated severely since infancy. Would it really matter if I weighed five pounds more when the ship could sink because of a flirting captain's inattention? A terrorist in a museum could target me. I could die of an aneurysm in my sleep tonight.

I lay back on my pillows, which Dante had arranged on one side of the bed for sitting up and on the other for sleeping, and shut my eyes. The ship shifted and groaned to starboard then lifted and rolled to port. Nice long heaves. I timed my breathing to meet the rises and falls. The room bell chimed. Dinner already? There should be a remote-control opener I thought, eyes still closed. Then came a knock. I cursed to myself.

"Okay, okay…"

Callista not so much entered as burst into my room. Her face looked more ashen and distressed than it had this morning. "I'm so, so sorry," she began." For a second I thought somebody else had been harmed, but the offender was a clipboard and a form that she thrust toward me. The words "non-disclosure" and "confidential" popped out.

"Officer Brandt asked to have you sign it." Callista sniffed as if ferreting a foul odor.

I quickly realized this was a binding contract.

Callista didn't know that one of my first jobs out of college had been as a paralegal for Monroe, McDonald, and Marin. I had done a temporary job for them—a Russian translation —and they asked me to stay on because the case was headed to trial. Harry Monroe took me under his wing and wrote a recommendation for my law school application. I was accepted at several just before I met David.

I took it to my desk, flipped on the light, and looked at it more carefully. The words "unfortunate accident" blurred. "What's this about 'further cooperation with security personnel'?"

"I think it's because you are a witness. And—" She hesitated for a few beats. "Rolf knows about your law enforcement background." She held her hands up. "I didn't tell him. He has a dossier."

"What the hell!"

She shook her head. "Welcome to the post nine-eleven world. They can get anything on anybody in a few minutes by entering the passport number." She swallowed hard. "Rolf said he was impressed with your résumé and he thinks you could be very helpful—like speaking Russian to Mr. Zlatogrivov and Mr. Lopatkino…maybe some others who wouldn't find you as threatening as someone from security." She took a long breath. "Look, we can use all the help we can get," Callista said in a strident tone. "Because we're landing in the US, we have to comply with the Cruise Vessel Security Act. As you know, our turnaround is less than a day and we can't afford to lose our departure slot for our first cruise of the Caribbean season. We're booked to capacity because it's Thanksgiving weekend." Callista's words raced as if she was having a manic spike. "We have no idea what your authorities are going to do to us. They can detain passengers, refuse to let any crew go on leave, even impound the ship."

"When did you hear all this?"

She inhaled noisily. "At last meeting an hour ago. The Fort is worried about the press."

"I'm not a journalist."

"You're the most notable passenger and could be a target for reporters…or…"

I bristled at the implication that I would try to profit from the story.

"When I first started this job, security problems revolved mostly around drunks—both guests and crew." Callista stood and paced the small space in front my balcony door. "These days the number one issue is terrorism—or fear of it. Last year the Orion Line lost twenty passengers in an explosion near the pyramids. We've had credible threats from extremists who would like nothing better than to disrupt the cruise industry. That's Rolf's main concern."

A few weeks before I boarded this cruise, the *Seven Seas* had been diverted to pick up a sinking fishing boat overloaded with Syrian refugees. Dante told me about the many unaccompanied children who reminded them of his own and I'd heard that some passengers donated warm clothing for the rag-tag group huddled on the forward crew deck.

"Does Rolf really think that there's a link between Tatiana and terrorists?"

"He refuses to discount any theory." She swallowed hard. "He's suspicious about Putin—Rolf always had a thing about Russians. He's sure they want to dominate Turkey to get a port on the Med."

"Russia's always searched for a warm-water port, although it's awfully farfetched to think that Tania would have had anything to do with espionage."

Callista held her hands palms up. "Apparently, her mother came from somewhere near the Turkish border—" She headed back toward the door to the foyer. "Okay, here it is: Rolf thinks you can help. The more information we have before we reach the USA, the better chance that the ship won't be detained."

I looked down at the clipboard. "Who else is being ask to sign these contracts?"

"There's a short list of people who 'need to know' and then there are those who might have critical information." She rubbed her forehead. "That's the one you're on."

"Actually, I hardly knew her."

"She put you on her clinic list."

"I only went with her to the doctor on two occasions and just to translate. The doctor knows everything that I do."

Callista gestured that she wanted to sit down. I motioned to the sofa. "This has been the—most—

63

horrible—day—ever!" She rubbed her temples. "I don't know how they can expect me to keep up the entertainment schedule all by myself as if nothing happened."

"What about Ellwood?"

"He broke out in hives in the middle of the pop music quiz and has been confined to cabin."

I pointed to the form. "What's this about an 'unfortunate accident'?"

"That's what they are calling it."

"If she had fallen and injured herself, that would be an accident. It also implies she is still alive."

"According to Rolf, she won't be legally dead until there's a death certificate, which won't be issued until we get to Florida." Callista raked her hair back with her nails. "Even when someone has fallen overboard, they aren't presumed dead till some landside official makes that pronouncement." She threw out her arms in supplication. "Can't you see we need all the help we can get!"

I closed my eyes, then whispered, "The gift of sorrow is empathy."

Callista blinked. "Was she in some sort of trouble?"

"Troubled, yes, like most young women her age—even more so because of her domineering father. After her mother died, she was forced to live the life her father prescribed. How would you feel if your father micro-managed everything—even when you were allowed to menstruate?"

"What?"

I pulled back the hair at the nape of my neck as if that would take back the errant words. "I shouldn't have said that."

I looked down at the paper, which was really more of a gag order than a confidentiality agreement. I started to speak, but Callista held up her hand. "It's more than Rolf. Captain Giambalvo said to tell you that he considers you more than a guest and he has allowed you to use his ship as 'your special resource'—that was his phrase. He said to ask you if, as a very special favor, you would be willing to offer your services as a special resource to the ship."

What a diplomat, I thought! This veteran seaman's role was often more ceremonial than technical, yet in the end he was master of the vessel— king, commander, the law and the father—none of whom would take no for an answer.

☐ ☐ ☐

Room service arrived just as Callista left with my signature on the document she had proffered. While it might govern my activities for my last few days on board, it did not prevent me from speaking to law enforcement; and while I had promised not to talk to the media, there were many other ways the story could leak. I cringed imagining the lurid headlines and photos of the contortionist's most sexually explicit poses. I hoped Tatiana's reputation could be protected. Besides, any breach on my behalf would both hinder my ability to remain anonymous at sea and compromise my credentials with the Empire Line.

Cozmin had opened the room service trolley's leaves and placed my desk chair in the middle. The cart was laid with a crisp white tablecloth. The yellow-banded china featured a sun motif more suitable to the Caribbean than the roiling Atlantic. Yellow rose buds saluted from a cut-glass vase. I pondered the cost of transporting them from Ecuador or Israel via the Amsterdam flower market to Barcelona, then loaded on a ship bound for Florida in the middle of November. Lifting the silver dome, I inhaled the buttery aroma of melting cheese on freshly baked bread. The wonton broth was soothing and the sandwich—comfort food for a sick child—quelled a hunger I did not know I had.

All day I had been an amalgam of enraged, confused, and impotent. Now that I was being offered a seat at the table—even one I normally would have shunned—the weight on my shoulders lifted slightly. Rolf had been right in assuming that I had skills that could be of use in the investigation.

I hadn't worked on a case for several years. When I interviewed with the Miami law firm, they asked if I was fluent in Spanish. "Sorry, no. I have college-level French, but am fluent in Russian," I said, thinking I'd blown it. The guy had brightened saying they were getting more and more Russian clients who were investing in real estate and had trouble getting them to understand the paperwork. I found business law tedious until one of the law school interns was doing pro bono work for a child advocate and asked me to assist. He was pursuing a claim on behalf of a foster child who had been mauled by a wolf hybrid whose owner claimed he only spoke Russian. Our meeting went well and I convinced him that it was cheaper to write a check for the child's emergency care than to hire a lawyer to fight the obvious. Then the birth mother inserted herself claiming the check belonged to her and the intern asked if I could explain the situation to her.

"Isn't that the job of the foster care people?" I asked.

"The problem is she is causing a scene in our reception area," he said. "I tried talking to her, but she screamed that I was touching her and I beat a fast retreat. These people will try anything for a buck. At least she won't accuse you of sexual harassment."

The mother was pacing and muttering. It didn't take an expert to realize she was unhinged. She was also painfully skinny and either high or craving something. "Hi," I said. "I'm just about to get some lunch. May I treat you?" My tactic was to get her the hell out of our waiting room, where several clients had moved to a far corner.

"Could I have a milkshake?" she asked in a high, thin voice.

I took her to a coffee shop and she ordered a chocolate shake, double-patty burger, and two cups of coffee. She did all the talking and I just nodded sympathetically. "They took my last baby. Now I have nothing," she said and then went on to tell me how two of his baby brothers had died in their cribs.

Bile rose in my mouth as she recited finding each child without registering any emotion. I decided she was the sorriest specimen of humanity that I had ever met.

When I got back to the office, I told the intern about this woman's run of bad luck and he said, "We have to call it in."

"Call who—and why?"

"We are helping with the representation of the child, not his mother," the intern said. "In Florida we have a duty to report any suspicion of child abuse or neglect."

"Even if the children are deceased?"

"One crib death, well okay...two?" He sighed. "Look, all you have to do is call an 800 number and they will follow up."

"Why me?"

"Cause she disclosed to you."

The person who interviewed her was David Lanier, the head of the law enforcement unit that handled abused and exploited children. Eventually he uncovered seven infant corpses in shoeboxes in the grandfather's garage. After the mother was convicted of serial murder—I had been called as a witness—David told me they had several child-protection jobs open.

"I'm not interested in police work," I said.

He explained they were with the Department of Children and Families and although the sheriff's unit cooperated, they served different functions. "We're more interested in prosecuting; you'd be protecting the children."

And so it began. All the cases were certainly more interesting than real estate, if not heartbreaking. Most were the result of poverty that led to ill health and pain, resulting in self-medication with illegal substances, lack of nourishment, inadequate education and few chances at a better life. The goal was to help parents get their children back—a Sisyphean task. Most weren't violent criminals and the goal was to remediate rather than punish. "If we jailed every parent that smoked pot," David said, "the schools would be empty."

He handled the more serious crimes like manslaughter and murder. "Every case is a story—often more fantastic than fiction. My job is to find the fragments of the tale and piece them together in a logical sequence. He was methodical, yet there was also an artful side—making intuitive guesses, untangling deceptions, and coming up with a plausible narrative. When I started writing novels, I used his techniques to plot my books, beginning with his decision-making flowchart.

I took a sip of mint tea before pouring the rest into my thermos tumbler so it wouldn't cool rapidly. I popped a feather-light pistachio mini-macaron in my mouth. Thus fortified, I opened my computer to my day-to-itinerary where I jot the date, the ship's position or port, how many pages I wrote, people I met—especially those with characteristics I might borrow for a fictional personality. I hadn't filled in anything since finding Tatiana. I took a long breath and began to type in the sort of notes I would make shortly after meeting with a family suspected of child abuse.

Morning show with Callista & Ellwood, I-95, Tatiana folded/twisted, laundry hamper, deceased, horror, dizzy, fall, captain, security, Callista visit, clinic, Olek, Papa Medved, translate, tragedy, solarium,

I started a new page titled: Questions.
Vance, affair?
Get Venice Biennalle date!
Cameras?
Witnesses?
Passenger?
Crew?
Pervert?
Callista
Gag order, cooperate?
Look up: Cruise Vessel Security Act
Dates of clinic translations
Terrorism?
Refugees?
Turkey
Russia
Mae Ocampo
Rolf Brandt
Dossier on me?

I pressed "Save As" and wrote "4-T"—for Tatiana, which separated my personal diary from this investigation. I deleted my notes about my writing schedule from the new document, but left in the trip's dates, itinerary, and who I had seen. With a simple search, I noted that Tatiana's name had showed up on eight different days. I lingered on my comments on "Venetian Gala," which took place each night the ship departed Venice—the first night on board for most new passengers. I'd seen Tatiana's show billed as the "Goddess of Flexibility." She wore a gymnast's version of a carnival costume complete with a gilded harlequin mask. She had wowed the crowd as she screwed herself into one implausible bend after another in an eerie blue light scored by the "Winter" section of Vivaldi's "Four Seasons."

The times I translated for Tatiana at the medical center also were listed: first for the UTI. Not long after that the clinic called me because they were treating her for a sprained toe and she didn't understand their instructions.

"Tell her she needs to stay off her feet for three days," Joyce, the nurse, said, signaling the number with her fingers.

"I must do my atrium," she insisted, explaining that it was only a few minutes to drum up an audience for that night's theatrical event. "Tell them just to tape it up as tightly as possible."

"Against medical advice," the nurse had muttered, and then more forcefully, "Tell her she is taking a risk, especially doing the full show."

Tatiana frowned at my translation. "I will modify."

I made a point to watch the performance and was pleased that she had scaled back some of the footwork and concentrated more on using her hands and twists.

The next time I was summoned she had lost her steely composure, openly sobbing when I explained her positive pregnancy result.

"Ask how soon I can get rid of it!"

"Nothing can be done onboard," Joyce had said in a tone that indicated she did not approve of abortion. Now both mother and child were gone.

My desk phone buzzed. I was startled because I so rarely received calls.

"Good evening, Mrs. Lanier, Officer Brandt from corporate security," he said with unexpected delicacy.

"Yes?"

"I'm sorry to interrupt your dinner, but I did wish to thank you personally for your assistance today."

"Yes, well…it was the least I could do…" I said, while thinking: He probably not only knows what I ordered but the calorie count.

"I realize the hour is late. Is it possible for me to stop by your cabin this evening?"

"Actually, no. I'm going to sleep early," I said because I needed time to order my thoughts and make more notes.

"Of course, but I'm sure you understand the urgency. "Is seven tomorrow morning too early?"

"Not at all."

"Would you be most comfortable in your cabin?"

The idea of his eagle eyes on my belongings unnerved me. I thought quickly. "I wanted to speak to Dr. Kotze anyway so could we meet in the clinic?"

"Excellent choice," Rolf said without a hint of sarcasm. "I wish you a good night."

▫ ▫ ▫

If people like Rolf were going to show up at my door—by invitation or not—I had to make my cabin more presentable. I dragged a suitcase out from under my bed and started folding everything I would not need as we approached Florida: sweaters, rain gear, dressy clothes, and city shoes. I'd meant to send out my laundry yesterday, although now I didn't want to risk not getting it all back in time, so I stuffed it all into the suitcase's outside compartment. Next, I rounded up all my research materials. My almost-finished novel takes place around the Shakespeare festival in Ashland, Oregon, amid legislative efforts to legalize cannabis, and includes a Romeo-and-Juliet romance between the daughter of a Mexican smuggler and the scion of prominent vintners. I had files on everything from gang murders to marijuana wholesale price fluctuations.

I took a swig from my thermos and burnt my palate. Panting, I took long swallows from the water goblet before wheeling the trolley out to the corridor. With half the closet emptied and most of the surfaces clear, I changed into black ribbed jammies, but the computer beckoned with more insistence than the bed.

I stared at my note file to figure out what was bothering me. The title "4-T" was too obvious. While a cruise ship seems like a party palace, the guiding principle is profit and I assumed someone was worried about what I might write about the murder. Maybe I was being paranoid because someone like Rolf could get an IT guy to hack my computer. I free associated: blini, caviar…Caspian…Kremlin…Lenin's Tomb, Tchaikovsky, Swan Lake…Odette!—the tragic heroine who's transformed into a swan. Odette824 (Bodhi's birthday) became the file's password. As a further precaution, I took out a fresh USB flash drive. Once during a severe storm at home, my hard drive was fried by a lightning strike. It cost several thousand dollars to recover my files, and even so, I lost some chunks of original story. Now I keep copies of my writing on multiple memory devices. When I am land-based, everything levitates to that elusive cloud. Onboard, I keep one set of USB drives in my room safe with duplicates in a plastic pouch in my tote bag, which Bodhi had decorated with manatee stickers and goes everywhere with me. The sinking of the *Costa Concordia* was a grim reminder to always have one copy with me at all times.

Following David's precautions with sensitive files, I also zipped the file, and saved it with a sentence as a password: "Thefogcomesonlittlecatfeet" from the Sandburg poem. Finally, I deleted the "Odette" file from my laptop.

I opened the safe where I kept my passport, wallet, a few pieces of decent jewelry, and my book backups. Just as I entered the code, I changed my mind. With a deep inhalation, I went back to the laptop to disgorge some jumbled thoughts.

David believed that love and hate were twin emotions. "Stranger danger" catches the imagination, although most crimes are committed by the nearest and dearest—usually the father or the man in the paternal role. I typed "FA"—social work shorthand for father—and listed what I recalled about Grisha Zlatogrivov: gymnast, Olympics, coach, medical school followed by questions: medicines, cures, routines, legal residence, citizenship, age, health, finances, substance abuse, addictions, gambling, romances, sexual orientation? My arms felt leaden and my head nodded forward. Sleep, I told myself, leaving the laptop's lid open so the bluish light would illuminate the room as I stumbled into bed.

I slept hard until a foot cramp roused me. As I sat on the edge of the bed massaging it, images from the previous day crackled through my sluggish brain. I reached for the lighted pen I kept on the end table. Fictional puzzles sometimes sorted themselves out in my subconscious, so it was not unusual for me to wake from a dream and take notes to remember them. Ghostly images emerged from a haze as I scribbled: Jerzy in the gym, Russians in engine room, the jerks who made the comments in the atrium...and... Vance! And who else...who else?

Two

The beginning of love is to let those we love be perfectly themselves, and not to twist them to fit our own image. Otherwise we love only the reflection of ourselves we find in them.
—Thomas Merton

Saturday, November 21
At Sea: Position: 814 Nautical Miles Southwest of
Ponta Delgada, Azores

After a cup of tea and half a croissant, I reluctantly took the mid-ship elevator back down to the Pacific Deck. Once docked, the bay doors were opened and a rolling ramp was deployed. Portable screeners checked every person and possession that came on board. Security officers used hand-held devices to scan ID cards, keeping a running census of who was on or off the ship at any given time. A photo embedded in the data visually confirmed everyone's identity.

I had paid little attention to what was behind the partition panels, which masked the view of I-95. This time, though, I tried to orient myself. The institutional linoleum tiles that led to the carpet by the passenger elevators were orange —a visual clue that this corridor crossed starboard to port at the narrowest part of the ship. Red flooring indicated that I-95 ran forward to aft on the starboard, or right side of the ship; while blue demarcated the left, or port, passageway because without a window to reference the ocean, most people couldn't figure out which direction the ship was going. The same system was used in the guest area with red or blue borders on the corridor carpets.

I jumped out of the way as a worker using a floor-polishing machine whirred past. A notice indicated that the medical center opened at ten on sea days, but as soon as I neared the door, Rolf Brandt opened it.

He wore the crisp white slacks and shirt of an officer with three wide stripes on each epaulette indicating his rank, which was equal to the chief technical officer and passenger service director. Mae Ocampo, the ship's security officer, only had two stripes and answered to the staff captain; however, Officer Brandt, who was the head of fleet-wide security, reported directly to the captain when he came on board to sort out issues and train staff.

"Thank you for coming, Mrs. Lanier," he said in a hushed tone. "Dr. Kotze will join us momentarily, but I wanted to talk to you alone for a moment." He waved his hand like a maître d' leading to a prime table. We walked across the narrow waiting room with industrial metal chairs and a bare floor, passed a curved reception desk, and through a door with a touchpad lock. The drab office was furnished with two chairs and a desk. The sign read: Joyce Barbarosa, CMSRN, indicating her Canadian nursing credentials.

I took the chair he proffered while he sat ramrod straight in the second visitor's seat, which he turned to face me squarely. "I wish to thank you for agreeing to assist us," he began in a manner which was more flirtatious than intimidating.

"I don't know how I can help."

"Miss Standish mentioned that you worked in criminal investigation, among your other considerable accomplishments," he said in an accent that combined German and upper-crust British.

"My husband worked in law enforcement," I said, "although I did investigations in my job."

Rolf's Roman nose had a sloping tip that in profile looked like it was modeled from an ancient coin. Damn! He was handsome. "Did I misunderstand?"

"It's hard to explain. The European system is different." Rolf tilted his head to encourage me to continue. I drew a long breath. "In Florida—like many parts of the United States—we have serious problems with child abuse. I once worked for the child protective investigation unit that cooperates with the county sheriff's department."

Rolf looked disdainful. "You look for lost children?"

"No, we investigate child abuse, which is a crime."

"These *are* criminal cases?"

"Hundreds are killed in Florida alone every year, most by family members."

"Hundreds? Of *kinder*? Were any of the children ever the victims of sexual assault?" I nodded. Rolf bit his lower lip inward. "The Fort has asked us to do a rape kit to preserve any evidence." He stood and paced for a few steps. "You know what that is?"

"Yes, I've accompanied children during the exam."

"But never after—" he stated.

"Those are done by the medical examiner, which is what I thought would happen to Miss Zlatogrivova's body when we arrive in Florida."

"They don't want to wait." He looked down at the mirror shine on his shoes. "It's because of the US Cruise Vessel and Security Act."

"I thought this vessel has a Bermuda registry."

"We are required to follow US law when the ship uses American ports. Since we're arriving in Ft. Lauderdale, your local police and possibly your FBI will try to take charge." He lifted his shoulder blades like a hawk about to unfold his wings and looked me up and down for an uncomfortable moment. "We— the doctor and I—wondered whether you would consent to be a witness." He waited a beat. "It was suggested that we find someone who is not a company employee and also someone with qualifications—and preferably female."

I turned aside to marshal conflicting thoughts about whether he was trying to charm me or con me.

"I'm sure that you also agree that whoever took Miss Zlatogrivova's life should be found as quickly as possible so that that nobody else is harmed."

"Of course."

Rolf bent closer to me. He smelled aggressively minty. "Have you ever been asked to identify a body?"

"I have."

I wanted to do something to help Tatiana although not if it meant any involvement with the Broward

County Sheriff's Department. I lifted my eyes. "Florida authorities might not consider me an unbiased witness."

Rolf shrugged. "Because of your lawsuit regarding your husband's wrongful death?" I wondered where he had gotten so much information so swiftly. He tilted his head and answered my silent query. "Callista is under a professional obligation to share information in a situation like this."

I'd told Callista about David after she'd shared the details of her brief, miserable marriage. "Yes, we've been in litigation for years. They have labeled it a publicity stunt; I call it justice."

"*Bitte*...if you please..." Rolf dabbed at his rheumy eyes. "All we are asking is for you to observe the examination."

Dr. Kotze walked into the reception area. He snapped open a file, bent its cover backwards, and steadied it with the clamp on a clipboard. "Please, come with me. We need this exam room. It's getting busy out there. They're all coughing. Were you in the theater last night?" Both Rolf and I shook our heads. "Several of the acts in the passenger talent show sounded more like seals than songbirds," he said with a forced smile.

"The dreaded cruise cough?" I replied.

We followed the doctor to the end of a hallway and he tapped out the keypad code. The room was lined with glass cabinets that displayed laboratory equipment and chemical jars. A floor safe presumably held narcotics and other medications.

"We are fortunate this happened on your watch," Rolf said to the doctor. "There aren't many who are so…*erfahren* to handle this." He reached out his hand as if trying to capture the English word that eluded him.

"Experienced?" Dr. Kotze asked.

"*Ja, das ist es!*" Rolf relaxed his normally stoic expression.

"You know"— the doctor directed his comment to me—"Afrikaans is a Germanic language. Then to Rolf, "Did you mean experienced with the type of death or rape kits?"

"The latter." Rolf pulled out his handkerchief and wiped his upper lip. "Just like any small city, we have situations…accusations…" he said to me. "It's prudent to have a way to protect evidence on board in case someone claims to be assaulted."

Claim? My stomach turned sour. Law enforcement used to be biased against rape victims when it came to rape. Some women refused to come forward because they didn't think they would be believed, especially without significant bruises that had been caused by a violent stranger. These days US authorities were more enlightened—or so I wanted to believe. I swallowed hard and breathed through my mouth because the medicinal smell and the cramped room in a lower part of the ship bobbing in the middle of the Atlantic was a nauseating combination.

The doctor tapped his paperwork. "Before we begin, I need to explain a complication in Ms. Zlatogrivov's medical…condition." He looked at me apologetically and said, "This situation voids confidentiality."

"What do you mean?" Rolf asked.

"She was pregnant."

Rolf placed his unusually large hands on his knees and inclined forward. "*Nicht Möglich!*"

"Yes, very possible." The doctor gestured with hands palm up.

"She was tested," I whispered.

"That father...he never let her out of his sight," Rolf said.

"Sometimes she slept in Olek's cabin—" I said.

"She slept with Olek?"

"No, she traded beds with him so she could have a private bathroom a few...necessary...days of the month."

Rolf wiped a feverish sheen from his forehead. If he were coming down with a cold, I'd surely catch it in such close quarters. "I don't give a damn where she slept—or with whom," Rolf said in a hoarse voice. "I want to know where the hell she was the night she was killed!"

"What about all the security cameras on board?" the doctor asked.

"We're reviewing them as fast as possible." Rolf pressed his thumbs into his temples. "It's a nightmare keeping them all running and usually there are a dozen or more out of service at any one time. Our priority cameras are in the casino and the exterior ones—in case of a jumper." Rolf grimaced. "The others—they fix them when they can." He clenched his fists. "We should try to find out who else knew about this."

"About what?" asked the doctor, who had been distracted by the camera comment.

"The pregnancy?" I filled in.

Dr. Kotze paged through Tatiana's file, then stopped and pointed to a notation. "I thought so," he said. "She had birth control listed in her medical file."

"What was she getting? Depo shots?" I asked because that way there would be no pills to hide from her father. "But that prevents bleeding."

"Which means she wouldn't need privacy once a month," Rolf said.

"She wouldn't have to tell her father that," I said softly.

"In any case," the doctor said, "she listed a pill: Seasonale."

"That's also continuous birth control." I turned to Rolf. "No period."

"They weren't very effective, were they?" Rolf muttered.

"Either she didn't take them as directed," I added, "or something else interfered with their effectiveness."

Rolf slicked back his hair. "So, let's suppose she told this man—the baby's father—that she was protected, then later that she was pregnant. He may have felt deceived, angry..." He blew his nose forcefully.

"It happens," I said because I'd seen much domestic violence that revolved around men who didn't want to become fathers.

A buzzer rang. The doctor lifted the phone on his desk. "Yes, shortly." He turned to us. "We're going to have to postpone. The clinic is already backed up."

Rolf held up his hand in a take-charge gesture. "How did she feel about this—this *condition*?" He turned from me to the doctor.

The doctor's large Adam's apple bulged in his skinny throat. "I already wrote her a medical excuse for some testing so she could remain in Florida and skip the first Canal cruise."

"For what reason?" the security officer asked.

"I put down an orthopedic scan."

Rolf cleared his phlegmy throat before asking his next question. "But it was really for…?"

"A termination," I filled in.

Rolf stared at each of us in term. "Who talked her into that?"

"It was her first response when she heard the news," the doctor said.

"I was there. She was adamant."

"She believed she had no choice," the doctor added.

Rolf opened his mouth, although before he could say anything, I spoke slowly and firmly. "That *was* her choice."

There was a knock on the door. Rolf, who was closest, opened it. Nurse Barbarosa stepped in, her pink highlights glinting in the glare. "Sorry, but they're falling like flies," she said. "I've been handing out antiseptic gargle, guaifenesin, and surgical masks by the dozen. I'm doing rapid flu tests and already two are positive for influenza A."

"Isolate them," Dr. Kotze said to her, then muttered to us, "This could turn into an epidemic."

□ □ □

Rolf and I left the medical center together. He halted abruptly in front of a door that was open a crack. "Could you spare a few more minutes?" He knocked, then pushed it open further. He grunted with annoyance. "This should have been locked!" I peered inside a small room with a table, and some charts. "Please." He gestured for me to go into the room and offered me the only chair, which I was happy to take after standing around in the clinic. "This is the pilot's room," he explained. "When the harbor pilot boards, he can leave his boots and coat here, prepare his charts, or meet with the navigation staff before going to the bridge."

"Have you seen them leaping on and off the ship? Looks dangerous."

"I've boarded and exited with the pilot several times." Tension drained from his face and his voice changed to that of an affable host. "The ship turns onto a heading to provide a lee on the boarding side, although when there's a lot of chop it gets rather—I think your expression is 'hairy'!" His smile seemed genuine. "Anyway, I wanted you to know that we will be eliminating any internet charges in case you want to do any research or make inquiries that might be helpful to us. In fact, we will comp your entire shipboard account."

"That's very generous."

He bent closer and for a moment I thought he was going to touch my hand, which at that moment I would not have minded.

"This is a nightmare for you," I said sympathetically. "I know the burden when something this serious is dumped in your lap."

He nodded. "You understand, maybe better than most." He held my gaze. "There's only so much we can do at sea, yet somehow I'm expected to find out what happened before we arrive."

"At least we know that whoever is responsible has to be onboard. Is there any evidence that might lead to a specific person?"

"We don't have a forensic lab." He sat on the edge of the table. "DNA should be embedded in everyone's electronic profile," he said oblivious to how he sounded with his German accent. "A baby could be in the database from birth."

"Will they test the fetus for paternity?"

"I don't know what your Americans will do." His lips formed a tight line. "Even if it matches with samples taken from her body, that wouldn't prove who harmed her."

"Maybe not the semen, but fingernail scrapings or a stranger's hair."

"It might not even have been the man who was with her last—if her assailant was a man."

"True," I answered. "You already said that you wouldn't have the lab results before we reach Florida."

For the first time, the security officer let his guard down. I saw his hand tremble and I briefly touched it just as the pager on Rolf's vest flashed.

He pulled away to check the number. "The bridge."

I looked down, feeling I'd taken a misstep. "Anything else?" I asked, getting to my feet.

He had a preoccupied expression, then asked, "Do you call it the 'circle rule' in the US?"

"I'm not sure what you mean?"

"Investigating first the victim's closest contacts and then expanding the circle." He opened his hands wider and wider.

"Yes. It's almost always someone in close proximity."

"Or in the same boat."

"I will talk to her friends—what we call 'sniffing around.'"

"That's where we begin, *ja*?"

☐ ☐ ☐

I felt empty yet had no appetite. The cliché about one's stomach being tied in knots might be the most accurate description. I had been dreading seeing Tatiana's body and the postponement only exacerbated my tension. I hurried to the sanctuary of my cabin, relieved that the corridor was empty so I didn't have to nod, smile, or pretend to remember someone's face.

Happily, my room was a shrine of sparkling surfaces. The curtains were looped back and the sun shone through recently polished glass. Dante had refreshed the flowers from my dinner tray and placed them in the middle of the coffee table. The fruit bowl had been refilled with my favorite Gala apples, pears, and seedless grapes. There were three fresh bottles of San Pellegrino on the counter. My personal neck and boudoir pillows were plumped on the sofa. The mirrors gleamed and the bedspread had been replaced because of a tea stain from a clumsy moment. On land, only the fabulously wealthy could afford this meticulous service. I had to admit this was one of the lures of cruising for me.

I opened the door to the balcony and was greeted with the sweetest of sea zephyrs—much milder than expected for mid-November thousands of miles from any landmass. The sea state was so serene a sailboat would be dead in the water.

A whistle screeched over the loudspeaker in the hall. I opened the cabin door to hear better. An official voice shouted: "Alpha Alpha Alpha! Deck Five. Starboard midship." Alpha meant a medical emergency. Deck Five was the Mediterranean—my deck—and I was starboard. I glanced down the hall and saw crew converging in the five- hundred area. The speaker came on again. I half expected it to say "For practice, for practice, for practice" because they often ran crew drills on sea days.

I reigned in my wild thoughts. Given the average age of my fellow cruisers—well over sixty—heart attacks and strokes could be expected, yet what if it was another murder? As I paced my cabin to relieve my cresting anxiety, the few steps in each direction became increasingly claustrophobic. Thinking a brisk walk on deck would calm my nerves, I headed for the aft staircase and scrambled two flights up to the Caribbean Deck. I pushed open the door to the promenade area with my shoulder, a ploy that works well when wind buffets the ship, although without any pressure, it gave way so fast that I stumbled over the water-barrier threshold. Two shirtless joggers rushed by in matching crimson shorts—must be Europeans, I thought because I was chilly even though this was the sunny side of the ship.

Who? How? Why? I asked myself as I loped forward in time with the ship's rhythm. A stream of unanswerable questions radiated through me with every step. I walked faster as if I could shed them in my wake.

Based on experience in child welfare, I would have bet that the pregnancy had triggered the violence. Many a baby-daddy flipped at the idea of being saddled with 18 years of child support, yet Tatiana had asked about abortion within minutes of hearing the news. Could this man have wanted her to keep the child? Or was he more worried about the information jeopardizing a career—or marriage.

I paused. A slate sky merged with the sea of a similar hue creating a glimpse of infinity. A trick of light in the salt spray brought Tatiana's face into focus. I remembered how she looked when I explained the results of her pregnancy test. Her nostrils had flared and her mouth had twisted as though she had smelled something rotten.

"*Ya ne khochu yego!*" she had said with undisguised disgust. "I don't want it!"

It reminded me of the vehemence some women felt when they discovered they had been impregnated in a shameful way—by rape, by someone they loathed, and especially if incest had occurred. Was that the reason she hadn't considered an alternative—if only briefly?

"Can't you just take it now?" she had asked the doctor. He had told her that he was not equipped. We assured her that it could wait until Florida.

I had assumed she would keep it a secret; now I wondered who she told. Some girls would tell a parent out of misguided spite. Grisha was temperamental enough to explode and hurt her accidentally, although most crimes of passion—if that was what it was—were more likely to be committed by a love.

I picked up my walking pace. What about someone who would not have supported a termination? Who could have offered his unconditional support and begged her to make a life with him? The fathers with whom I had worked had been with people who lived marginal lives and men who avoided responsibility like the plague. My heart beat faster and my respiration became more erratic. People who worked—or traveled on ships—were generally doing fine. Still, even someone with money could be a creep. In recent years, celebrities and politicians were being unmasked as serial offenders—you couldn't tell by the hype and veneer, which is probably why so many women were duped.

I thought about Vance. Although an unlikely suspect on the surface, there *had* been something wrong with his affect, although—to be fair—shock came in many forms and his preternatural calmness could have been a coping mechanism. One whiff of his Clive Christian cologne was a big turnoff—at least to me. Something about the lemony-jasmine combo seemed to magnetize the little old ladies who followed in his wake as did his slick art sales pitches that promoted Kinkade and Kandinsky in the same sentence.

I stopped and leaned against the rail trying to remember where I had seen Tatiana cozy up to him. Entertainers and certain levels of staff—like the shop and spa personnel and the officers—were allowed to use the passenger venues as long as they were in uniform, or if off-duty, wearing appropriate attire and name tags. Vance always sported a custom-tailored suit and Tatiana had an array of gossamer gowns with slits that revealed her ivory legs. I recalled passing behind them on an upper tier overlooking the atrium when we were overnighting in Livorno. I was standing just behind them as two tenors were performing a short concert of operatic favorites. During their lilting rendition of Bizet's *Pearl Fishers* duet, I had noticed Vance slipping his arm around Tatiana's waist and giving her an affectionate squeeze as the tenors hit the sweet notes, "*Oui, c'est elle! C'est la déesse.*"

Vance translated, "Yes, it is she! It's the goddess." She had slipped into his embrace, her limbs soft and melting. My thought had been: How adorable! And, maybe I had misjudged him because I had supposed that he preferred men. Although you never know what someone was capable of like all those terrorists whose neighbors thought they were just unobtrusive people who "kept to themselves." To me, Vance's persona was more lightweight than lethal.

How could anyone who knew this sweet soul have harmed her! Dilating the circle of potential killers from the few men she knew well opened up the field to any of several thousand men on board who could have fixated on her—even fantasized that she would welcome his attention—and when rebuffed… In a few days, almost every passenger would be dispersed to the four winds, their cabins scrubbed and disinfected, their very essence erased. "We'll never know the unknowable" was one of David's infuriating axioms because it was both true and vexing. He had been influenced when his college roommate had insisted he go to a lecture by the Dalai Lama. After that, David found meditation both relaxed and provided insights. He spouted phrases like "learning to embrace your anger" and how kindness always triumphed over hate and "if you think you are too small, try sleeping with a mosquito." Of course, Bodhi was David's choice of a name because he wanted his son to be compassionate and optimistic—traits I continued to encourage. Sometimes I wondered if he had been the survivor would he have been able to transform his fury and find the peace that had eluded me.

My forehead felt as if it was going to explode with the impossibility of ever finding an answer. I rummaged in my tote for my migraine medication before remembering that I had hardly eaten all day.

□ □ □

Everyone must have slept in on this lazy sea day, had a late breakfast, and now congregated *en masse* for an even later lunch. I made one full pass of the circuitous buffet to avoid an impetuous choice. The luncheon's theme was "South of the Border" and the make-your-own-taco station was decorated with Mexican *papel picado* doily banners. Standing in front of a pyramid of fresh cactus—an unusual mid-Atlantic provision!—a chef was peeling and slicing the fruit to order. He offered me a piece that dripped with juice.

"Mmmm!" It was perfectly ripe, cool, with an unexpected peachy taste. He gave me a toothy smile and placed a serving on my tray.

At the hot station, I selected a mushroom-and-leek quiche, green beans with crumbled bacon, then added a dollop of hollandaise to some poached salmon. All the window seats were taken, so I carried my tray toward the beverage station, which was so noisy with clanking ice and glassware that most people avoided it.

Before I had unrolled the silverware from the lime-tinted napkin, a server named Kester asked, "Arnold Palmer, right?"

"How do you keep everyone's preferences straight?"

"Not everyone. You are a special lady."

Callista once said, "Ship life makes the memory sharper." She explained when someone is separated from most of responsibilities for family, their uncluttered brain has space for names and faces. "Besides, it's short-term memory because every week you can purge to make room for a new set."

"*Dobryy den.*"

I looked up just as Oleksander Lopatkino slid his tray across from mine and took a seat without inquiring whether it was all right. "Good afternoon to you, too. I am so very sorry for your tragic loss," I said in Russian.

"It can't be possible!" The deep dimple on his chin bristled with twenty-four hours of stubble. "Who would harm my *dorogoy kotehok*?" His back, usually as rigid as a skater about to perform a triple axel, was hunched like a beggar.

"Darling kitten…" I echoed softly. "I can't imagine how you're—"

Three gongs heralded the captain's afternoon announcement. "This is your captain speaking. We are maintaining our southwesterly course at an average speed of eighteen knots. The weather is partly cloudy with a slight chance of showers and an unseasonably warm high of twenty-one Celsius, seventy Fahrenheit and a low of eighteen Celsius and sixty-four Fahrenheit. One important message: A patient in the medical center requires blood transfusions. If you are blood type A positive—that is Alpha positive—or AB positive—that is Alpha Bravo positive—and you are carrying a donor identification card, please register at the clinic on the Pacific Deck. Thank you for any assistance you might offer. Good afternoon from the bridge."

"There was a medical emergency on my deck an hour or so ago," I told Olek. "I wonder if it's that person."

"All the crew, we carry the cards. Me, I'm very rare. AB negative. They know to call me."

"I'm actually A positive, but I am not permitted to donate because I once had hepatitis."

Kester delivered my iced tea and lemonade combo. "White coffee?" he asked Olek.

"*Terima kasih*," the entertainer thanked him in Indonesian.

I had never spoken more than a few passing words with Olek previously. He had seemed aloof.

Callista had mentioned he resented playing second fiddle to Tatiana since he had once been the star.

"My Tania...she was perfect in every way," he said with an exaggerated moan.

"A beautiful girl," I agreed. Suddenly my salmon look anemic and unappealing. I replaced my fork. "How did you meet?"

"At Cirque in Montreal. They were building *Konditori*. The theme was a cafeteria of the sweetest elements of the universe."

"I've never seen that one."

"It was a long time ago. Tania was only thirteen." He closed his eyes. "One day I was asked to evaluate a young performer and told to wait in a private rehearsal space. Then this man—Grisha—came in wheeling a small case like you put overhead on an airplane—what do they call it—?"

"Rollaboard?"

"Yes! That size. I asked him what he wanted and he said he had been told to leave the case in that room. As soon as the door closed, the case's top popped open." Olek lifted his arms out to me like a supplicant. "First one hand fluttered into the air, then a shoulder, then an elbow, then very slowly, like a flower opening to the sun, she unfolded herself and entered into my life—and my heart—forever."

His voice fell into the barest whisper. "The box, it was only this long and this wide." He gestured about three feet by two feet. "And she wasn't a small woman. I am only a bit taller."

"I hadn't realized that."

He saw me sizing him up. "I'm one point eight meters...so she would be...in US...about five feet, nine inches."

"It's almost impossible to imagine how she managed it."

Olek closed his eyes. "One of a kind..."

"So that was the beginning of 'the girl in the box'?"

"At first it was a large Fabergé-style egg. In *Konditori,* I was the stork who delivered it to the candy shop wrapped in a sack. We flew over the audience, me with ten-feet long mechanical wings, then I lowered the egg to a revolving glass stage and flew off with only the cloth in my beak. The orchestra played a music-box song as the egg slowly cracked and she emerged in a shimmery baby chick costume. It was magical every time—like birth itself!" He pointed to himself. "Every time...*Gordyy.*"

"Proud? Like a father." I gestured for him to eat.

We picked at our food. Olek was with Tatiana almost every day. If she needed to release pent-up steam, she might have complained to him.

"I expect you were in a difficult place between her and her father."

Olek looked up at the ceiling, his long, loosened hair—which he usually tied behind his neck—dusted his bony shoulders. "You have no idea! I tried to tell him that the only way he could keep her would be to let her go."

"In what way?"

"She hated to perform. No—that's not what I meant, she was fine once we were a few minutes into the routine. But the more he pressured her, the more nervous she became. When she was younger, she was more carefree, the more prominent her role, the more she froze."

"So, the more he pressured her, the worse it became," I said, using the technique of validating to prompt him on. I speared my cactus fruit with a knife.

"What's that?" Olek asked.

I offered him a slice. "*Khorosho*."

"Yes, surprisingly good." I cut him another slice. "Are you saying that she had stage fright?"

"Yes. Many great artists like Andrea Bocelli, Renée Fleming, even your Barbra Streisand have it." I nodded for him to continue. "Grisha—he made it worse—sometimes laughing at her, other times yelling, and once…" He rubbed his temples. "Once I saw Grisha try to slap it out of her!" He released a heaving sob. "*Pochemu? Pochemu*? Why?"

"You sound like you really cared for her."

"Always. From the first moment I saw her I knew—although she was too young. Then, after my accident, they wanted her to train with a new partner. It was a disaster. She didn't trust him and they had to take away the gasp elements."

"What's that?"

"It's what makes an audience's gasp because it seems so unbelievable. That's what we could do together—night after night, show after show." He smiled shyly. "Then one of our friends, who does a chair balancing act, was offered a ship contract. Seems crazy to do that at sea, yet he's been very successful. He explained that the performances were shorter and not anywhere near as strenuous as Cirque because the expectations are lower on a moving ship.

The money—not so good—but free food and cabins."
He waited a beat. "And safer—not so many chances."
His hand reached out and held mine tightly.

Every fiber wanted to pull back yet I pounced.
"You were lovers." A statement, not a question.

He lifted his head and stared at me with glistening
eyes. "How else could I anticipate every flutter, every
glance? How else could she trust me to catch her in
mid-air?" All of sudden his back straightened and he
half rose from his chair.

An officer with three stripes on his epaulet and a
regal bearing slowed as he came toward us. From his
uniform, I knew he was a very senior officer, but I
couldn't place him.

"Staff Captain Castanga," Olek said as a greeting
and also to inform me.

"Sorry to disturb you, Mrs. Lanier and Mr.
Lopatkino." He gestured for Olek to sit back down.
"Officer Brandt has been trying to reach Mrs.
Lanier."

"I've been out on deck."

"Of course, madam, but the clinic has been so
overwhelmed with blood donors, he wondered if you
could meet him there at fifteen hundred. He tapped
his watch face. Three o'clock."

"That would be fine," I said.

He touched his right hand to the brim of his hat
and moved past the beverage station and out to the
corridor.

Olek exhaled. "My boss."

"Don't you work for an entertainment company?"

"Yes, but on board I answer to the staff captain. If you break a rule, he's the one who will give you the boot."

"I thought the captain had the final say."

"Technically, although the staff captain is the ship's sheriff, priest, and judge."

"What about Mae Ocampo and security?"

"They also answer to Castanga."

"Including Rolf Brandt?"

"That *mudak*!" He misread my expression as not understanding the word. "You know, asshole." He clenched his fists. "He's only temporary, from the Castle. So, I'm not sure.

"Why don't you like Rolf?"

"He's a two-faced son of a bitch. Did you know Agata?"

"Sure, in the spa."

"She's the only one who knew how to work on my injured shoulder. And she did wonders for Tania. Brandt heard a rumor that she did 'special favors' for some of her clients—you know what they call a 'happy ending'?"

"Yes."

"Well, he wanted to catch her, so he offered her a big tip—" He snorted. "She knew enough to refuse him, although he canned her anyway." Olek sucked in his bony cheeks revealing the outline of the skull beneath. "That Nazi ruined her life because his pride was wounded. Tania was furious." He grunted at a memory. "Tania had such a funny way with words. She'd ask me to make an appointment with Agata cause 'my knees are screaming' or 'my neck is firing bullets.' She said that Agata had the golden touch."

He drummed his fingers on the table. "Did you know that she was stage frightened?"

"What? Oh, you mean 'stage fright.'"

He stood and gestured for us to leave the buffet area through a sliding glass door that led to a terrace.

"Most people are tense before a performance," I began as soon as we were outside.

"With her it was like a disease you always have—what's that called?"

"Chronic?"

"Yes, chronic. She tied herself up in knots inside before she did it on the outside. It became even worse when the head of corporate entertainment was coming on board to evaluate everyone before the January contract renewals." He looked over his shoulder where two women were at the rail waving to someone on the deck below. He took a step away from them. "After my accident, they discovered I had high blood pressure. When the doctor gave me the medication, he said I might perform better because of its side effect: it takes away the stage fright. I didn't think I had that problem until suddenly I was able to do some of the more daring routines that I had given up after my accident. I had convinced myself that my body wasn't up to it, although it was more mental than physical. Once again I had the sense that I could conquer the world. The better I got, the more Tania feared she was one inch from disaster." He tossed his head as if to rid himself of a tainted memory. "If she started to panic, her father would try to snap her out of it by pinching her ear or pulling out some hair." His face flamed. "That's why I suggested she try my tablets. They worked miracles. Is there any chance they could have harmed her?"

"I doubt it, but you need to tell somebody. In Florida they will test to see if she was poisoned or given drugs to knock her out."

"You mean the rape drug?" Tears filled his eyes. "I shouldn't have offered them."

"You meant no harm. The case is much bigger than that now."

"The point is she didn't ask me anything about them because she was so used to swallowing whatever Grisha gave her." He wiped his eyes with his fists like a little boy. "The way she was found—without clothes…makes me *psikh*—crazy!"

"Do you want me to tell the doctor that she took something for stage fright that wasn't on her prescription list?"

"Just a half a pill—she was so little—that's all she needed." He looked at me warily. "Do you have to tell them I gave them to her?"

"What's wrong with the truth?"

"You're right. I have no reason to be ashamed. I just hope they can find out who did it. When they do, I want to be the first to gouge out his eyes!"

☐ ☐ ☐

When I got off on the Pacific Deck, Rolf was waiting to get into the elevator. When he caught sight of me, he stepped off backward. "The emergency case is not going well," he said, massaging the sides of his nose as if to relieve sinus pain.

"I got your message a few minutes ago. What's happening?"

"Marius—Dr. Kotze—says it's a perforated ulcer and our consultants at the Cleveland Clinic in Ft. Lauderdale want us to evacuate her." He opened his mouth to speak but sneezed hardily, then stifled the next. "We have a contract with their telemedicine division." He opened the clinic door partway. "I won't be able to join you here because we're having a conference regarding a potential evacuation."

"But—"

"Officer Ocampo will take my place. Probably wiser to have another woman in the room anyway." He cleared his throat noisily. "Also, I might be coming down with that flu." He opened the door the rest of the way and as I walked through, he closed it behind me.

I heard Olek's Nazi epithet ringing in my ears, but the man who headed down the corridor seemed bent by the weight of the death and concerned for the critical patient. I suspected he was more of a marshmallow than a martinet. Everyone was wary of any form of law enforcement. I was accustomed to distrustful families, guarded words, and guilty glances. "I'm from the Department of Children and Families and I'm here to help you" was met with both fear and scorn. As much as I'd liked Agata—my massage angel too—it was possible that she was dismissed for a valid reason but blamed Officer Brandt to save face. In the US, she could have filed a sexual harassment complaint, but lax maritime labor laws did not favor a young Filipina woman. As David used to say, "There are no winners in the battle of the sexes."

All the seats in the waiting room were taken. A deckhand was setting up more stacking chairs. There were bottles of water and pitchers of apple and orange juice on the receptionist's counter as well as one tray of tea sandwiches and another of mini éclairs.

"I'm AB, actually," a frizzy-haired woman was saying, "but they said they still could use me."

"I know the woman who needs the blood. Her name is Claudia," said a woman with a British accent. "She's been complaining of stomach pains for a long time. She's on our trivia team—and quite good, especially on American football." The listener's head bobbed to keep the gossip flowing. "She lives in Albany, New York, and her husband Jerry just retired from a state job—something to do with pesticide regulation. This is their twenty-fifth cruise with Empire and they got upgraded into a mini-suite."

I was impressed with how much the woman knew, although in this artificial hothouse, friendships bloomed quickly and faded within hours of disembarkation.

"Oh, I know them," a woman in a many-pouched photographer's vest chimed in. "We were on the same barhopping tour in Venice. Her husband tried to order her a soda after the first stop, but she said how many times in her life would she be able to sample wines in Italy. I suppose he was right, because she felt dizzy and they returned to the ship early."

The nurse behind the counter called, "Mrs. Frazier, we're ready for you." The woman with AB blood stood up. "Next victim," she said with a grin. "It's a privilege to help, don't you think?"

Callista entered the clinic and nodded in recognition when she saw me. She raised her voice to silence the buzz in the room. "On behalf of the captain, we are honored that so many of you have volunteered." She held up some cards. Please take one of these before you leave, even if you can't donate for some reason. It's a coupon for credit in the gift shop as our way of thanking you. A bottle of champagne will also be delivered to your cabins."

"What time will the pop choir rehearsal be tomorrow?" a man standing to one side asked Callista.

"Two-forty-five in the Colonnade," she replied automatically. Then she gestured with her chin for me to follow her to the corridor.

"Thanks again for agreeing to be…a witness."

"I didn't exactly rush to volunteer like these donors."

Callista rubbed her temples. "It's one of those there-but-for-the-grace-of-God-go-I' situations, isn't it?"

"Rolf mentioned an evacuation. How is that possible in the middle of the friggin' ocean?"

"That's hardly definite. They have to make certain they are considering all the contingencies so if the worst happens—" She sucked in her lower lip. "Will you tell Marius something for me?"

I blinked. "Who?"

"Sorry, Dr. Kotze. He needs to be told about how she got…" She patted her tummy as if saying "pregnant" might be a jinx.

"Do you know who the father is?"

"No, it's not that. She stopped taking those pills for a while because she thought they were giving her headaches." Callista exhaled a groan. "She said the funniest thing: 'The communists haven't invaded the summer house in too many months.' I didn't know what the hell she meant until she explained that it was a Russian expression for getting your period! She thought that if she stopped those pills, her body would regulate itself. I don't think she thought she could become pregnant until after her periods resumed."

"That's what some women think after they've had a baby, but you're fertile a few weeks before your period returns."

She blew out another a long sigh. "Anyway, tell Marius what I said."

Callista made a gotta-go gesture, then whispered. "I think she was afraid of something…or someone. It could have been her partner."

"Olek? What makes you say that?"

"She had begun to fear rehearsals."

"Why?"

"She said he was angry at her for making so many mistakes lately and wanted her to spend more time strength-training."

"If he thought she was out of shape, then there's no hope for anyone else."

"Right, her conditioning was superb, but she told me that she was often light-headed and was terrified it could happen in a performance." Callista shook her head. "I told her that she shouldn't keep to such a stringent diet. Do you think it could have been low blood pressure or blood sugar?" She looked down at the carpeting. "Or the…baby."

I hadn't realized that they were so close, maybe because the performer was younger and didn't speak English. "When did you find out?"

"She told me the same day she took the test."

"How were you able to understand each other?"

"There's an app!"

Apparently everyone else knew about these. "No point in learning a language anymore," I said more to myself.

"It's amazing. Everybody on the ship uses them. There are dozens of languages amongst the crew. You speak normally and it both says the translation and writes it out." She closed her eyes. "And…well…for some reason we were on the same wavelength." She gestured that she had to get going.

As Callista headed out, I stood for a moment and stared toward the flapping vertical curtain that partially veiled I-95, not far from where I'd last seen Tatiana's ashen leg and golden braid. The clinic door opened as the lady with AB blood departed. I slipped inside. Guests were licking chocolate from their fingers and laughing at a joke that belied the serious reason they were there. The critically ill woman— Claudia something—was only a few doors down. Maybe they would have been more subdued if they had known that the body of a murdered entertainer had been moved from the chilled morgue and was lying nearby.

▢ ▢ ▢

"Good afternoon, Mrs. Lanier." I was surprised by Officer Ocampo, who had come in behind me.

Joyce Barbarosa gestured for us to follow her. She led us to a darkened examining room. For the second before she flicked on the light my heart raced because I thought Tatiana might be in there. Mae Ocampo, the head of security for the vessel, gestured for me to sit. I took one of the two chairs. I pointed to other, but she remained in a military at-ease stance.

Most of the security officers appeared to be from India, although Callista had told me they were Nepalese. "They're former military—from the famous Gurkha regiment—have you heard of them?"

"That's right. They come aboard as a cohesive group with their own chain of command."

"They served in the British military and carried a tribal sword or something."

"The kukri—it's curved and deadly, although it's not standard issue on ships!" She grinned.

"Isn't Officer Ocampo Filipina?"

"Yes, and with a very impressive background. Mae was first in her class at the Philippine Military Academy—their West Point—and has further training in cyber warfare. Before she took this job, she worked on computer security for the fleet at the Castle headquarters."

Officer Ocampo coughed.

"I hope you aren't coming down with the cruise crud," I said to bridge the awkward silence.

"I receive all the inoculations, Mrs. Lanier."

There was something about this petite woman's ramrod posture and lowered chin that I found paradoxically both endearing and austere—just the qualities I needed for a character in my latest book: a good-hearted matron in a juvenile detention facility. I decided to encapsulate some of Mae's mannerisms when I did my final revision.

"We're finally ready." Joyce called into our tiny cell and led us to the emergency operating room.

Dr. Kotze was gowned with a surgical mask pushed down below his chin. The nurse passed out latex gloves. I hesitated. "Just a precaution in case you accidentally touch something."

"Sorry to have pushed this back all day"—the doctor's apology was directed at me—"but we do have a rampant virus on our hands."

"No worries," I said. "We're all going to the same place."

If ever we needed a light moment, this was it, but the joke was lost on the others in the narrow room where the body of Tatiana Zlatogrivova was laid out on one of the regular examination tables that was draped with a large white sheet, making it seem as if she were an offering on a banquet table. Another sheet covered her completely.

"Doctor?" Joyce asked with her hand on the doorknob.

"Yes, that's fine. I'll call when I need you."

"Normally a nurse would witness the whole rape kit procedure," the doctor said, "but she's needed with the blood donors, so I've only asked her to step back in when I start taking the required samples."

"Do you usually have two witnesses?" I asked.

"This is a unique circumstance," he replied. His meaning was clear: The other victims had been alive.

He shifted toward Mae. "We're trying to store enough blood for the next thirty-six hours. Is there word on how the plans for an evacuation are proceeding?"

"If the cold front doesn't get this far east, it might be possible because Monday we'll be only two hundred miles south of Bermuda. If we divert slightly north, we'll be within helicopter range."

"Can the ship handle that kind of delay and stay on schedule?" I asked, knowing that they were scheduled to turn around in Ft. Lauderdale and leave the same evening for a Panama Canal cruise.

"Diversions for weather are always factored into our timetable," Officer Ocampo said, "because we try to give our guests the smoothest possible sail. When we're ahead of schedule, they just slow the vessel—if we're behind, they can speed up."

We all fell silent for the same reason. In order to avoid the ghostly shape in the room, my eyes were riveted on the doctor's prematurely receding hairline.

I took a deep breath and was assaulted by the repugnant smell of compost mingling with medical antiseptic and the industrial mint of janitorial products. I covered my nose and mouth and inhaled the faint scent of gardenia in my hand cream.

The doctor opened a jar of Vick's VapoRub, swiped some on his finger, and coated his upper lip. "Trade secret," he said and passed it to Mae, who mimicked him before handing it to me.

He turned to a medical cart. A large carton with an unbroken seal was waiting on a sterile blue drape. "Following US protocols, we use a Physical Evidence Recovery Kit—or Perk kit. At the end, I'll need both of you to sign the procedure sheet. As I said, normally, we do this with just one witness—but the Castle insisted that someone other than an Empire employee observe so that we could not be accused of withholding evidence to protect the company."

He began organizing the tubes and containers for fluid samples, bags for collecting clothing and other physical evidence, swabs, and a large folded piece of paper.

"How often do you do this, Dr. Kotze?" I asked.

"Rarely," he said as he continued to lay out supplies in rows on the surgical tray.

"Mostly crew or guests?"

"Guests, actually. So far it's been mainly American women."

"Because…?"

Mae jumped in. "They are the most knowledgeable about what constitutes rape," she said to me, then turned to the doctor. "We need to educate the crew better. No matter what I say, the ladies think their job is at stake."

"When you have free-flowing alcohol and those inane adverts for 'whatever happens here, stays here,' it encourages irresponsibility." The doctor's usually modulated voice verged on anger. "The worst is when a passenger accuses a crewmember. No matter what really happened, someone loses his job."

I knew he was talking about a female guest accusing a male crewmember, but I wondered about Agata. If she had been raped by someone—say a passenger—or Rolf—would she have submitted to a medical examination? And if she had, what laws protected her?

The doctor broke into my thoughts. "I understand this is not your first time observing a kit."

"My cases always involved...children." I closed my eyes slightly, remembering the last one—just a few weeks before David was killed. Poor kid had sexually transmitted warts on her genitals that her drug-addled mother called her "flowers." Her parents had allowed men to "play games" with her in exchange for drugs.

The doctor put his mask in place and picked up an edge of the sheet that covered the body.

"First, please get an all-over impression, Mae, because you may be asked to compare with the photographic evidence. Rolf has the ones you took at the scene, right?"

"Yes, and they've been forwarded to the C"— Mae started to use the nickname of headquarters in the UK—"To London."

The doctor turned to me. "I've been taking photos daily to document the changes of coloration, which was requested by the US authorities."

"Is that what you call livor mortis?" Mae asked.

"Very good."

"I took a class in forensic pathology many years ago," Mae said.

"Then, as you know, when the heart stops, blood settles in the capillaries and this results in the bluish coloration. However, at pressure points the blood pools and the color darkens." He waved to the draped body. "For instance, we notice some reddening of the peripheral margins, which was caused by refrigeration."

I pressed my back to the wall and took a deep whiff of the Vicks, then shifted my weight to accommodate the ship's increased rocking. As a vibration shuddered from my feet and up my spine, an acrid taste rose in my throat.

"Last year we had two drowning victims," Mae continued. "They were quite—pink."

"That's due to higher levels of oxyhemoglobin. Also, certain poisons change the skin color as does the cause of death. I've seen two cases of septicemia on ships—both crew—and they had a mottled bronze-like color to their livor."

"Do you remember the suicide who overdosed?" he asked.

"I don't believe I was onboard," she said.

"Oh, right." In full-professor mode the doctor continued, "Some drugs like sulphonamides cause a pronounced cyanosis. Interestingly, I could have prescribed Bactrim for her recent infection, but since she once had a reaction to it, I switched to Cipro…"

The doctor's voice droned nauseatingly; he was procrastinating. The form beneath the sheet morphed into a memory of my father before he was laid out in his coffin. My mother absently touched his cheek and then his mouth—before his jaw was wired shut—gaped. The mortician had babbled something about a reflex. I still have dreams of apologizing to my father for burying him prematurely.

After that, I avoided showings until it became a necessary part of my job. Their names—my failures—are engraved on my heart. First there was Jamal, who'd swallowed prescription drugs he'd stolen from his foster mother thinking he'd get high with his friends. Then Suzette, D'Vaughn, Kiki, Traydon, Scarlotta, and Qiana—all killed by a parent, relative, or in Kiki's case, an older brother. Nine-month-old Qiana was drowned by her stepfather. In the hospital, they'd found multiple welts on her buttocks and there were red ants crawling in her diaper—she'd been wailing incessantly from the vicious bites, when her stepfather—high on meth—flipped out. Not a single one vaccinated me against the horror of the next little body...least of all for David's.

When I blinked away my teary film, the doctor was folding the drape like he was preparing for origami. Tatiana's face had the pale blue of a tropical sea. Her golden braid was draped discreetly across her breasts to conceal her nipples.

"Both of you were at the scene and saw the way she was coiled in the laundry trolley," the doctor began. "Her buttocks were at the bottom and her legs protruded out from the linens that covered her. Please note that the top of her trunk has remained blanched and waxy except for that thin red margin I mentioned. The discoloration you see in the lower pelvis is due to the livor mortis, not trauma." He gestured to her legs. "Notice they are blotchy. This does not surprise me because when I examined them after she fell during a practice, she had many contusions in various states of healing. Her act—was just that—a painful performance with a forced smile. Her many hematomas are because her damaged capillary walls allowed blood to seep into the surrounding interstitial tissues."

"It looks like she was beaten." I gestured toward larger purpled blotches on her thighs and forearms.

"Those are Tardieu's spots—post-mortem hemorrhages. The coroner will have to study her medical records to figure out not only the cause of death but what marks are remarkable and what might be due to her ah…unusual profession."

"Could it have been anything besides murder?" Mae asked.

"I don't see how, although some of the findings may have been caused by an inherited condition."

"What do you mean?" I asked.

"Remember when you translated for us the first time and I asked her whether she'd ever been tested for Ehlers-Danlos syndrome?"

"Yes," I said, although I hadn't paid much attention. "What is that?"

"A defect of the connective tissues that results in reduced amounts of collagen—the 'glue' that adds strength and elasticity to support the skin, muscles, and ligaments. In her profession it would make her even more supple. It's inherited, so maybe her mother, who was also a contortionist, had it."

The doctor moved to the end of the table and waved his hand above Tatiana's knees. "The last time I examined her I noted this same discoloration, but it was much less obvious—it's called spontaneous ecchymoses—and it could be an indicator of that syndrome."

"I've seen similar bruises on children who we thought were being abused," I said. "Could some of them have had that condition?"

114

"Doubtful that they had EDS—as it's abbreviated—because it's fairly rare."

"Are there any noticeable injection sites?" Mac asked, changing the subject.

Dr. Kotze took a step backward. "What do you mean?"

"We found a sharps disposal container in the father's stateroom and are cataloging the vials of injectable medication."

Dr. Kotze looked to the ceiling. "She did mention some steroid use—just not how recently." He bit his lower lip. "The Russians are more cavalier about performance enhancements, even in competitions that require testing."

"Because she didn't work directly for Empire, she wasn't subject to our random drug testing program," Mae said. "Every crewmember is tested on a rotating basis. One of my staff has to observe while the sample is produced, seal it, and bring it to the clinic for testing."

"What happens if they're positive?"

"They're sent home at the next port. There are no second chances."

"I will need the list of all of her medications," the doctor said to Mae, "and I'll have to send the actual containers too."

"We've already collected everything from their cabin, including a case filled with syringes and bottles—most with Russian labels. I have a list of the ones we could understand. Mae pulled out her mobile phone and read: "Dexamethasone, Kenalog…Ser-a-steem…" She squinted and enlarged the image. "Sorry, Ser-o-stim, Zorbtive, Nutropin, Aristospan…"

"What the hell?" the doctor shouted. "Some of those, like Kenalog, are corticosteroids—" The doctor ran his gloved hand through his thick curly hair, then realized he had compromised sterility, tore off both gloves, and reached for a new set. "Serostim and Nutropin are human growth hormones!" He snapped on a new glove.

"Why would an adult take growth hormones?" I asked.

"Some people believe it prevents aging or boosts energy." Dr. Kotze swallowed hard, trying to compose himself. "Maybe he experimented on himself. I sure as hell hope he wasn't giving it to Tatiana. She was already having some issues that could have been caused by steroids—which she denied taking."

"What kind of problems, doctor?" Mae asked.

"Hair loss, hoarseness, and frequent infections. She'd been on treatment for a severe UTI since Barcelona. I think that's the first time we asked Mrs. Lanier to translate."

I nodded. I had worn a mask when I met her because she had presented with a high fever and chills and was relieved when the diagnosis was not something contagious.

Mae blinked. "U...T...eye?"

"Urinary tract infection," I filled in. The sexually active teens in my caseload had them frequently due to poor hygiene combined with promiscuous activity.

"Luckily she responded quickly to a short course of ciprofloxacin." The doctor shook his head. "On one hand, she had an exemplary diet—as organic as possible and she was deathly afraid of GMOs—but apparently these quack drugs were just fine!" His face wrinkled in disgust. "Toxicology will have to sort out the chemical soup in her system."

I glanced at Tatiana hoping she might magically waken long enough to answer a few questions. With her long braid and celadon-green skin, she could have passed for Sleeping Beauty.

"There's no obvious trauma," Mae stated.

"If she hadn't been found in that—that basket, my preliminary assessment would have been either an intentional or accidental overdose."

"Could she have been smothered?" I had known more than one child whose parent claimed he died from SIDS had been covered with a pillow.

"She's negative for signs of cyanosis or petechial hemorrhages in the eyelids; no blood oozed from her mouth, although in some cases of homicidal smothering, death is due to reflex cardiac arrest leaving very few signs."

"Petechial what?" I asked.

"Tiny spots on the skin caused by broken capillary blood vessels," Mae responded.

The doctor tilted his head in surprise. "*Very* good. How did you know that, Mae?"

"I trained as a paramedic in the Philippines."

"Your credentials will be valuable in an inquiry."

There was a knock on the door and Joyce slipped inside. "Bermuda accepted the transfer. The bridge is setting up the evacuation."

"How's the patient holding up?" the doctor asked.

"Stabilized. I talked her husband into getting some rest."

"Could you assist me now?"

"Yes, doctor."

Dr. Kotze turned back to the examining table. "Let's do the kit."

☐ ☐ ☐

"Nurse Barbarosa has certified by her signature that she witnessed me breaking the integrity seal on the box before you arrived so I could fill out the preliminary forms," Dr. Kotze said. "To the question about how any hours it's been since the 'assault,' I wrote 'unknown.' Where it asked if she showered or bathed since, I wrote 'unlikely.'" He cleared his throat. "I think I we can presume that this examination is being conducted within the requested one-hundred-twenty hours of a sexual assault."

"If one occurred," the security officer added.

"Which is the reason for the exam," the doctor said with a hint of annoyance.

"Why that time frame?" I asked.

"The paperwork presumes the victim is alive and that she hasn't washed, laundered her clothes—and that there haven't been more sexual encounters." He nodded to me. "As you know, a coroner would usually do this, but the rape kit will give us fresher evidence."

I concentrated on the box with the orange biohazard notice as Nurse Barbarosa held out a new pair of latex gloves from the kit to the doctor, then exchanged hers as well. She picked up the box and read off the registered number: "Kilo, Forty-two dash Nine, Six, Zero, Mike, Quebec, Ten, Foxtrot." The doctor confirmed that a page of stickers repeated the same number. He picked up the paper marked "Patient Consent Form" and scribbled "N/A Patient deceased." He opened an envelope marked "Survivor" and fanned out a number of pamphlets. "Joyce, maybe you might want to keep these in your office."

He handed them to the nurse who placed them on a counter, careful to only let the paper touch the metal to preserve sterility for her gloves.

"I've already done the initial physical exam to assess injuries, lacerations and any obvious broken bones and will include those findings with the kit. I've noted all contusions, broken skin, and let's all be alert for possible injection sites. The box will include a copy of the first set of photographs taken by Officer Ocampo."

"And your subsequent ones to show deterioration?" Mae asked.

"Yes, of course." He paused. "First sample."

Joyce read from the instructions. "Oral." She lifted a drape off a tray of implements. "The first swab goes back into the package, the second gets rubbed on a slide, which must be air dried." With a scissors, she cut down the shaft of a cylindrical container on a dotted line and angled the blades forward to create a wider opening. "Flap aeration," she announced. The doctor stood over Tatiana's head and held out his hand. Joyce tilted the tube so he could grasp the swab's wooden end. Holding Tatiana's jaw open, he rubbed the swab around the outside of her mouth, then back and forth on the upper and lower gums before pressing it into her cheeks deeply. He reached for tweezers with flat ends and lifted her tongue before rolling the swab's tip underneath, swiped inside her cheek, then placed it into the transport tube. Joyce marked its label and placed it in an envelope that she closed with a tamper-proof sticker.

"Please initial here under 'Collector's initials.'" Joyce handed the doctor the pen, then took back the envelope, pressed it closed and affixed a pre-printed sticker with the kit number. "You witnesses will sign the master form for chain-of-custody verification."

The doctor placed some Tootsie-Roll shaped cotton dental rolls in Tatiana's mouth to keep her jaw open.

Joyce opened the next package. "Buccal."

This stick had a brush-like end that the doctor used to scrape the inside Tatiana's cheeks.

"What's the difference between buccal and oral?" the security chief asked.

"The buccal is for DNA to differentiate the victim from a potential assailant," Dr. Kotze replied. "The next step normally would be trace evidence on clothing." He turned to Mae. "Everything in the laundry hamper—including the linens on top of her—was secured by you, right?"

"They're in evidence bags and locked in my safe."

"Bring them to Joyce after we finish and we'll send them in the kit's clothing envelope."

While they conferred about how to get all the evidence together, I stared at a newspaper-sized piece of folded white paper. When a child came in for rape kit, a member of the child-protection team would undress her over the spread-open paper. Any hairs, pieces of grass, dirt from shoes, or other telltale evidence would be collected on the paper, which was then folded back up and placed into the prescribed envelope. I remember one terrified little girl—less than five—shivering before she was redressed into a child's hospital gown, the snowy paper crinkling under her. Crimson spots splattered the paper and she stamped on them, making footprints with her bare feet. The exam revealed both vaginal and rectal tears that had required stitches under anesthesia. Both the nurse and I wept during that procedure. Ironically, the child's name was Miracle.

"Was any blood found anywhere on her body or in the laundry hamper?" I asked.

"I noted some rusty spots on one sheet," Mae answered.

Joyce shifted her feet impatiently. "I'm going to have to change Mrs. Greenberg's drip in a few minutes."

"Let's wrap this up," the doctor muttered.

Joyce read from the list. "Next is fingernail scrapings, pulled head and pubic hair, plus pubic-hair combings." She opened a larger kit envelope and removed two smaller ones marked "Right Hand" and "Left Hand." She held up a sheet of paper. "Do you want me to read the collection instructions?"

"Not necessary." She handed the doctor a plastic fingernail scraper. "They're filed to the tip," he muttered. He put the minute scrapings from the right hand into a paper bindle before repeating the procedure on the other side. "Doubt these will be useful."

The nurse peeled off another evidence seal and used it to bind the envelope. I knew what was coming next and was relieved that Rolf wasn't in the room. Everyone else had medical training, and as they say, this was not my first rodeo.

The doctor bent closer to her crotch. Like many young women, Tatiana had chosen the pre-pubescent look. My heart clenched thinking of the young girls who had been subjected to the same exam while awake and aware.

"Nothing much to work with here." He tossed the pre-packaged plastic comb in the envelope.

I supposed she wanted to look better in those form-fitting costumes was my first thought because she always seemed so innocent to me—which was ridiculous now that she was pregnant, and dead.

"Tweezers," the doctor said.

"The hair is supposed to be hand-pulled," she whispered.

He bit his lip as he plucked a few tender blond wisps and put them in the unfolded collection bindle. "I've already noted various scrapes and healing cuts in the pubic region, perhaps from shaving, and a few strip-like burns on her inner thighs."

"Probably from waxing strips," the nurse said.

The doctor stood and rolled his shoulders to relieve a cramp.

"Head hair," Joyce said, handing him the tweezers.

He yanked at a blonde filament so hard his arm flew back in an arc.

"Peri and—"

"I know!" For the first time, his composure wavered. I turned away from the table. "Just help me turn her."

The nurse and doctor tried to do this discreetly, but Tatiana's lifeless limbs flopped at unnatural angles. They recomposed her lying on her stomach with her head turned toward the wall. Her tight, boyish butt was the blackest part of her torso. "As you can see, there are no noticeable contusions or lacerations on this side either but the areas of livor mortis are much darker." The nurse unwrapped two long swabs and moistened the tips with the bottle of sterile water that came with the kit.

He dipped the stick between her legs. "This is an area where secretions often pool."

"Don't you use fluorescent light to find stains?" I asked.

"Sorry, no Wood's Lamp on board." He spoke toward the nurse in a facetious voice. "Remind me to order one."

My face burned as if I had been slapped.

The doctor pointed to the camera on the counter. "Officer, would you take a few pictures while she's in this posture?"

Dr. Kotze struggled to spread her rigid legs. The world's bendiest girl would never be supple again.

"Vulvar swab and smear," Joyce said in a hushed tone.

I turned my head to avoid the wiping and inserting.

The doctor clenched and unclenched his hands before using the force necessary to access the secret folds. His motions slowed as he wiped her inner and outer labia. He reached behind his back to hand the nurse the moistened swab but released his grip too quickly. It fell to floor. "Damn it to hell!"

"You can use the one from the penile set."

The doctor repeated his maneuver without moving his left hand, which held open the delicate vault, and inserted two swabs simultaneously and with more force than I expected.

"Can you manage a cervical exam?" Joyce asked.

"*Hel nee*! He cussed in Afrikaans. "I'm not going to shove a speculum into her. They can do it with cameras in Florida without harming tissue." He stepped back from the table. "What's left?"

"There's a urine collection bottle." She waited a beat. "We still have her UTI sample. I'll send it along with an explanation."

"Doctor, I'm confused," Mae said in a bolder tone than usual. "I've processed many rape cases. Normally there are signs of a struggle, bruises on the arms, finger indentations, fingernail scratches, bite marks, bloodshot eyes…"

"She's right," Joyce added. "No bleeding, no marks in unusual places except for what looks like discolorations from aging contusions from her gymnastics."

"Nobody is classifying this as a rape yet," the doctor said. "We know only that she is sexually active and in her first trimester of pregnancy. They will do a more invasive internal exam at the autopsy, which is why I didn't want to risk muddling the evidence. You're right, so far there are no signs of forced penetration, although that can be hard to discern in an experienced adult woman."

"What about DNA?" Mae asked.

"What about it?" The doctor shrugged. "If there is any, it still could be from consensual sex. Semen can be detected for at least a week, which is one of the main reasons they asked us to complete the kit onboard."

"Or...she could have had more than one partner," I added. One of the most unusual cases I had was a set of fraternal twins with different baby daddies, according to the DNA tests.

"Something is bothering me," the officer said. "My first photos showed a dark smudge under her nose. Now it's gone."

"Could have been a smear from makeup?" Joyce asked.

"There was some crusted blood in her nasal passages and I noted some swelling there as well. Probably early cold or sinus symptoms like half the population on this floating flu cesspool," the doctor said, sounding irritated.

Joyce took a step back. Dr. Kotze always seemed as if nothing would ruffle him, but he was obviously frustrated. David had a similar seen-it-all temperament. He used to say, "One loop at a time unravels everything much more neatly than trying to pry the knot loose."

"Also, there was a stain on the sheet in the laundry basket that could have been blood," Mae added softly.

"What about...a seizure?" I offered.

The doctor cocked his head. "Not impossible. She could have bit her tongue or her lip and I could have missed it."

"Good call," Joyce complimented me. "A seizure could cause her to lose bladder or bowel control, which would also leave a stain."

A knock on the door startled me. Joyce opened it a crack. "Yes?" she asked the unseen visitor. "Just a moment." She closed the door firmly. "Mae, Rolf wants you to contact him at five-seven-seven-nine." She indicated a phone on the wall.

Mae stared at her gloves. "It's okay," the doctor said. "You can sign the paperwork without the gloves."

While she made the call, Dr. Kotze flicked the drape open and covered Tatiana gracefully. The nurse tidied the folds on her side of the table.

"Yes, I understand, yes, thank you, yes, I'll tell them." Mae hung up the receiver. "They are definitely planning to evacuate Mrs. Greenberg to Bermuda. And—"

"Yes?"

"They want the rape kit and all the specimens and…" She gestured to the body.

"To go to Bermuda?" Dr. Kotze's voice dropped. "I can't believe the Castle would try an end-run around the US authorities." Directly to me, he said, "How's your FBI going to take that?" Then, to Mae: "Not to mention what the Bermudan technicians are going to make of the all the shit her father pumped into her?" His South African accent burst with contempt. "And why? To make her faster, stronger, ever more amazing." His dark eyes widened as his pupils dilated. "I'd wager he also gave her something for the pain he forced her to endure."

"Narcotics?" I asked.

126

He rubbed his gloved hands. "That man is like a mechanic for a high-performance car. He probably shot her up with whatever she needed to get through the next show."

"Like a race horse," I said, "only doping them is illegal."

Officer Ocampo's pager sounded.

"Please, if you will just sign the paperwork…" The doctor said to her. "We'll close up the slides and pack the box." His hands quivered slightly as he handed me the pen. Joyce pointed out where I needed to sign on several pages. "Mrs. Lanier, on behalf of myself and the—" He made a gesture meant to include the group present and the larger ship community, "I thank you for your cooperation. I also want to apologize for putting you through this thoroughly unpleasant experience. You're free to go."

Passing through the now-empty waiting room and into the corridor, I inhaled deeply, but all I could smell was Vicks. The doctor's mood swing should not have surprised me as much as it did because we'd all clenched our feelings through the ordeal. In retrospect, he had tamped down emotions more fulminating than I would have expected. Maybe because he had been masquerading as an impartial clinician?

Not quite ready to face chattering elevator mates, I turned and paced the other direction. The ship lurched violently. I propped myself against the wall near the passenger elevators to steady myself and closed my eyes. So far, I had attributed something beyond friendship to Olek and Vance—no, more than that—they had volunteered their feelings. Was the doctor's reaction because of the senseless loss of a beautiful and talented young woman or had he—like so many other men—been enthralled by her act? There was no reason why the doctor should have been immune to her eroticism—or her sweet nature.

I unwrapped a foil packet from my pocket—a wet wipe that I use to clean surfaces to avoid the bugs that fester in close quarters—and wiped the Vicks residue from my upper lip. I took my first deep breath without the camphor overlay and tried to focus.

"What's the immediate takeaway?" David would ask his team after an abuse exam. He told us to immediately make exit-interview notes because there could be vital clues in obscure details that are quickly forgotten. "Nothing may make sense at first; only later do you see the patterns."

I pulled out my phone—useless for calls on the ship—but the note feature still worked. I pecked out:

- Meds father gave her
- Painkillers?
- Pregnancy
- Passenger/stranger?
- Did anyone dislike her?
- Was someone jealous?
- Surveillance camera recordings?
- Looked happy/peaceful
- Olek?
- Vance?
- Doctor?
- Nurse knows more than she says

I heard a spitting sound, then smelled something burning. I walked in the direction of the sizzle that seemed to be coming from the gangway area, which was almost blocked by the ship-to-pier rolling walkway. Clang! I peered into an open doorway and saw something flickering on the opposite wall. I took another step toward a shaft where a workman was soldering a wire on the top of the lift that handicapped passengers used to reach the wheelchair ramp. I remembered that when we were in Ponta Delgada, the embarkation queue had been held up while two muscular crewmembers hefted a man in a wheelchair up the stairs because the lift was out of order. I supposed that he was repairing it at sea so it would be in service when we reached Florida.

Something clanged. I watched as the worker turned the wheel that secured the watertight lock on the hull door. As air rushed in, I realized he was opening it a crack to ventilate the smoke. He started to turn in my direction. I scooted aside since I shouldn't have been in a crew-only area and hurried to catch an elevator door that had just opened, then concentrated on how good a long, hot shower was going to feel.

□ □ □

While the ship's movement rarely bothered me, it was intensified in a closed space with no visual reference. In the shower, I kept one hand on the grab bar for equilibrium. I wasn't sure whether it was the ocean's motion or the maelstrom in my mind that had me so off-balance. I had been able to push my revulsion into a temporary compartment during the intimate examination of Tatiana's corpse. Now it slithered out like a boa constrictor and compressed my chest. She was gone because some cruel, sick, crazed person *on this ship* had stolen her life—someone nearby, someone I may have seen a few minutes or hours ago, someone I knew or someone who knew…*me.*

I lathered my hair with shampoo and controlled my respirations by counting inhales and exhales. As the water cascaded from the massaging showerhead, I remembered what David told me when I had tried to fathom how a father in my caseload deliberately scalded his daughter. "Everyone is motivated by either self-interest or passion. Everything else is either an accident or unintended consequences." This was part of his "bucket theory." He explained, "People like us start out with a 'full bucket' because all our needs have been met since infancy and we've been able to satisfy most of our wants for love, health, security, education, fulfilling jobs, supportive friends and family. However, most of the people we deal with in law enforcement or child welfare have buckets so shot through with holes that they're downright sieves. They're hungry—for love, attention, validation, and whatever necessities they've been denied. In fact, many of them are literally hungry." After that, I asked everyone I worked with if they knew whether their clients were "food insecure" because much of what we attribute to pathology goes back to never having a full belly, eating cheap junk food, and the subsequent health and emotional issues.

Thus, if hunger is the fulcrum of behavior, nobody on this ship is suffering! Of course, there was hunger to be loved, to feel needed, to be important—to have power. "The powerless abused child becomes the powerful abuser of children" was another of David's truisms. Talk to most criminals about their childhoods and you will find a legacy of sadism and violence. He would hear a news story about a shooter in a school or a serial killer and shout, "Arrest the parents and find out what they did to him."

As I rinsed off, my reflections darted to Papa Medved. Could the trite phrase "We always hurt the ones we love" apply to him? When I last saw him, he was still in shock. A new thought penetrated the water drumming on the tile: All those meds. What if he simply had miscalculated a dose? Yet I couldn't imagine that Grisha could have removed her clothing and abandoned her body.

I wrapped myself in a cozy spa robe pondering yet again how anyone hurt their own child, and yet I had known parents who had brutalized their children with beatings, rapes—unmentionable tortures. Few were killed purposefully, but many died as the result of these injuries. Statistically, though, the perp was more often a mother's paramour than the genetic father.

At first I could not summon a germ of compassion for the abuser. I wanted vengeance. "I thought that too at first," David had said. "Then there was this guy I had to visit in prison that had tortured two adopted children, poured acid on them, then left them in a landfill to die. The boy lived." David had closed his heavy lids. "When I interviewed him, I didn't ask if he had done it or how or why. Maybe I was channeling my inner Freud"—he had laughed sardonically—"so I began with questions about his mother and—" Then David has given me his "soul stare" and told me for the first time his mantra about being unable to despise someone when you know his life story. Over time, I had found some truth in this—although had never been quite as accepting as my husband with his exceptional heart.

What had Grisha's life been like in cold-war Russia? This was the Soviet Union where my grandfather had—in my grandmother's words—"been disappeared" and never found. I did some quick math. Tatiana was around 24 and her father looked in his fifties, so assuming he had been 30 when she was born, his birthdate was close to 1962—the year of the Cuban missile crisis. Tatiana had said something about him being removed from his family and sent away to a state gymnastics school. Institutions were rife with abuse. Another case of the abused child growing up to be an abuser? What would infuriate him the most—possibly incite violence? Could it have been because of the pregnancy?

I sat at the combo desk/dressing table and pulled out the hairdryer from the drawer. It only took a few minutes to dry and brush my geometric Sassoon-style hair, which looks a hell of a lot better on Keira Knightley than me.

So, who could be the baby's father? Olek had been forthcoming about their sexual relationship, so he was first on my list. Vance. Seemed more like the auctioneer's wistful dream, but I had seen them touching in public and she hadn't pulled away. Yet

Olek and Tatiana had chemistry—at least on stage. Their performance demonstrated phenomenal, almost inhuman, physical abilities, with twists and poses that were rawer and more sensual than anything you might see at a ballet. Because this was a family ship catering to many nationalities, religions, and sensibilities, Olek and Tatiana dressed in unisex costumes and matching makeup. Their routines had an edginess with a robotic, asexual vibe—that is, if the audience could ignore the flagrant display of female anatomy turned inside out. Because, quite frankly, most of what a contortionist does is just plain weird.

I put on a diaphanous caftan and opened the balcony door. A tropical mist enveloped me. It was hard to believe that this was Thanksgiving week. I took deep sips of the silky slipstream. Callista claimed salty air contained negative ions that accelerated the body's ability to absorb oxygen and balance serotonin levels. "Nature's anti-depressant," she called it. "I'm more alert and energized aboard a ship than anywhere else."

"Perhaps that is why I can write a book more swiftly at sea," I said.

"I agree," she said. "When your body is balanced, your mind can take wing."

Best of all was sleeping on board. Ever since David died, I've dreaded crawling into a cold, lonely bed. I let Bodhi sleep with me for the first year, but while I loved it, I knew I was ruining his ability to sleep alone.

"The sound and sensory feel of waves alters brain patterns," Callista had said, during a sales pitch on the Rise-and-Shine show to get the current crop of passengers to re-up for another cruise. "Research proves that motion lulls one into deeper, more refreshing sleep that rejuvenates both mind and body." Turning to her sidekick Ellwood, she had asked, "How did you sleep last night, mate?"

"Not nearly long enough," he answered with a practiced yawn.

"Didn't you adore being rocked to sleep like a baby?" She smiled directly into the camera. "And what about you slowpokes still in bed? You could spend the day in your cocoon, couldn't you? I guarantee you will find your land bed wanting and soon you will crave lying down in mother nature's cozy cradle." After that she launched into a sales pitch for Caribbean cruises for a winter break.

Usually all that sea and sky and nothingness calmed me; now I wanted nothing more than to be home cuddling Bodhi on my lap—if he didn't wiggle off complaining he wasn't a baby anymore. I sighed—only a few more days. If I didn't get back to my book, I'd lose the momentum. I went back inside and stared at my computer. The book—all fantasy and fluff. It could wait. I caught sight of my pillow and realized how weary I was. Best to succumb to the urge. I slipped between the crisp sheets, closed my eyes, and let the ship do its magic.

☐ ☐ ☐

I awoke in a dim room with a stiff neck. I had passed out flat on my back. My stomach rumbled. The combination of adrenalin and mental exhaustion demanded caloric input. I contemplated calling room service and ordering a white-sauced pasta, a crisp wedge salad, accompanied by an icy glass of Prosecco, but I also needed to be around people who weren't consumed by the tragedy. The commotion at The Terraces acted as a privacy curtain most of the time; even so, there were always people who wanted to share the table and I was in no mood to chitchat with a stranger. If I could have chosen a dinner companion, it would have been Callista, but she was much too busy with the evening entertainment roster. I could go to the dining room, the venue of choice for most of the passengers for whom the leisurely multi-course meal was the high point of sea days. The maître d' would try to dissuade me from eating solo by promising to seat me with a "most interesting gentleman," although I wasn't up to several hours of impeccable service. If I just wanted an appetizer and a salad, it would disturb the precisely-orchestrated routine. And I didn't want anyone lumping me with the narcissistic guests the crew labeled, "Cones on the Throne."

The solution was Florentina's, the specialty restaurant that cost an additional fee. Not that it mattered, yet I was pleased that, according to Rolf, I was being comped. The boutique restaurant was tucked into the bow on Baltic Deck, just under the Solarium. At lunch, pizzas from the wood-fired ovens were popular and they had trendier toppings like goat cheese and sun-dried tomatoes than the poolside pizzas. At dinner, the menu featured regional Italian dishes prepared with authentic ingredients and freshly-made pasta.

I dressed in black velvet slacks, a gray silk blouse, and a black velvet hoody that would do for a post-prandial stroll on the promenade. I looped a paisley scarf in shades of gray that I'd purchased in Provence around my neck.

"*Buona sera*, Signora Lanier." Vito flourished a hand. "Would you care for a window seat?"

"Just a table for one, *grazie*."

"It's a quiet night," he urged me forward, "so take the corner table."

"*Grazie*," I said, seating myself in the "Godfather spot." Earlier in the cruise Vito had explained that Vito Corelone ("my fictional namesake") always sat at the table with his back to the corner. "That way nobody can surprise him from behind." Tonight, that was a comforting thought.

I settled into the chair upholstered in a rich brocade shot with gold threads and relished the hushed ambiance.

"A Bellini?" Vito knew my favorite cocktail.

"Just a glass of Prosecco."

"*Molte bene*". He handed me the menu encased in a wooden folder lined with ruby velvet. The assistant waiter placed a basket on the table containing an herbed focaccia, grissini breadsticks, and rosemary flatbread; and little plates with Parma prosciutto and mixed marinated olives. He sprinkled an herb mixture into a saucer and poured a shimmering strand of jade-and-gold olive oil from a brass jug. "This is our award-winning Segesta unfiltered, Sicilian extra-virgin," he said and then exhaled loudly. "Oof!"

I laughed, as was expected, just as a bus boy delivered a bottle of chilled San Pellegrino. I popped a plump black olive in my mouth and studied the pasta selections: Spaghetti allo Scoglio, Penne con Brasato di Manzo, and Manicotti alla Florentina—all seemed too heavy, and although I knew I could special order almost any pasta with any sauce, I wasn't in the mood to wait. A shadow crossed my table.

I looked up to a grinning Vito and an abashed Dr. Kotze. Vito grinned like he had found the missing piece of a puzzle.

"I just wanted to say good evening," the doctor muttered. Vito was beaming and waiting. Dr. Kotze shuffled his feet. "Enjoy your dinner," he said, moving aside, but Vito blocked him.

Anything I said short of asking the doctor to join me would have been rude. I tilted my head to indicate the empty chair to my right. "I haven't ordered yet, doctor."

"If you are sure…" he said, taking his seat. "And please, I much prefer Marius."

Vito sighed with relief as he pulled back the doctor's chair. "Your usual martini?"

"Just fizzy water for me," he said. "I may have to work tonight."

Marius looked sharp in his officer's jacket with the three stripes and large star on the epaulets. Earlier in the day he had worn scrubs in the exam room and the aqua color had given his pale face a sickly tint. Now, in the restaurant's diffused light, he looked ruddier and more relaxed.

"What are you considering?" he asked.

For a second, I thought he was asking about the case, but he was merely studying his menu. "Just a salad and a pasta. The tomato coulis with the shrimp is lighter than the braised short rib that comes with the penne. "

He gave a muffled whistle. "You come here every night?"

"No, although the menu is the same fleet-wide."

"I confess that I always have the lobster three ways." He smiled shyly. "It supports the family business."

"What's that?"

"We export South African lobster tails."

"I grew up on Maine lobster, but I prefer the tails—all the flavor and none of the work."

"Mind if we steal that slogan?"

"Are you still involved in the business?"

"Not now, although my uncles own a fleet of lobster boats that work the western coast of South Africa and the Cape peninsula. I used to work for them on holidays."

"Although your mother wanted you to go to medical school."

He laughed. "I see you've met my mother."

Our waiter returned with the chef's complimentary appetizers. "Good to see you again, doctor."

"Thanks, Salvatore."

"Will you be having your usual?"

"Si! You know me too well."

"Caesar salad, lobster three ways, and tiramisu?"

Marius nodded. "And—"

"Extra anchovies."

Salvatore pivoted to me. "Wedge salad with balsamic vinaigrette and"—I beamed at the doctor—"A few anchovies on the side."

"Kindred spirits!"

"Then the manicotti."

"Very good, Mrs. Lanier," he said, collecting the bulky menus.

Marius sipped his water. I removed my glasses and pressed my thumb into the indentation on the right side of my forehead.

"Headache?"

"Just tension."

"It wasn't fair to put you through that ordeal, although I'm grateful that you were willing."

"A compliment I could have lived without."

"I talked to Officer Ocampo a few minutes ago. You remember when she mentioned removing all the medications from Mr. Zlatogrivov's cabin? Well, it occurred to me that she should have left his personal scripts. She claimed she asked him which were his since many had only Russian labels and he said that none of it mattered anymore."

"She was his whole life."

"That's what worries me. Mae has assigned a soco to keep an eye on him."

"What's happening with Mrs. Greenberg?"

The doctor frowned. "Joyce shouldn't have broken privacy by saying her name. I think she forgot you weren't crew."

"Another compliment?" I said, then, "Is she going to make it?"

"Dicey situation. She needs to be in a major surgical center."

"Don't worry about me, though, I've already forgotten the name." I grinned. "I sometimes have trouble keeping tracking of the characters in my own novel."

"I hope it doesn't take place on a cruise ship in the middle of the Atlantic."

I make it a practice never to discuss my writing because I believe it dilutes creative energy, but I didn't want to be rude. "No, in a small town in Oregon where it suddenly becomes legal to grow marijuana."

"Is it titled 'Cannabis Capers'?"

I made the mistake of laughing while sipping water and had to dab my mouth and chin. "In a manner of speaking."

"A mystery or romance or…?"

"A bit of each."

"Why don't you come to South Africa and write a lobster tale?" He grinned. "Pun intended."

I finished mopping up and reached for a breadstick. "Is there much treachery in the lobster tail world?"

"There's all sorts of crustacean crime. Pirate boats sometimes go over catch limits, work during the closed season, don't throw back females when they are 'in berry' or sell illegal soft-shelled specimens."

I smiled easily for the first time that day. "I must say I'm shocked!"

The doctor removed his wire-rimmed glasses and started to wipe them with an edge of the tablecloth. "The truth is that if we don't protect the sustainability of the resource, they won't exist in a few years. There's far more demand than supply."

"Sounds like a lucrative business."

"They've done all right, but it's like farming—relying on fickle mother nature."

Our salads were served and we both ate without speaking for a few minutes. I stared out the window where a half-slice of moon rose in the distance, illuminating a crooked path for the ship to follow.

We both looked up and started to speak simultaneously. "What does—?" I asked.

"When did—?" he began.

The doctor gestured to me to go first. "What does 'in berry' mean?"

"The eggs are called berries because—well, because they look like a cluster of berries. We don't want to disturb a new generation by taking that female."

"Is that the same thing as coral?"

"Yes, very good! Believe it or not, lobster reproduction and migration are fascinating. They can travel amazing distances."

"Just like you."

"I wouldn't mind being called fascinating," he said with a shy lowering of his chin.

How had this so quickly turned into a flirtation? I laughed awkwardly. "That too, but I meant that you—on a ship—traveling around the world." He looked puzzled. "You migrate long distances like the lobster, but on ships."

"For a moment I thought you meant ah…re-pro-duc-tion." He enunciated every syllable for effect.

I held up my wine glass, tilted it in a wordless toast, and took two long swallows.

"Sorry, I couldn't resist; migration pretty much sums up my life." Marius squinted as he laughed. "I must say that you are a very impressive woman."

There is no good way to respond to that so I took another sip. He did the same while giving me a penetrating stare over the rim of his glass. "I mean the way you conducted yourself during the…that difficult exam. I protested including any passenger—even another doctor, but I was wrong."

"To be frank, it was an imposition, although not for the reasons you might think. One of the worst parts of my job was not being able to unsee the brutality. I'm trying to prevent my son from seeing violence on the news or in movies as long as possible. There are alarming statistics on how many murders and violent acts children view in a year."

Our moment of affability vanished. I drained my glass of Prosecco while looking past him into the far distance. "I know this must be some ridiculous form of denial, but I can't shake the thought that Tania committed suicide."

After a long pause, Marius replied. "I *know* she wasn't unhappy. To her everything was beautiful, every day more interesting than the next. To her there were a million colors of water and innumerable scents in the air. She wanted to experience everything! She loved the ships, the ports, all the people of the world—their skin tones, their different languages and songs. She wished she could capture what she saw, even though she didn't have a camera—not even a mobile phone, so I loaned her a camera and she started photographing one place in different lights. You know what she selected?—a life preserver hanging by the children's pool with the words 'Seven Seas' on it. In some of her shots, it radiates an eerie green light; sometimes it reflects pink from the dawn. Children in the foreground sometimes are in sharp focus, other times blurred. She had an eye—and she knew it. Unlike so many people who are shy about their talents or feel they must act modestly, she felt true pleasure in her accomplishments and had a thirst to improve. You could see that in her act—always a little better, a little harder, and a bit more spectacular. Sometimes I watched the audience watching her and how they were with her every twist, rooting for her, worried for her. She was...she was magical."

He glanced at me and then back at the window because he knew that I knew that he'd given away his secret. Marius was in love with Tatiana. For a second I felt a pang of envy, then chided myself. Vance, Olek, and now Marius—all adored Tatiana. Did they know about each other? Were any of them jealous— one of the most dangerous emotions and often the fuel for rage.

And how many more admirers could there be?

□ □ □

Friends—especially my closest friend Margot— assumed that shipboard life offered opportunities for romance and they were not shy about probing. Their fantasies; not mine.

"There isn't an eligible man under eighty," I protested, and I was not far off.

Suitable men in their thirties or forties were too busy in their careers and families for cruises more

143

than a week at a time. The few I saw were part of extended families celebrating their parents' Golden Anniversary or taking a babymoon before birth kept them home for several years.

"What about the crew?" Margot had asked.

"Plenty of eye candy," I admitted, "and they are paid to be polite and attentive, but it is verboten to date passengers."

"Yet it must happen…" she prompted.

"I wouldn't know," I said, cutting her off. There was no point explaining that careers at sea were just that. Officers' families were often on board, but most staff had contracts ranging from six to ten months. Like the military, the only way to rise through the ranks was to pay their dues at sea. Also, there were almost no Americans in the crew except for some of the art auction people, including Vance, or employees from the Fort taking a supervisory turn. I had yet to meet any American medical personnel—they just couldn't make a competitive salary on board. So far, all the doctors I had met were from Canada, Scandinavian countries, Australia, and South Africa.

I glanced back at Marius. His mind had drifted off toward Tatiana because he was avoiding eye contact with me. His banter was only to get his thoughts off the subject, just as I had made a lame attempt to do the same. He'd not only just lost someone for whom he felt deep affection, he'd also had to steel himself to do the rape kit. Whatever revulsion I had felt, his had been far more intense. I felt a clutch in my chest for him and his loss but also a twinge of care for him. I was touched by his sorrow but Margot would have insisted it was something else.

The waiter who served the main course respected our silence. He knew about the murder. While there had been an aggressive attempt to insulate the passengers, news passed through the crew's grapevine faster than the internet. Many might have been questioned by security or asked to be on the alert. Had the cabin stewards and the laundry been given a description of what Tatiana might have been wearing? I hoped they were searching for her clothing. The killer could have trashed her garments or he could have been a weirdo who kept lingerie or other items as trophies. Finding them would be a major clue.

The doctor picked at his lobster tail with the graceful hands of a pianist—or surgeon. He was not my "type"—or at least not at all like David who'd had the build of a surfer, thinning blond hair that always brushed his collar, and pale blue eyes. Marius was short, slender, with shiny black hair, brown eyes, and rounded shoulders. He wore wire-rimmed glasses and had more than a five-o'-clock shadow. Still, I liked his intellectual appearance and kind mannerisms.

"Do you ever tire of eating lobster?" I said to break the silence.

"No, but Tania wouldn't touch it, said they looked like giant bugs." He shook his head as if to clear a thought. "I still can't believe it…"

"I have another question." He looked away for a second, before trying to appear interested. "When you mentioned some…spots…on ah…her body…that you didn't find, what did you mean?"

"That there were no signs of those petechial hemorrhages in the eyelids, which r-ruled out"—he stuttered, and began again—" ruled out smothering. Also, there was no cyanosis; no blood oozed from her mouth." He blinked several times. "The problem is that sometimes a smothering death may be due to reflex cardiac arrest, leaving few clues."

"So, it's a possibility?" He nodded. "Mae said something about bleeding."

He took a slow sip of water. "I couldn't find any reason for the blood Mae mentioned seeing, although a small spot on her face that could have been blood shows up in the photos she took at the scene."

"I didn't notice it at the time either, but then everything went blurry for me," I said, remembering only her legs white as bone sticking out in that gruesome position.

"You saw for yourself. There wasn't a single blemish on her body except for the bruises from her work." He stared at the back of his hands. "Mae delivered the linens to send with the kit. There's definitely a small red spot and a lighter smear."

"Could someone have wiped between her legs?"

"I looked again to be sure. Her legs and thighs were spotless. And I double-checked her eyes and nose. I found the remnants of small clots that could have come from a nosebleed or even blowing her nose too forcefully."

"She could have hit her face during a rehearsal."

The doctor placed the cool water glass against his right temple. "Until the bedding is tested, we won't even know if it's her blood—or someone else's."

"By then thousands of passengers will have dispersed all over the world," I said with a gulp.

The doctor's pager buzzed. He gave me an apologetic glance and went to the phone at the maître d's stand.

"Joyce," he said without sitting down. "She's a brick." He wiped his lips with his leaf-colored napkin. "The last transfusion didn't go well." He gave an apologetic bow. "She needs a hand. Our patient is a very difficult stick."

The doctor nodded to our waiter, mumbled a few words to Vito, and was gone.

Three

*Truth, like gold, is to be obtained not by its growth,
but washing away from it all that is not gold.*
—Leo Tolstoy

Sunday, November 22
At Sea: Position: 1364 Nautical Miles Southwest of
Ponta Delgada, Azores

My sleeping brain tried to incorporate the ringing into a dream as a jangly carriage return on a manual typewriter. I had just realized I'd been typing all day without any paper inserted. I awoke with my heart pounding and reached for the receiver on the end table.

"Please, madam, would you come to see me?" came a faint plea in Russian.

"Are you ill?"

"I just need to talk to someone who will understand me."

"*Da, konechno*. Of course. I'll be there within the hour."

Grisha Zlatogrivov gave me his new stateroom number. "I will leave the door unlocked."

According to my clock, it wasn't quite seven, although there was more sunshine peeking through the drapes than I'd expected, until I remembered that it was actually eight. One bonus of sailing west was reaping an extra hour almost every day and arriving without jet lag.

Frankly, I wasn't anxious to give solace to this man who not only had been Tatiana's tyrannical coach, but he may have injected her with performance-enhancing drugs. I pondered the gruesome possibility that he had caused her death—by accident or intent. My experience in the nasty streets of south Florida informed me that a parent was often culpable. One father had shot his teenage son because he had mud on his boots and justified his actions by saying, "I gave him life so I had a right to take it." While Grisha might not have been addled by drugs, poverty, or mental illness like so many of the parents I had known, he reminded me of a puppeteer pulling marionette strings. He was Svengali to Tatiana's Trilby, Dr. Coppélius to Swanhilda, Professor Higgins to Eliza Doolittle.

I dialed room service and ordered a cheese omelet, a croissant, raspberry jam, "Early" Grey tea, and freshly-squeezed orange juice, then pulled the curtains back, squinting in the reflected light. Dark clouds in the shape of a pregnant woman loomed above the southeastern horizon. A veil of sadness gripped me: Tatiana's baby was dead in her womb. A tiny boy…or girl…not much bigger than a fig.

In less than ten minutes Cozmin arrived with my tray; he knew better than to be chatty in the morning. I placed a teabag in the carafe of hot water then took a swallow of my juice. A burn of acid made my gorge rise. I hurried to the balcony for fresh air. The ship was cutting a wide swath toward Florida. I kept my eye on the bobbing horizon and took long lungfuls of air that felt like seltzer.

"Do you know why looking out to sea is so calming?" Callista once asked me before going on with another of her pseudo-scientific theories. "Because you can see the enemy coming for a long way off."

"The days of the armada are over."

"Agreed, but it is an atavistic holdover. That's why people love houses on hilltops—they can see if an invading army is heading their way."

"And prepare the kettles of hot oil to pour on them!"

"Seriously, it is one of the only facts I recall from university." She straightened her spine, tilted her chin forward and spoke in a supercilious voice. "I'll have you know that is why people plant grass in even postage-stamp gardens: It gives them a faux horizon."

"So, they can watch for hostile pizza deliverymen?"

"No, seriously, it's called '*La magie des perspective infinies,*'" she said in an excellent French accent.

When I'd sailed with her the first time, I'd been impressed with her stage presence and checked on her bio in the ship's bulletin. She had trained as an opera singer. "I wanted to be the next Kiri Te Kanawa," she said when I was seated next to her at the captain's table one night. "Eventually I had to get a real job."

It turned out that most of the cruise director's staff had a background in entertainment. Not only did Callista have excellent stage presence, she conducted the passenger choir, taught early morning Zumba, and was featured in the crew talent show singing an aria from *La Traviata*. Because it was her job to be social, we chatted often and found we had much in common. I'd had an aunt who was in the chorus of the Met; her father taught Russian history at a university. We were close to the same age. Her brief marriage had ended when she realized she wasn't "cured" from her preference for other women. That confession led me to tell her exactly what had happened to David. After that, we could tell each other anything, or so I'd thought because I was sure she was withholding something about Tatiana.

I ran my fingers through my flyaway hair as disparate details bumped around in my mind. Before going to bed, I'd taken the flash drive from the safe and listed the meds that had been mentioned. Under "Injectables" I'd listed: human growth hormone and steroid; under "Oral Meds" I wrote Cipro (UTI) and Seasonale (birth control). Something about the blood stain pricked at me. I went inside, poured myself a cup of tea, and opened my computer. The steam from the tea burned my lip and I set the cup down while the computer booted up. I opened my last document and started a list under <u>Blood</u>: Nose (clots), Vagina, Urethra, Anus, Scratch…. My head pounded.

I went back outside and felt the weight of the wind, which was logy with humidity. Way too warm for November and most of the clothing I'd packed. I realized I was stalling because I really didn't want to listen to Grisha. But I'd promised.

I tried the tea again and this time it soothed my throat. I flaked off the point of the croissant, however it tasted like sawdust. I lifted the silver dome over my omelet surrounded by dainty slices of fruit. The watermelon was green, the pineapple woody.

I gave up and went into the closet and surveyed what now looked like a funereal wardrobe. Black worked in every season so I had five pairs of black slacks that I teamed up with various tops and scarves. I picked the lightest pair, added a gray-and-black paisley tunic that had survived more than a month without cleaning, and tugged on my Propét sneakers with the elastic-and-toggle design that eliminated laces. I grabbed my tote and tossed in a notepad, a bottle of water from the mini-fridge, a hat, two Empire pens, my ID/cabin card, a travel tissue pack, and looked around for anything I'd missed. Before we went out into the field, abuse investigators were trained to think defensively—in other words, to prepare as much as possible for anything that could go wrong. Not that you could ever prepare for something like what happened to David. I went through David's checklist to carefully guard important files and reminded myself to turn off the laptop, unplug the memory stick, and zip it into an inside pocket of my tote, rather than leave it in the "safe" that could be opened by any soco. What else? My phone was useless onboard, but David would have wanted me to take it—so I did, if only for comfort.

□ □ □

Grisha's new stateroom was in the passenger section on Baltic Deck, fitting for a Russian I thought. I hesitated as I neared B-303, which was propped open by a brown shoe. I inhaled and knocked.

"*Spasibo, shto prishli tax skoro!*" Grisha called out thanking me for coming quickly even though I had hardly rushed.

He was now in an oceanview cabin with the view partially obstructed by a lifeboat. I asked how I could be of help. "*Kak ya mogu byt' pomach?*"

He pointed to the single armchair before realizing it was covered in discarded clothes. He waved me aside, bundled them, and tossed them toward the desk. Apparently, no room steward had visited recently because every surface was littered with papers, clothes, empty soda cans, beer bottle. Trash basket overflowed and partially eaten plates of food covered the bed, desk, and even the floor.

"*Ya proshu proshcheniya,*" he apologized waving his arms at the mess. Grisha's shoeshine-black hair, which was usually pulled back into a ponytail, drooped across his chest. He wore saggy black exercise pants and a black tank top that flattered his muscular back and arms. His bare feet revealed yellow toenails that curved like claws. A feverish patina of sweat glistened on his chest, feeding the stink emanating off his unwashed body.

"You have children?"

"Yes, I am a mother."

"Then you can imagine... I have lost everything—my son, my wife, my daughter. Who would want to hurt my *christyy tsvetok*—my pure flower? For what reason should I now live?"

I stared out the window, past the lifeboat, up into a sky of whirling clouds and slanting rain. "I didn't know you also had a son."

153

"Maksim came just a year after Tania." He panted. "In five months…" He closed his eyes.

The air in the room was a stifling. I placed my hand, redolent with the lavender scent from the soap I'd bought in Provence, discreetly by my nose. "I'm so sorry."

"He was the strongest baby ever. He could pull himself up when holding my hands."

"I'm so sorry. Was he sick?"

"Not for a day—then he didn't wake up." He smoothed his hair with his fingers. "After that, Galina was never the same." He squinted at me. "You know Tania's mother was a gymnast, yes? Almost made the Olympic team." He placed his head between his over-sized hands. "Maksim…Tania….Galina…Yegor…poof!" He sprang up and made a zig-zag gesture. "Like lightning! One day Galina was pulling a grocery cart and she collapsed in the street. By the time the ambulance came she was gone."

"Her heart?"

He shrugged. "Galina's family, they all are followed by the devil."

"Why do you say that?"

He jumped up from the edge of the bed where he'd been perched. "I met Galina through her older brother Yegor, who was the youngest member of our *vershina* team—the one the world contenders were picked from." He raised his arms toward the ceiling. "Yegor mastered the Arabian double front before anybody else."

"What's that?"

"A half twist that turns into a double somersault."
His voice caught. "One minute he was showing how
to do it from a tuck, pike, or layout...his hands shot
up as he stuck the landing, then he just...just folded
into himself. I reached down to help him up, but he
was gone..."

"Was it the same as with Galina?"

His lips drew into a tight line. "Nobody really
knew for sure about either of them." Grisha's
expression contorted in crushing pain.

I'd lost one person without warning; he's lost
three—no four! A wave of nausea warned that
another migraine loomed. I needed to take my rescue
medicine early for it to be effective, but I couldn't
leave now.

"All these people you loved...they all died
suddenly," I said softly. "Now Tania." I reached out
my hand and Grisha grabbed it between both of his
and kneeled at my feet. He kissed my wrist and began
to weep. His trembling reverberated to my bones.
"How can I help?"

"Did you know that they are sending my
malyshka to Bermuda?" He wept into my hand. "My
baby!"

I kneeled beside him. "They want to know if she
was poisoned."

"My little girl—a Litvinenko?"

It took me a moment to realize he was referring to
a former KGB spy whose tea was tainted with a
radioactive pill in London. "No, nothing like that."

"They packed up all my bottles."

"Blood work is checked in all suspicious deaths."

"That's not what that German *ublyudok* told me." Grisha stood and backed away. "That bastard is the one who wants to send her to Bermuda!"

"Maybe you misunderstood. What language was he speaking?"

"Russian!" He gave me a crooked smirk. "Didn't you know that he's fluent!"

"Really?" I said, thinking: Then why the hell did they need me to translate?

"*Da*. He was born in *East* Germany—Rostock."

"I thought he was from Austria."

"Everything from his mouth is bull-sheet!" He spat toward wastebasket but missed. "His mother is from Vena—you know?"

"Vienna?"

He nodded. "He said that because you Americans prefer to think of edelweiss and singing nuns." He grimaced. "Anyway, Russian was mandatory in the schools there until the Wall fell. He speaks a very stilted version, like he never used it with a real *Russkiy*. Probably he resented being forced to learn it. Whatever." He shrugged. "I've always felt—how do you say?—bad viber-ay-shuns from him."

"It's his job to find whoever who hurt Tania."

"Before Flor-ee-day? *Nevozmozhno*!"

"There's a chance…"

Grisha propped himself against the window to steady himself. "The Castle just wants to dump her—like trash." He stared out at the silvery sea.

I had good reason to dread giving a statement to the county sheriff, so Bermuda offered advantages to me. I knew the odds were against finding the perp. "Everything might be easier in Bermuda."

"Ha! Those little men riding scooters in shorts? They're a joke!" He cleared a spot to sit on his bed. "Don't you understand what they are doing? The Americans will be all over the ship like ants on honey. In Bermuda they will just stamp a few documents and that will be the end of it."

"But—"

"This ship flies the Bermudan flag," Grisha said with disgust. "And the Empire Line is chartered out of Malta. They'd set up a branch on Mars if it would help them avoid restrictions."

He had a point. Having a "Flag of Convenience" gave the cruise line the least amount of regulation. The reason ships like the *Seven Seas* were under the authority of Bermuda was to keep them out of the legal reach of American or British regulations. Like the Bahamas, Panama, Liberia, even tiny Vanuatu and Cyprus, Bermuda's liberal labor laws also did not require a minimum wage or taxes on profits. If a ship sailing to or from the US stopped at one other country, it could be registered anywhere in the world.

"Still, once we arrive in Ft. Lauderdale the ship will be subject to American law."

"Not if the victim is no longer with us!" Grisha punched the bed, sending a dirty dish flying.

Nothing that I could say would make a scintilla of a difference because I'd teetered on the same precipice. It's like it is the moment when you wake up from surgery when the anesthetic has worn off, but you can't swim away from the pain long enough even to ask for help.

"Papa Medved," I said softly. "You must take a good long shower. I'll get room service to take away

157

all this—*musor*—and order some tea." Grisha stared at the floor like tired child. "I'll try to find out more about what is happening."

Wordlessly, he headed for the bathroom and shut the door with a bang.

I summoned the room steward and headed for the atrium to be alone in a swirl of passengers checking to see what they owed on their on-board accounts.

□ □ □

A polka band was playing on the atrium stage while dancers in poofy skirts and tight slacks oompah-pahed. The audience gathered on the various tiers above clapped to the music. I maneuvered past them to take the center crystal staircase up to the promenade deck and pushed the door that led outside. It didn't budge on my first try. I used both hands and a knee against the force of the wind blowing directly starboard at the flank.

I had been ready to condemn Tatiana's father but by the time I'd looped the deck once, I understood that he was the product of a harsh Soviet system. His only escape had been the sport that placed his family in a privileged position. To keep his daughter safe, he had to groom her to succeed, made more critical by the tragedies that had befallen his family. Could the devil haunting Galina's kin be a genetic curse like that syndrome the doctor had mentioned? First the brother, then the wife, even a baby. Tragic as they were, they had nothing to do with homicide. His pain was from bereavement, not guilt. He would have passed David's litmus test.

158

"When the parent has done something wrong, listen carefully. They don't ask about the child's condition; they complain about how bad the situation is for *them*!" He called it the "woe-is-me rule." He'd said, "When you hear the parent—or parent-substitute—whining, slinging snot, and asking, 'What's going to happen to me?' or 'Why does everything go to hell for me?', they've done something wrong. The parent who asks, 'How's my child feeling?' or 'Does she have her teddy?' or 'Is her cold better?' is the one who has nothing to hide."

Grisha's most pressing problem was that his daughter's body was being taken from him. The visit had been worth it for me because empathy had replaced suspicions and I mentally moved him from the perp to victim.

❑ ❑ ❑

I leaned my back against the rail. The crosswind porcupined my hair.

"Hello stranger!" came the perpetually cheery voice of my favorite person on board. "Walk with me," Callista said, heading toward the bow.

I lowered my head as we walked upwind. Without taking purposeful steps, we would have been blown backward. "Are they really sending Tania with the medical evacuation?" I asked.

"That's what I've heard." She frowned. "I just came out of a meeting with the socos and IT people. They're trying to upload everyone's ID photos—passenger and crew cards, passports, every image that every crew photographer has taken in the last six weeks even though our internet connection is about as fast as bubbling mud."

"They could send storage drives with the evacuation."

"How did you know that's the backup plan?" She laughed at her own pun, which took me a few seconds to catch. "Every photo ID in the world is now searchable, giving law enforcement a virtual global lineup. If they're crazy lucky, they might match someone onboard with a known stalker or psychopath."

"That's a disturbing thought." I touched her shoulder to steady myself. "Anything yet from the security cameras?"

"Rolf says that they've been through hundreds of hours of video. So far nobody's seen Tania entering or departing any stateroom but her own."

"What about the cameras near where the laundry cart ended up on I-95?"

Callista tried to smooth back her curls. "The two most likely cameras have been out of service. Rolf's coming down hard on security, IT, and maintenance."

"I wouldn't want to be in his crosshairs."

"You're not the only one. Poor Ellwood has been on sick leave since…since we found her."

"Why?"

"He's freaking out and is terrified of Rolf."

"Don't you find that odd?"

"He was told that Rolf called him a—let's just say something nasty and homophobic."

"Who's taking Ellwood's shifts?"

Her shoulders sagged. "Who do you think?"

Two joggers passed us for the second time. Callista waved for me to follow her. She led me up the forward steps to a covered landing. There were ashtrays and a bench set up to accommodate smokers. Nobody else was there so we sat down.

"What are your thoughts at this point?" Callista asked.

"Let me ask you something first." The cruise director tilted her head expectantly. "Marius. I think he...maybe had a crush on her."

"You're not off base." She kneaded her lips before she spoke again. "Let's face it, we all had a soft spot for Tania. Her...vulnerability—well, it's how you feel about a charming, talented child. She was endearing." She rubbed her chin. "So far I can't find a single motive."

"They make a big deal out of that in crime novels, but in the real world there are just horrible, damaged people who are controlled by their most primitive brain or fueled by drugs or driven by some sick passion."

"It has to have been one of those weirdos," Callista said with a shudder. "There are a few creeps on every voyage. Everybody has stories of being stalked, people who take a friendly smile as an invitation to sleep with them. All the young crew women—especially the entertainers—have been harassed." She looked out to sea. "You know who have it the worst? The female cabin stewards. Some guys get a kick out of not answering the door and having them walk in on them stark naked. One type hides behind the door and pounces on the steward when she walks in."

"How does the ship handle that?"

"It's tricky. If the guy hasn't touched the woman, they'll get one of the head male housekeepers to either do the cabin or have two at once so there's always a witness. If he's tried to get physical, he's put off at the next port."

"I didn't realize that was a thing."

"Most of the problems stem from passengers over-partying. Security usually delivers a warning. If it persists, the person is put under supervision—like a soco stationed at their door—and then escorted off at the next port. At that point, they go on the no-cruise list."

"How frequently does this happen?"

"Every few weeks. We routinely offer self-defense classes and ways for the crew to indicate when they don't feel safe. It's tricky though, because if you so much as touch a hair on a passenger—especially an American—they threaten a lawsuit."

"I don't want to sound like I'm blaming the victim," I began, "but I keep going back to one of my first evenings on board earlier this summer. It was a formal night and photographers were doing portraits by the fountain. I heard catcalls and laughter coming from the Pirate Cove and checked it out." I cringed at the memory. "Tania was posing in a chair with her right leg hoisted behind her head, and her left tucked in front of her. She wore glittery black stockings, a garter belt, and a red bustier, which made her breasts almost tumble out. Men were invited to be photographed sitting in the wing chair and she would repeat the pose on their laps. It was supposedly a joke pose because the guy didn't know where to rest his hands. Most flung their arms out in a helpless gesture; a few held onto one of her legs as she propped her butt against them. Others ducked her stilettos."

"I know." Callista grimaced. "Tania was paid extra for that by the photography contractor because of the high percentage of sales."

"All you need is for some psycho to take the laughter the wrong way."

Someone wearing chef's garb lit a cigarette as he walked up the steps. He looked sheepish when he saw the cruise director. She gave him one of her camera-ready smiles. "Just leaving." We moved inside and stood by the elevator bank. She pushed the UP button with her elbow, a crew technique for minimizing germ contact. "Now I'm expected to paste on a smile and judge the tango contest." She snorted with annoyance.

"Once I took a course on profiling," I said. "Stalkers are often smarter than average, have low self-esteem, and refuse to take a no for an answer."

"Got plenty of those losers on board."

"Won't the photographer have the names of every guy who posed with her?"

"Doubtful, but he has every picture." Callista deflated. "I don't think we'll ever know. Just too many…too little time…"

"Has anyone asked why Tania's shows have been cancelled?"

"The official story is that she's recovering after a fall during rehearsal."

The elevator door opened. A woman using a walker stepped out tentatively. Callista helped the rear wheel over the threshold. "My ride," she said as the door closed.

I rubbed the back of my neck as if it would send a bolus of blood to energize my thoughts. Callista had seemed more of an apologist than a truth-seeker. Her training was in jollying and pacifying and pumping up passengers to forget their cares and have a grand time. Peering into dark hearts was not her forte, although it had been mine when I was an investigator—and even now as a novelist.

If I were Rolf, I would cancel the crew's shore leave during the Ft. Lauderdale turnaround. Since all crew passports were held by security, it would make it difficult for the guilty party to jump ship and head back to Tallinn or Timbuktu. But what bothered me the most was that I would have thought Callista would have been more passionate about seeking justice for her friend.

□ □ □

"This is your captain speaking," blasted from a speaker above my head. "I'm sorry to report that our attempts to stay in fair weather and calm seas, which took us slightly off-course in order to avoid some of the squalls, have come to an end. In order to avoid the choppy bits, we would have to change our heading from Florida to Nova Scotia, where it is currently minus five degrees Celsius, twenty-three Fahrenheit. I assure you that Ft. Lauderdale at twenty-two Celsius and seventy-two Fahrenheit is a better option and the foul weather won't last long. From fourteen hundred on we are expecting intermittent rain, worsening until the early hours of the morning and clearing tomorrow. After that, we can look forward to fair sailing. Please use the handrails in the corridors and especially on the stairs. Now I will hand off to Assistant Cruise Director Hawthorne."

"Lovely ladies and gregarious gents..." I recognized Ellwood's exaggerated Aussie accent, and felt relieved. "For all you hardy sailors, tonight's dress will be smart casual with extra points for fancy fleece or faux fur. Our ironic—I mean iconic—beverage special will be the Ultimate Cooler featuring Grey Goose, watermelon syrup, passion fruit purée, and cranberry juice. You will not want to miss the final hilarity of comedians: Joey and Lou in the Parrot's Perch and the sublime songstress Rachel Chevaux in the Empress Theater."

I ducked into a nearby ladies' room and noticed a stack of barf bags on the counter, a signal that we really were in for rough weather. Not quite ready to closet myself with my computer, I headed for the tables outside The Terraces for a snack. Dutifully, I went to the hand sanitizer station, spritzed it onto both hands and rubbed them well before perusing the lavish offerings. I selected a plate of sliced fruit, added three types of cheese, and a hard roll. My stride widened as I walked outdoors, a sure sign that the ship was pitching more than usual. I found a quiet table by the glass wall that acted as a wind break.

"Nice to see you on deck," Cozmin said.

"I didn't realize you also worked up here."

"Only a few hours in the afternoon. Tonight, though, is going to be dizzy-bizzy." He gestured to the ocean. "Lots of soup, salty crackers, and ginger ale."

"I'll try not to bother you."

"You, never!" He tilted his head. "Your usual?"

Smiling, I said, "I'm going to miss you, Coz."

A strident voice caught my attention. Ellwood was listening to a very animated woman wearing black yoga pants and a camel-colored cashmere tunic, who was muffled in a Burberry scarf. "I *do* see your point," Ellwood said in an exaggerated obsequious voice. "Even so, that's a matter for the purser."

"Don't you think I tried him first?"

Ellwood caught my eye and gave me a "help-me" glance.

I rose slightly in my chair and waved for his attention. "Oh, Woody! Do you have a tiny sec for me?"

Although I knew not to call him that, it made me sound more like another demanding passenger to give him an excuse to disengage.

"They always try their best to come up with a satisfactory solution," he said.

"They *claim* the ship is full and so moving to another suite is not possible, but I *know* they always have a few in reserve for just my sort of emergency."

"I believe they offered you several of the reserve cabins," he said defensively.

"They're all way below my category!"

"Weren't you offered a credit to offset your inconvenience?"

"I don't *want* a credit, I want a quieter room! I can't sleep because of the clanging in the pipes."

"I am happy to go to bat for you, but I can't make any promises."

"What about the mini-suite of the lady who's going to be evacuated?"

"Yes, well…" I saw his eyes roll heavenward. "I will make some inquiries. Please check with passenger services in a few hours." He turned toward me. "Now, Mrs. Lanier, how may I assist you?"

"Do you have time to join me for a moment, Woody, dahling?" I said in a stage whisper.

"A reprieve!" he muttered as he took a seat. "If I am walking about, it's open season and passengers are welcome to attack me; if I am sitting at a table, the unspoken rule is not to approach."

"Are the passengers that predatory?"

"You have no idea…"

Cozmin delivered my drink. "What would you like, Mr. H?"

"What I'd like is a dirty martini with extra olives, but I'll settle for regular coffee."

Cozmin winked at him. Ellwood said, "He's going to bring me a latte macchiato."

"Does crew have to pay extra for those too?"

"Theoretically, if we order them. I only asked for a coffee." He leaned back and closed his eyes.

"I wouldn't have your patience with a passenger like that woman. She looks familiar. On formal nights does her husband wear a kilt?"

"Yes, but he shouldn't. He has double chins on his knees!"

I covered my mouth to stifle my laugh. "Are they Scottish?"

"No, Anglo-wannabes. They don't dare cruise with Cunard or they'd be unmasked." He gave a wicked grin. "The chutzpah! She's a grave-robber trying to grab a better cabin if only for a few days."

"What's wrong with hers?"

"Nothing, but she's done a few back-to-backs and is probably nearing the thirty-day mark. That's the 'sell-by date' for most cruisers—present company excluded, of course."

"What do you mean?"

"After a month on board, passengers go 'off'—they're spoilt. They are tired of the entertainment, the food, their stateroom, and the service, and they start nitpicking. All she is angling for is some extra attention and an on-board credit. The purser will put a few hundred dollars in her account and she'll be thrilled. For people like her it's a sport."

"How *are* you?" I said in a serious tone. "I haven't seen you since…"

"I only left my cabin for the first time this morning." Cozmin delivered the latte in a tall glass cup with luscious layers of coffee and cream complete with a leafy design in the foam. Ellwood gave an exaggerated sign of contentment. "Coz, you're the best!" he said between wracking coughs.

"Have you been sick?"

"I think the medical term is 'flipped out.'" He rubbed his chin. " I can't explain it but it felt like something exploded in my face." He rubbed his chin. "I still can't banish the image of seeing—her. It's burned into my retinas."

"Yes, I know."

"The crazy thing is that we'd been working together for several weeks. Callista had this idea to add a new sketch to the crew talent show, which we do on the last night of every cruise. We were going to debut it on the Canal trip."

"You mean something with Olek and Tania?"

Ellwood nodded. "You've seen Tania's famous box routine, right?"

"Of course."

"Callista came up with the idea of stuffing me into this ginormous suitcase with Tania struggling to bring it center stage. Then after some silliness with bumps and knocks, she opens it and finds me wedged inside and she has to untwist me. Instead of stepping out gracefully like she does, I fall down, have cricks in my joints. It was going to be hysterical." Faster than a wind changing direction, his face drooped and he squeezed his eyes shut.

I touched his arm. "You see it even when your eyes are closed." He nodded in agreement. "You keep replaying the moments before when you were scouting a location, then what you saw, then the rest is a swirl of fragmented images."

"How did you know that?"

"Post-traumatic stress disorder—what's called PTSD."

Ellwood covered his face with his hands. "Callista insisted I work a few hours today. She said I'd feel better if I was distracted, but it's like trying to have a phone conversation and hearing your own voice reverberating on a one-second delay. I can't think straight."

"I know what you're going through."

"I've got to get the hell off this rust bucket. I'd do anything to get on the evacuation helicopter."

"You have something called 'fight or flight.' Flight seems the easier alternative—in this case literally. You need a break."

"I've been given leave to skip the next cruise and stay in Miami."

"That's only a few days from now. You'll make it."

"Not if I have to pass another of those freakin' laundry hampers!"

"I know. I cringe every time I see one."

"How can Callista stand it?" He took a long swallow of his coffee. When I looked confused, he said, "You really don't know?" He smacked his head with his fist. "Hell, it's not a secret—they're both technically crew so they weren't doing anything wrong."

"What do you mean?"

"They were lovers."

I gasped. "Are you sure?"

"We play on the same team in more ways than one."

"I knew that much but—"

Seeing my surprise, Ellwood said, "We have to be discrete."

No point in asking him why Callista hadn't confided in me. For a moment I felt betrayed and then could think of numerous reasons both before and after we discovered the body for her to be secretive. ""Everybody loved her," I whispered.

"Except some sicko bastard cone." He swallowed hard. "Any creep with a credit card can book a cruise.

And this one will vanish the second he's down the gangway."

"Whoa!" came a chorus of people around the pool as a sudden wave washed over the edge and splashed a few die-hard sunbathers. People jumped up to retrieve possessions that were sliding across the rolling deck.

The next wallop came a few seconds later. I grabbed my fruit-and-cheese plate, but my glass toppled to the floor. "Good save!" I said to Ellwood who had clasped his coffee glass with both hands. The bow rose again and slammed down hard. "The captain wasn't kidding. Just how choppy are those bits going to be?"

"Somewhere between a force six and a seven, with winds gusting to about thirty knots."

Living near the seacoast in Florida, I was familiar with the Beaufort wind force scale and knew that a ten was a gale and a twelve was a full-fledged hurricane. "Doesn't sound that bad."

"Normally, we would divert around this patch, but because we're trying to get closer to Bermuda, our course can't be varied by much."

This time I felt the early warning signs of the uplifting deck and braced for the downward thud. The last stragglers in the pool area headed indoors. "If this keeps up, will they still be able evacuate?"

"You never know. We could be in a dead calm by tomorrow." He checked his watch. "Almost time for my next gig," he said but didn't move. "So, this P— STD…" He caught his gaffe and gave a naughty grin.

I chuckled. "Not as bad as that, but here's the point: PTSD is real and it has triggered chemical changes in your brain. It's like your body's smoke detector is shrieking and you can't turn it off."

"Yes!" Ellwood shuddered. "How did you know?"

"Been there."

"It's...making me nuts."

"I'm glad you're taking a break. Where will you stay in Miami?"

"With a friend," he said, between attempts to clear his throat. "He's a concierge in a South Beach hotel."

"A little hanky-panky could be just what the doctor ordered."

"In my case, it's going to be more hanky then panky." He gave a half smile.

"A friend of mine is a terrific therapist who does a lot of work for the Dade County Sheriff's Department. Those guys are always dealing with grisly accidents and crime scenes and they are just as vulnerable as anyone else." Ellwood bent forward. "I'll email her and copy you."

"Thanks." Another coughing fit took over. "Damn cruise cough! Everybody worries about getting a norovirus, but these respiratory attacks are more common. Tania had it a few weeks ago and didn't miss a single appearance. I gave her all my Sudafed and now—"

I reached for his arm. "Did you ever give her anything besides Sudafed?"

"No. Why?"

"I meant something for pain—an Excedrin or migraine drug or...?

"Grisha had all that crap yet nothing for the common cold."

I stood as he did, holding onto the chair to steady myself though another crash and bump. "And, Mr. H," I said using Coz's nickname for him, "As impossible as this sounds, this too will pass. I promise."

□ □ □

The minute my computer flickered on, I typed a frenzy of impressions. Even though my visit with Grisha had lightened my suspicion of him, I wanted to sort out my conflicting feelings about Ellwood. He claimed he'd been upset—well who hadn't been? Nobody else had cloistered themselves. Was it PTSD or....guilt? He hated the nickname Woody. Why? Because of its sexual connotation? Perhaps bullies had used it or a dominating parent or even a doting mother. David believed that shame was the cause of most self-destructive behaviors like substance abuse, while guilt was the sign that a psychologically healthy person was trying to correct a mistake. "When parents shame a child, his whole sense of self is eroded," he used to lecture the new hires. "Even worse, it is the genesis for anger, rage, and other irrational behaviors that are directed toward others. Guilt leads to remorse and restitution. However, a deep well of shame explodes into abuse and violence." This seemed counterintuitive to me until he explained, "While you'd think the hurt child would have promised himself never to put someone else through the same pain, keep in mind the cycle of abuse whereby the powerless victim grows into the powerful tormenter."

The irony was that he had died trying to protect an unfortunate young man from being bullied.

I looked out my sliding glass door. Waves heaped upon each other sending up geysers of sea spray that blew back toward the ship, which was heading directly into the wind on the fastest course for Bermuda.

"Nah," I said aloud, as I tried to discard my brief suspicion. Everybody enjoyed Elwood, who was handsome in a boyish way, charming, talented, and especially light-hearted about his sexuality. In this instance I also could rule out jealousy. Yet how had I missed the fact that Tatiana and Callista were lovers? Maybe because the cruise director was so gracious, so warm, so funny with everyone that she never radiated anything personal. One hazard of entertainment jobs was that a charismatic smile meant to charm an audience could affect someone who was a bit lonely or unstable into believing that it was directed at them. It's a syndrome that gives teenage girls crushes on stars and motivates stalkers.

Thinking back, I realized that Callista had taken it far harder than anyone else—even those who professed to have loved her. How had Callista felt when she learned that Tania was pregnant? Angry? Resentful? Had she supposed that Tatiana was faithful to her or had they agreed to not be exclusive? Who else had she seduced? Grisha's "pure flower" was far more experimental than I would have guessed. In fact, I would have been surprised if the next confession of ardor came from the captain.

Perhaps I shouldn't have been so cavalier with my amateur diagnosis of PTSD. Even though traumatized people with PTSD sometimes became so enraged they committed crimes, I wasn't certain whether the discovery of a body could actually cause the syndrome. To refresh myself, I googled: <u>PTSD diagnosis</u>. Ellwood couldn't stop remembering the incident—check. He had *avoidance symptoms*—wanting to get off the ship, staying in his cabin—check. *Arousal triggers*—like seeing the laundry hampers—check! What could cause him to want to harm her? I couldn't remember the details of shame-and-blame, but people did hold grudges against those who had shamed them.

I tried to conjure a scenario between Elwood and Tatiana. They had been rehearsing the suitcase routine. Perhaps she had done some of her more erotic contortions close to him, even using him as a prop like twisting herself in a knot on a man's lap. Elwood was so flagrantly gay that she might have come on to him as a tease. To him, it might have seemed as if she was taunting his inadequacy and he felt humiliated. Humiliation that could have ignited a simmering rage—causing him to snap and kill her. I was having trouble selling myself my own theory, still many a culprit is the one who "discovers" the body. To hammer home his "shock," he sought refuge in his cabin. Even better, his understanding superiors already granted him leave in the United States and would relinquish their hold on his passport. Instead of going to South Beach, Ellwood could get on the first plane to Brazil or Bora Bora. Then, after a suitable time, he could return home to Oz.

Could... "Never fall in love with your theories," David had warned, "because they only pan out in detective stories."

David was considering leaving his job to teach criminology, with an emphasis on child abuse and crimes of passion. We talked about me helping him write a book. Nobody I ever knew had a mind so intuitive and analytical, but even he couldn't have sorted this without forensic tools.

I stared at my computer screen and typed my final thought: Unlike most everyone else, Ellwood never said he loved Tatiana.

I started a new list titled "Father." Nothing percolated. All I felt was commiseration. If I knew anything, it was how losses in one's life could pile up incrementally. A strong soul might cope with a few—especially with a support system—but Grisha lived in what David used to call the "tragicsphere"—a hell-on-earth where everything that could go wrong for a family did. I bristled at any idea that people were predetermined to follow a certain path whether to the moon or the gutter, yet over time I came to see his point. Grisha had pinned all his dreams on his daughter—protecting her in every possible way. If I could imagine Ellwood becoming irrationally angry, her father had far more at stake. When we had our son, David warned me not to fawn over every little accomplishment because those who only feel loved on the condition that they perform well are at high risk for depression or even suicide, which seemed extreme to me. Yet maybe that was why I now couldn't shake the feeling that Tatiana had taken an overdose, although Sudafed would hardly have been the pill of choice.

I stood up and stretched by the sliding door to the balcony, which was fogged with salty spray. I tried out another hypothesis about shame. Let's say that Grisha found out about the pregnancy, berating and belittling, reducing Tatiana to crumbs as only a parent can. Maybe it was a particularly Russian skill, even though I had seen my grandmother criticize my mother and watched her usually proud demeanor melt into a puddle. If Tatiana felt ashamed, afraid, and alone, she may have felt cornered. If suicide had been on her mind, the solution was never more than a few feet away: she could have jumped. Statistically, though, women preferred pills and she had easy access to her father's stash. If she had been rebelling against her father, would she have done it in their cabin? She sometimes slept in Olek's cabin, so that was another choice. That didn't get her into the laundry hamper. Let's say anyone of those people— or even someone else—found her body in their room and panicked. Lots of people would have preferred to move the corpse—whether they were associated with it or not. The wheeled laundry hamper brimming with dirty linen was a clever way to transport a body, although it would look odd for anyone but a room steward to be seen with one, so it would have to be done stealthily, likely in the middle of the night.

I stepped out onto the balcony and felt the violence of the wind stream being sliced by the bow before it jetted down each side of the hull. So much turmoil underneath, yet all through the ship, mostly unseen, more than a thousand workers had jobs to do from the commander on the bridge to the engineers in charge of generating electricity or converting sea water to drinking water. In the bowels of the ship, a crew washed everything from passengers' panties to cooks' uniforms to a never-ending tide of towels and bed linens. Cooks trimmed vegetables, whipped sauces, sliced slabs of meat, carved ice sculptures, and prepared dough for rolls, pizza, even artisanal pretzels. This mostly-unseen navy fascinated me. Passengers only ever were in contact with the tip of this servicing iceberg: a few officers, social directors, waiters, and room stewards. When we arrived in Florida, the room stewards would have only two hours to make every stateroom fresh and welcoming without a smidgen to reveal that someone else had used that bathroom for the last two weeks—or had died in that bed.

My focus shifted from who was with Tatiana last to where she had breathed her last. Could it have been in poor freaked-out Ellwood's cabin? Callista didn't have a roommate, so maybe he didn't either. They had been working together on the crew talent show skit so maybe she went there because she knew he worked such long hours and she wouldn't be found for a long time. Despondent over the pregnancy or something else, she took pills. He freaked when he found her, tried to move her body in a hamper, but was frightened by something and ran away. So, maybe the real reason he'd holed up in his stateroom was to have plenty of time to scrub it thoroughly. By now every sign—even the laundry cart tracks—had been obliterated by zealous cleaning and the corridor maintenance crews.

One of the oddest facts so far was that the contortionist's body had been so…pristine. Death was messy with blood, vomit, feces, sweat, and other traces of the cause. There could have been time to fix her up. The sort of evidence usually found at a crime could have been churned in our wake. People lost items overboard all the time. Dirty towels, soiled clothing, pill containers, cocktails—all could flutter overboard a bit at a time without being a large enough target for the ubiquitous cameras. Warnings not to leave clothing or wet towels on balconies were everywhere because no clothespin was a match for thieving mid-Atlantic whirlwinds.

"Everyone makes a crucial mistake, our job is to find it," David taught. So far there was one obvious smear. Smears arise from a deliberate human intervention. Tatiana could have wiped between her legs like many women do after sex or someone else had tried to cleanse that area. While forensics would uncover the chemistry of the stain, there would be no way to tell if the encounter had been consensual.

Shafts of sunlight were gobbled by the chomping waves. Even through the closed door it sounded like a mighty train was heading toward the ship. Shutting the sliding door silenced it to a muffled roar. I heard another announcement over the loudspeaker in the corridor and opened the cabin door to hear it better.

"…Also cancelled tonight will be the balloon drop and midnight pool party.," chirped Callista in her join-in-the-fun voice. "Not to worry, they are on schedule again for tomorrow when the weather should be the Caribbean kiss we've all been anticipating. And don't forget the gala champagne-for-all art auction in—"

"Hello! Hello!" Coming toward me was the smiling face of Dante pushing a laundry cart. I ducked back into my cabin. The sea swell helped plop me in the arm chair. Those damn carts were all over the ship! I had seen them backstage bursting with fluffy can-can skirts when Tatiana had shown me the silks apparatus. There were several carts by each of the pools marked for fresh and used towels. And the shop girls used them for toting merchandise to "impromptu" sales in the atrium. So many carts....so many people...

I felt lightheaded and knew I had better eat something because I tolerated rough seas best with a full stomach. I contemplated my options. The Terraces were the worst place to be in a headwind; the stateroom was feeling claustrophobic. That left a sit-down meal in the dining room, which was a good option for a stormy night because the restaurants were at the most stable part of the vessel: mid-ships on a middle deck.

I saved my new notes to the flash drive, replaced it in my tote bag, then I went into the bathroom and picked up Floris's Malmaison talcum. Once the favorite scent of Oscar Wilde, it was now discontinued and this was my last can of the spicy geranium scent. I closed the computer and lightly dusted the area around it with powder, blowing off the residue. Washing my hands, I wondered what David would think of my cartoonish attempt at espionage. If nothing was disturbed, I'd admit that my paranoia was silly, yet as ordinary as everything seemed onboard, someone had died and nobody knew how or why.

□ □ □

The Treasure Island dining room was almost empty, probably due to woozy stomachs.

"Will you share?" the headwaiter asked me. The convention at lunch was to agree to join a large table.

"Be happy to," I said. I needed a break from my inner conflicts. Besides, I was interested in whether there was any gossip about the absent headline performer.

I was the last one to join seven others, who introduced themselves. The ladies to my left were Gwen, Cathy, and Michelle—a mother and two adult daughters traveling together. Gwen was a decorator on a European buying spree for her North Carolina gift shop. The others were two couples from British Columbia: Terry and Vicky, Hugo and Olive.

My turn. This was tricky. Dale sometimes triggered "like Dale Lane, the writer?"—flattering but also a trap. I didn't like to lie or be pummeled with questions. Not much better was when someone asked, "As in Chip n' Dale?" or they referred to the Chippendale male strippers, the race car driver, or Roy Roger's wife. It also was best to avoid saying I lived in Ft. Lauderdale. Superficial shipboard acquaintances sometimes breeched traditional boundaries when they bonded over a mutual interest in Italian grappa or movie trivia. Invitations to visit when in Missoula or Mobile were bandied about because nobody ever showed up in those places.

181

However, Ft. Lauderdale is a major cruise port and I've lost track of how many have asked if they could spend a few nights post or pre-cruise at my place.

"Donna Lanier," I said, "from Pennsylvania."

"Oh where?" Michelle asked. "My husband grew up in Pittsburgh."

"Swarthmore," I replied, which is where I went to college. "What port did you like best?" I asked the Canadian gentleman across from me to deflect further questions.

"We're keen hikers," Terry began. We did Cinque Terre, trotted up Vesuvius, made it to the top of Brunelleschi's dome in Florence first thing before the crowds. Oh, and we climbed up to Montserrat."

"We had to take the tram down," his wife Vicky replied, "otherwise we would have missed the boat." She leaned back, satisfied they had bested the group.

But no, the travel competition heated up. "In Turkey, we realized it was our fiftieth country," Michelle said. "My bucket list is to do a hundred, so we're halfway there."

Nobody could top that, so we concentrated on the menu, which featured mushroom ravioli in vodka cream sauce, shrimp po'boy sandwiches, Caesar salads with grilled chicken or steak, and a vegetarian curry. The waiter mentioned three soups, firehouse chili, and a few appetizers including game pâté, egg rolls, and prosciutto with melon.

"A double of the ravioli," Hugo said to the waiter, "and a side of chili."

"Hugo, really, is that wise?" Olive chided her husband, then to the table, "Hugo turns green if he stares at ice in a glass."

It was Vicky's turn to order. "I'll just have a steak Caesar, medium rare, and a cup of hot water."

"Just plain water?" Olive wrinkled her nose.

"Cold liquids solidify fats in your stomach, while hot liquids aid in digestion.," she replied. "We learned that in Hong Kong. Really helps with digestion."

"It works wonders for my regularity," Terry said.

His wife blushed. "Sorry, TMI!"

The waiter then turned to me. "I'd like the melon first and the pâté second."

"I should have thought of that!" Gwen said. "I love to graze by having two appetizers."

Olive was the conversation turner. "Anyone else going to the art auction this afternoon?"

"I'll stop by for free champagne," Michelle said, "although there's no way in hell I'll bid for any of that—" Her sister Cathy poked her arm. "Most everything is worthless."

"No," Gwen corrected, "just worth less than they promote in the spiel."

Hugo gave his wife a light warning glance, but Olive ignored it. "We've been very pleased with our prior purchases. They have something to suit every décor."

"What do you think of the auctioneer?" I asked.

"Vance?" Vicky chimed in. "*Adore* him. I've gone to all his lectures, still my favorite was the one on modernism." She gave a self-deprecating laugh. "I thought it referred to present day, but Vance explained it began in the middle of the nineteenth century."

Cathy sputtered while sipping her Chardonnay. Her sister patted her back.

The whole restaurant started clattering, first as soft as a rattlesnake in the bushes, increasing to a metallic jangle. Hugo looked to the window wall. "Getting a lot wilder out there."

"Whoa!" Cathy said, catching the stem of her wine glass that didn't stay put as she tried to replace it on the table. "We're in for a Nantucket sleigh ride."

"I doubt we've harpooned a whale," her mother said with a chuckle.

"Whatever! I love it when it gets rough."

"Yeah, and you like roller coasters too," Michelle said, obviously not as keen as her sister.

The ship seemed to settle into a steadier pattern just as the first course was served.

"I admit the auctions are entertaining," Michelle said, "like the casino or bingo, even so people shouldn't expect to be investing in fine art."

"My sister knows of what she speaks," Cathy said. "She's one of the auctioneer's shills."

I looked up from my plate.

"It's not illegal," Michelle said defensively. "The company has the right to set the price. A few of us agree to be first bidders to build the excitement."

"And get free prints in exchange," Cathy added.

"Just souvenirs," Michelle replied with a shrug.

Olive straightened her back. "I decide how much something is worth to me and I never go over my limit." Hugo's cough contradicted her. "What I *say* is my limit and what my *real* one is may differ, darling."

"How can they claim something 'unique and collectable' when anyone can buy a duplicate for the hammer price?" Gwen asked. "And what really gets my goat is when they sell those mystery pieces, where the painting is shown only from the back. I mean, why in the world would anyone buy something sight unseen?"

"Those can be great deals," Olive answered. "They're always offered at a rock bottom price. Not only that, you are free to reject it if you don't like it once you see it."

"In any case, the frames, matting, and glass are worth at least as much as the bid," Vicky said in her friend's defense.

"*Caveat emptor*," Gwen replied in a silky voice. "Just beware when they offer you a Picasso or Rembrandt, or even a Dalí." She used the Catalan pronunciation: "Dull-lee."

"They have a Picasso on an easel in their gallery now," Olive said. "It's a museum-quality print appraised at more than thirty-five thousand dollars."

"Which is a little rich for our budget, my dear," Hugo said to his wife and then to the table, "But they *are* genuine."

"That may be true," Gwen said, "however, a few years ago, someone who bought a Picasso on a cruise ship sued the company."

"How could they? You have to sign a sales agreement not to sue before you even get a paddle," Vicky said.

"All I know is this guy bought a Picasso clown print, which the auctioneer said was a great deal at forty percent of the appraised value," Gwen continued. "When the buyer got home, he did some research and found that Christie's sold the same print—the exact same number out of a series of two hundred—for around six thousand dollars. With taxes, buyer's premium, and shipping the guy on the ship paid over thirty thousand!"

Cathy looked like she was going to add something but thought better of it.

Vicky glanced at her watch. "We're going to have to hustle to get a good seat."

"No dessert?" Michelle said a bit maliciously, since Vicky was a generously sized woman.

"They'll have chocolate-dipped strawberries to go with the champagne," Vicky replied, missing the barb.

▢ ▢ ▢

The art auction business on board always perplexed me and I found the repartee at lunch a good indication of the dual way it was perceived. The Hemisphere Lounge was the second largest venue on the ship after the Galleon Theater. Copies of historical maps lined the walls. Comfy chairs were upholstered in a fabric that featured antique globes. Two stick-thin auction assistants in black dresses, white sailor collars, and patent leather stiletto heels flanked Vance, who wore a tux. Michelle sidled up to Vance, who beamed at her and handed her a numbered paddle.

The Canadian couples were seated side by side in the second row. Gwen stood in an aisle farther back waving to me. "I've saved you a seat." I slalomed through the crowd in her direction. "Have you been to one of these before?"

"I've watched a few from the sidelines."

"What's *your* opinion of the auctioneer?"

I shrugged. "He's a sweetheart but not my type."

"All style and no substance." In a lower voice she added, "Michelle sees right through him but Cathy—" She looked around for her daughter who was lingering near the sign-up table. "I warned her, and she still fell for him."

"I didn't think he is supposed to ah, fraternize with the guests."

"Apparently, those rules don't apply to him. Beaux Arts is an independent company that pays Empire a percentage," Gwen said. "Anyway, it's no longer an issue. As soon as he realized she saw it as more than a harmless flirtation, he announced that his fiancé was onboard."

"When was that?"

"Somewhere in Greece. She was all mopey in Mykonos."

Out of the corner of my eye I saw Cathy standing right beside Vance. He was smiling at her. His hand casually reached for her waist and he whispered something in her ear. She melted into him and I saw his lips graze her forehead. Not exactly what her mother had just reported. Puzzled, I looked over at Gwen, but she was waving for Michelle to join us.

The lights dimmed. The theme from *Star Wars* blasted. A spotlight highlighted Vance as he strode across the stage. A few—including my new Canadian acquaintances—stood up waving their auction paddles in the air. A second spotlight illuminated a landscape on an easel.

"Welcome to our Champagne gala auction. By request, we begin with Branislav Cervanka." He gestured regally toward a canvas of three trees; each looked like a giant leaf planted in a hilly ground. "As those who've attended my appreciation lectures already know, this Czech painter melds the line of Toulouse-Lautrec and the palette of Matisse. Most contemporary artists won't risk using such vibrant colors, yet Cervanka has achieved the perfect balance. The appraised value is fifteen thousand dollars; we'll begin bidding at sixty-five hundred—less than half!"

The comingling of illustrious names with their mass-market artists was an ingenious form of salesmanship. Someone started the bidding and the price rose rapidly. Vance called out, "Eleven thousand two hundred and fifty!" His hammer fell with a pompous plonk. "Congratulations Number One Forty-five."

The audience applauded. Vance said, "Thank you for showing respect for the collector."

Gwen moved over and Michelle took the seat next to her mother. A few seconds later, Cathy sat in the chair next to me.

"Next we have a stunning giclée by—does anyone recognize this French painter's signature romantic poses of women?"

"Durant Chappelle" ricocheted from several places in the room.

"You very attentive students are in luck because we are selling not one—but three of his paintings. Feast your eyes on the ethereal lady in gold on the portico. In the distance is a sea so vivid you can smell the saltiness. The piece in the middle features a deliciously languid woman with cinnamon skin waiting…waiting for what? My favorite, if I might be permitted to have one, is the pianist in the black dress, her hands blurring as she plays what song? In my mind, I hear Gershwin's *Rhapsody in Blue*." He gave an exaggerated sigh of satisfaction. "Remember each one is a hand-embellished giclée on canvas and personally signed by Chappelle in ink."

Michelle turned toward me. "Do you know what giclée is?" I shook my head, surprised that I had never heard the word before. "It's a French term meaning to spray or squirt, which is how an inkjet printer works." I stared at the pictures with renewed interest. "Then they are 'enhanced,' which means that the artist—or one of his minions—paints on some texture or highlighting."

Gwen bent in. "Vance said that Peter Max puts at least one dot of paint on every piece himself to 'authenticate' it."

There was some confusion on stage because several bidders were selecting the "paintings" they wanted. Michelle said, "The gimmick is that one person wins the bid and then they allow anyone else to buy the others at the same price."

"How does that make sense?" I asked.

There was another rumble from the core of the ship followed by a jerky motion. A few champagne glasses teetered off the small cocktail tables.

"Ride 'em cowboy!" Vance called. "Everybody still with me?" Waiters rushed in to wipe up the messes. "No worries. We have plenty more bubbly."

"He cuts quite the figure," I said to Cathy, curious as to what she would say.

"I've enjoyed getting to know him better. When he first met me, he thought I was a prime sales prospect."

I knew Vance wined-and-dined potential big-spenders. "I can see why, you're a beautiful young woman and isn't that a Valentino pants suit?"

"Vintage." Cathy held a finger to her lips. "E-bay." She pouted before gushing, "I don't know what my mother said, but he was always upfront about having his fiancé on the ship."

"Harmless flirting never hurt anyone."

"Besides, he really isn't engaged; it makes it easier to manage some of the more 'aggressive ladies.'" She tossed her auburn ponytail. "Anyway, she's leaving in Florida." I waited. "She and this other guy from IT are shifting to the *Empress of the Pacific*."

"Is she also in IT?

"No, she's a dancer—from Russia."

My stomach rolled the opposite direction of the ship's motion.

Two cabaret performers, who were doubling as art assistants, set a large painting covered by a drape on a double easel. "On my count," Vance began, "one, two, and…"

"Three," shouted the audience. The drape fell with a flourish.

"Ahhh…" Vance prompted the audience to echo.

"Here we have one of the most collected artists in the world. Sadly, he is no longer with us, making his luminescent art even more of a collectable treasure."

190

"The *kitschmeister*," Gwen muttered.

I blinked at the maudlin scene of a thatched roof house illuminated by a glowing fireplace within, a winding brook mirroring a sunset, and an arched stone bridge. Even I recognized a quintessential Thomas Kinkade of shopping-mall fame.

"Here we have the very essence of hearth and home, a serene vision of what matters most. The windows of our very lives will be lit with the irresistible glow of a place that says: welcome." Vance's smile was even more saccharine than his sentimental patter.

"But you're also leaving the ship," I said, swiveling toward Cathy to pump her for more about Vance.

"For now." She lamented dramatically. "Poor guy, first he finds out she's leaving the ship—and he made it sound like he was the dumpee, if you know what I mean. And then got news that one of his family members was killed in an accident." She mistook my attempt to stay silent for disbelief. "No, really, I found him in tears. He was so broken by the news, he was beyond comforting."

I looked up at Vance prancing and pontificating. Cathy read my thoughts. "The show must go on…"

"Of course."

"He asked me come back for a Canal cruise in a few weeks."

The smell of spilled champagne mingling with the minty mop-up spray was an off-putting combination. "I need some air," I said to my companions and stood up.

The crowd was tightly packed and the center aisle was clogged with wheelchairs, so I squeezed my way toward the front and exited through the door closest to the stage.

The corridor was littered with wheeled pallets holding stacks of paintings. Two assistants were looking for something.

"CH-204 and 206 are the same Chapelle painting as 205," the taller one said.

"Don't see it here," the other answered in a Scottish brogue. "I think they're still in the starboard art locker."

"Look in section Seven Zero Seven Kilo Foxtrot," the tall one instructed, almost stepping on my toes as he passed me.

He didn't go far. Using a magnetic card, he unlocked an unmarked door less than three feet wide. The light flicked on revealing a narrow space about twenty feet in length and six feet wide. Nobody would have guessed there was a closet tucked in between the ship's side and the wall that lined the passageway running from the photography display to a restroom near the elevator bank. The inside was outfitted with shelves and spacers that held four levels of paintings on their sides. A skinny ladder offered access to the highest shelves. Against the opposite wall, dollies were tied to hooks so they wouldn't fall as the ship listed.

One assistant walked to the far end and wrestled something out of the corner. He turned it, rejected it, and pushed it into one of the banks of shelves. He ran his hands over the edges of the next row of paintings until he alighted on the one he wanted. Then he hefted it into the cart and wheeled it out.

I watched as he headed back toward the Hemisphere Lounge. He was pushing a yellow laundry cart.

□ □ □

One of my favorite places on the ship is the viewing area at the butt end of Gulf Deck. *The Seven Seas* is a Panamax class of ship that is narrow enough to fit through the original Panama Canal locks. In the summer the vessel spends most of its time in the Mediterranean; the rest of the year it departs Fort Lauderdale for partial Canal transits, which means it does not continue into the Pacific Ocean. The aft exterior of Gulf Deck is outfitted with a horseshoe curve of varnished teak benches with a view of the ship's foamy wake. In the past six weeks, this is where I headed when I hit a rough patch in writing. To cleanse errant thoughts, I reminded myself our ports of call in the last six weeks as they receded in the mist: Ljubljana, Barcelona, Cartegena, Korcula, Messina, Santorini, Civitavecchia—so evocative, so lyrical. This time, though, another word buzzed in my brain like a mosquito dodging my mental swatter, interrupting my meditative flow: Vance.

"Apologies, madam," a deckhand said. "We are closing this deck due to the weather." As he opened the door for me to proceed to the inside passageway, it shuddered against the wind.

The ship lurched and I grabbed for the handrail bolted to the corridor wall. It took me a few steps to catch the new rhythm: a sailor's lope with long, angled strides. The more motion, the wider my steps. I headed up to Baltic Deck so I could continue ruminating in the glassed-in aft area that was part of the spa. Hardly anyone ever used the heated stone loungers that faced the wake.

I took a shortcut through the library where I could hear mahjong tiles clacking. A curl of smoke wafted from Winston's, the indoor smoking venue. I glanced through the glass wall to see if I knew any of the nicotine addicts. Rolf caught my eye. He held up his pointer finger as a request for me to wait a minute.

"Mrs. Lanier," he began when he met me by the atrium railing, "I wonder if I might have a word?"

Rolf tilted his head in the universal "follow-me" gesture. He used a card key to open the tiny Empire Circle office where future cruises could be booked at a discount. The walls were decorated with vintage travel posters. He took the seat behind the desk and I sat in one opposite him.

"I don't want you to think I'm a smoker," he began. "I stop by the lounge because it's a hotbed of ship gossip."

"Has anyone mentioned—?"

He coughed to clear his lungs. "No, so that's a relief." He fumbled for a tissue in a classy leather dispenser and blew his nose. "The topic today was digestion—how the last meal went down and—I am serious—how it came out. I wrinkled my nose. "What was delightful after a week becomes tiresome after a month and the picking of nits begins."

I laughed. "Nitpicking."

"It means—what?"

I pulled on a sheaf of my hair. "Nits are the eggs laid by hair lice. Picking them out is a laborious task, not that I would know!" Rolf grimaced. "Don't worry, your English is excellent." I waited a beat. "And apparently so is your Russian."

"Not as fluent as yours. Thanks for checking on Mr. Zlatogrivov."

"He's very upset about sending his daughter to Bermuda?"

"Unfortunately, our policy is to offload the deceased at the next port of call."

"I am sympathetic to him, but I agree that it would be easier to avoid US involvement as much as possible," I said.

"Yourself included?" A slight shift in his gaze revealed he knew more than he let on.

"I'd rather not have to deal with the Broward County officials—and they would prefer never to have any further dealings with me."

Rolf didn't press the point. "I tried to tell Mr. Zlatogrivov that once Empire gets clearance from Bermuda, we will be repatriating his daughter to Russia, but he didn't seem to hear me."

"Grief deafness," I said. "He's shut down his senses for self-protection."

"I wasn't aware…" Rolf said, then contemplated in silence for a minute.

I felt a frisson of excitement in the close room without any logical reason why I found Rolf so appealing. The ever-wise Margot might have joked that I always went for the law-and-order type, although David tried hard to soften his image so families and children would confide in him. Rolf was more European, more…debonair might be the best description, and while I also found him a bit arrogant—and had resented his role in firing my favorite masseuse—he was the highest-ranking security officer onboard and had to project a commanding image. He had cared about Tatiana, which is why he avoided being in the room for the rape kit.

The walls of the tiny office seemed to tilt as the ship juddered, lifted, and settled back hard—waking me from my brief fantasy. I'd have to tell Margot because she would be thrilled that I might be coming out of my self-exile.

Rolf cleared his throat. "The weather ahead is improving."

"Is the evacuation on?"

"The patient's stable, although we might not be able to send her husband with her."

"Why?"

"He's one of your super-sized Americans. Must be a hundred and forty kilos." Rolf stared at the ceiling as if looking for divine help. "Even so, some good can come from bad. I'll have to stay in Florida to help with the paperwork. Happily, I can have my son fly over for Christmas and I'll take him to Disney."

I decided against asking more about the boy. Instead, I said, "May I ask you something about the security cameras?"

"That's classified information."

"I only wondered whether you've been able find anything that relates to Tania."

"Not yet. It's a massive job because there are more than a thousand cameras." His thin lips drew up into a semi-smile. "This isn't one of your *romans*—novels. We may never know what happened." He knitted his fingers together.

The room was becoming stifling, but I had something else on my mind. "Did you know that the art gallery uses laundry carts to transport their paintings?"

Rolf unfolded his hands, placed them on his knees, and leaned toward me. "Why didn't I think of that!"

"And I guess this won't come as news to you, I saw Tania and Vance together—they looked like more than friends."

"Well, *he* isn't the papa!" Rolf gave a strange, throaty laugh. "He *appreciated* her like he would a sculpture, but she didn't have any *feelings* for him." Rolf had a brief run of sneezes, a variation on the cruise cough that was going around. "How should I say this? The officers all tiptoe around the auctioneers because the company receives a respectable percentage of sales. Mr. Sharkey is one of the biggest rainmakers." He tipped back in the desk chair. "Also, he's not subject to the same prohibitions when it comes to mingling with passengers. Still, we keep an eye on the auction staff." He winked at me. "Let's just say that he's very popular with some of our guests—that is our *male* guests."

I thought about Vance's professed feelings for Tatiana. Could it could have been just a bit of playfulness, pretending to be that couple? Despite

Cathy's pipe dream and Vance's fantasy fiancé, Rolf had just confirmed my initial intuition.

A new thought bubbled up. "At least Tania could confide in you—in Russian."

He watched me through his heavily lidded hawk eyes that glared gold in the desk lamp's light. "Once the Wall fell, I tried to forget everything I learned." He sat up straight. "Although Russian can be quite, ah, sentimental—under the right circumstances." His eyelids were half closed and he bit his lower lip, a gesture that revealed vulnerability. "You and I..." he began tentatively. "...More in common...so we should understand..."

I remained impassive, sensing a ploy to diffuse any prejudice I might have had against him because of Agata or other negative rumors.

"This case...it won't be solved before we land, if ever." He placed a finger on his nose.

"Sometimes even when you see it happen right before your eyes, it doesn't help you believe or understand or..." Rolf's jaw clenched, and then his words whistled through his teeth. "I too...my wife...gone in a flash." My hands clutched the sides of the chair. "Like your husband."

"What do you mean?"

"We had to check on you before we could ask for your assistance," he paused for a long beat. "I am very sorry."

"Your wife, was she ill?"

"No....no....a car..." He gave a croaking laugh. "A Smart car, little harmless looking thing. We live in London; she's from Belgium and she was always forgetting to look to her right—even though they have that printed on the curbs for stupid tourists. So, she crossed the street and walked right into the path of the Smart. It swerved to miss the baby carriage but got her in the back. Both went up in the air. She came down on her head and the carriage—they say it did a loop—but luckily the baby was strapped in and he didn't have a scratch."

"When was this?"

"Four years ago." He closed his eyes. "Never goes away, not for a second."

"Your child?"

"A boy, He goes by his English name, Ralphie."

"He…wasn't injured."

"No, and he was only two, so he doesn't remember Vero. He lives with my wife's sister in Brighton. She's single, a teacher, and devoted to him." He looked at the ceiling, blinking as a strategy to contain tears.

Then silence. I assumed I was supposed to commiserate and share, which seemed like a ruse because he had some sort of file on me. "That was a gambit, right?" I said, trying to fold my anger into hospital corners. He angled his head in feigned innocence. "You showed me yours, now you want me to strip."

"I beg your pardon."

He looked more guileless than conniving. You have to have felt a certain exquisite and unrelenting barbed sorrow that never, ever, not for a second lets the wound heal completely, to see the tender spot in someone else. Rolf was not faking, even if he probably had an ulterior motive.

"My husband worked in child protection," I began. "One of his cases was a boy of fourteen, but he looked like an adult. He was heavy—really fat—over six feet tall—and black with a big bush of hair." My hands suggested how large it was. Jimbo was autistic and lived in a group home because he could flare up and needed strong counselors to calm him, even medication sometimes. Mostly, he was a sweetheart, hugged, held your hand, and sang beautifully—if not too loudly. He was very artistic and if you showed him a picture of a train or car or even a house, he'd render it perfectly from memory."

"Idiot-savant, like in *Rainman*?"

"We prefer autistic-savant, although he is something like that." I gulped. "My husband David—he had removed Jimbo from his parents because he would wander out of the house and scare people, so they chained him to his bed. He was in very bad shape when he came into foster care and David was the one person who could calm him. So, one day he was called because Jimbo had punched a hole in the wall and they worried he might hurt someone. David went right over, but he didn't know they had also called the police."

Whatever people imagine about a crime or an accident is always tinged with a blurry buffer that spares you of the horror of a real-time moment. There was probably no recording of Rolf's wife and child being tossed by the car nor of her landing or the other cars screeching and clashing or of his baby's stroller flying up and miraculously landing on its wheels. There is, however, mobile phone footage and body-cam tape of police believing that the big, boisterous, flailing and screeching Jimbo was coming at them in a threatening fashion and of David—half his size—arms flailing and his inaudible protest not to shoot. And then, David, being David, throwing himself on top of Jimbo to protect him as six bullets penetrated his head and back, the blood pooling all over the terrified boy who thought he was dying but didn't have a scratch. David was gone before he had finished saying, "No! No! He's—"

I said some version of this as fast as I could spit it out. Rolf nodded and said, "Friendly fire."

"I *hate* that term!" I groaned. "Stupid, crazy, unnecessary…everybody who knew the kid wasn't worried about him. He was just a big, lonely baby. David would have calmed him with chocolate milk and soothing words."

"I know…" Rolf stood and came behind my chair. For a moment I thought he was going to touch me. Even though I couldn't see him, I felt the movement of his outstretched arms stir the room air. "If I am still angry every time I see one of those ridiculous half-cars…" I felt his hand on the edge of the chair. "Who cares for your little boy?"

"His grandmother."

Rolf inclined his head so I could see his face. His mouth had gone slack and his forehead was glossy.

"One moment more…" He swallowed hard. "I just wonder what you do…where you put…your…rage?"

The question felt like a slap. I recoiled and turned away. Nobody had asked me before, not even the therapist I saw for a while at the insistence of David's well-meaning friends. The whole notion that someone

201

could help was like trying to repair a plane that had fallen from the sky and scattered into a million pieces. Whatever was left was devoted to Bodhi and earning enough money to protect us from the next disaster. I didn't answer because I could not. Rolf's usually stiff spine had lost all his military starch. He hadn't expected an answer; the question had been rhetorical.

His voice was low and slow. "I just wanted you to know that we've stayed at the same vile hotel." Then he gave a wry smile and moved toward the door. "After that, ship life isn't so bad, is it?"

He opened the door and I relished the rush of cooler air. "Again, we thank you for your kind assistance."

◻ ◻ ◻

I took the elevator to the bottom of the atrium. A trio of Croatian violinists were playing the Winter section from Vivaldi's *Four Seasons*. I was more sympathetic than upset with Rolf's ploy. Time was running out and his career could be at stake. He had made one macho slip by repudiating any chance that Vance could have fathered Tatiana's child, a possible admission that he too either was in love with Tatiana—or bragging that they had been lovers. Somehow, neither Rolf or Vance seemed her type, although she hardly had been selective.

Just as I turned into the forward elevator bank, I heard a strangled cry. I spun around but saw nothing. A weak "Help" seemed to be coming from above the middle elevator door. The outside door was opened a crack, revealing that the elevator was stuck three-quarters of the way up with the cables dangling. When I looked up, I noticed fingertips trying to keep the inside door open a crack.

"I'll get help," I shouted, and rushed back the way I had come.

At the edge of the atrium balcony, I saw Rolf surrounded by a bevy of mature women. "Rolf— Officer Brandt —there's an emergency! Elevator bank," I shouted and he hurried past me.

A woman in a wheelchair was just about to push the UP button. "*Halt!*" Rolf commanded. "Everyone, please go to another elevator or take the stairs. These are now out of service."

The woman stuck inside sobbed, "Please, please, get me out."

Rolf spoke a few garbled words into a two-way radio. "Madam, help is coming," he boomed. "How many are you?"

A man with a French accent responded, "Three of us."

"Your names?"

"She is Harriet Cunningham. I'm Pierre Dubois and—"

"Ernst Ziegfield" called another male voice.

"Now Madam Harriet," Rolf said, "what I want you to do is sit down on the floor, okay?" There was as scuffle and a clunk.

"Now, gentlemen, can one of you press the door-open button while the other tries to pull it further?"

The crack opened to several feet revealing folds of a skirt, sneakers, and pink socks.

A man wearing a green jumpsuit arrived. "The elevator crew is on its way."

Rolf moved to the edge of the abyss. "Get me a chair," he ordered the maintenance man.

"It's moving!" Harriet wailed.

"That's just the ship," the voice named Ernst said with a Boston accent.

"Would one of you gentlemen kindly sit down beside the lady?"

"*Mais oui*," Mr. Dubois said. He was wearing flip-flops and shorts revealing skinny, hairy legs.

"Will this do?" a crewmember asked as he placed a settee next to the officer.

"Good choice," Rolf said without losing his focus. "Monsieur Dubois, I'm going to ask you to come out first."

The trapped man's legs dangled down to Rolf's chest. "Now if you just slide forward a bit more your feet will land on this bench. There are three of us who will grab you. Just scoot a bit forward while still sitting. That's it. Now duck your head down. Right. I've got your hand and give your other to—"

"Ricardo."

"*Wunderbar!*"

The man awkwardly ducked under the lintel, then jumped, landing unevenly on the settee. Rolf helped swing him to the floor.

"Oof!" he said with relief. He turned and saw the gaping hole with no visible end and clapped his hand over his mouth. "*Quel bordel!*" He turned to Rolf. "The lady…" He made a wide gesture with his hands.

Rolf looked up at pudgy ankles in pink socks and back at the bench. "Won't be safe." He walked backward, reviewing the situation. Suddenly he began to sneeze. Maybe he is allergic to me, I thought, breaking the tension I felt.

Callista arrived. "What the hell is going on?"

Rolf blew his nose. "We have one gentleman out with two more to go." He used his head to point out the passenger in plaid shorts. "Please introduce yourself to Monsieur Dubois and review his experience."

"Got it," she said. I assumed "review" had something to do with lawsuit prevention.

Two more men arrived, one with a bald head and wearing an officer's white shirt. His name tag identified him as Nels, Safety Officer.

Harriet began to moan. "I can't jump!"

Nels formed a huddle with Callista, Rolf, and the elevator man. "One of us could climb in the elevator with a ladder, open the ceiling hatch, and assist the passengers out on the deck above," Nels suggested.

"Won't work for the super-size," Rolf muttered.

"Harriet, this is Callista, your cruise director. What's your favorite beverage on board? Ultimate cooler, Long Island iced tea, sangria, cappuccino...?"

Pierre perked up. "Do I get one too?"

"*Tout ce que vous voulez, cherié,*" she said to him

"Jack D-daniels," Harriet blurted between sobs.

"Whatever you want, sweetheart.!" Callista signaled to somebody on the fringe to get the drink.

Nels positioned four men facing the open elevator shaft. "Miss Harriet," he called. "We have a team out here to absolutely ensure your protection."

"Okay," the trapped woman choked.

"What I want you to do is to lie on your stomach with your head facing away from the door. Just do exactly what I say. Do you hear me?" Harriet groaned a weak assent. "And you, Mr. Ernst, kindly make certain her head is in line with her feet. Now Miss Harriet please place your feet in the opening. It's best if they can hang out a bit."

Callista called, "Harriet, as your cruise director, I'm here to lend you some immoral support. We have a double Jack Daniels on order."

The crowd that had formed chuckled. Callista reached over her head but could not touch the woman's feet. She waved for the men to bring the bench closer and before the safety officer noticed, she jumped on it. She patted Harriet's sneakers. "Harriet, nice runners. This is me, Callista. I'm right here with you."

The safety officer twirled his finger. Callista nodded that she understood. "Now a little roll onto your tummy. I know, that carpet must be disgusting, but you'll be off it momentarily." Callista rubbed Harriet's ankles as she slowly turned. "That's it. Now Ernst, could you please sit down beside Harriet and make sure she doesn't lift her head."

"And Harriet, one more thing—we have the current winner and runner up of the crew swimmers contest to assist you. Wait till you see the muscles on these gorgeous specimens of manhood."

Nels tapped Callista's calf and helped her off the bench, then said, "Now!" Two men tugged on Harriet's chunky legs. Callista pushed the bench forward just as gravity propelled Harriet's substantial buttocks downward. She landed so hard there was a cracking sound, although the bench didn't give way.

"You're just fine!" Callista said as if to imprint the thought. "How do you feel?"

Harriett rubbed a red spot on her cheek. "I don't know."

Callista handed her a cocktail. "This should help."

In the fuss over Harriet, I missed Ernst's swifter exit. He was wearing a Hawaiian shirt, Bermuda shorts with suspenders.

"I need to get your full names and stateroom numbers so you can get a generous cruise credit for your trouble," Callista said as she steered them to the nearest cocktail lounge.

Orange cones and safety barrier tape were being installed around the elevator bank. A workman handed down Ernst's cane and Harriet's purse. Rolf took them and turned to me. "Those folks have won the lottery."

"What do you mean?"

"They'll be asked to sign a release of liability in exchange for a full reimbursement on this cruise and fifty percent off the next one." He pulled out his handkerchief preemptively.

"Yes, well, that seems more than generous for fifteen minutes of inconvenience."

"You can't imagine the diagnoses of post-trauma and back pain and migraines that will arise once they get home and see their lawyers." He readied his handkerchief. "Ah…ah…ah…"

Before it got to his nose, I saw a thin trickle of blood draining from one nostril.

□ □ □

My computer had been violated. There were so many smudges in the powdery residue that a fingerprints specialist would have been orgasmic. Even if someone had downloaded everything to a portable hard drive, all they had was my novel-in-progress, email correspondence, photos of Bodhi, and my latest—and rather plump—royalty statements. Access to my banks and investments was blocked by two-stage password protection. Last year my wallet was pickpocketed in London's Covent Garden, nevertheless I felt more disturbed by this intrusion, even though I had half expected it.

I had nothing to hide, so why go to all this bother when they simply could have asked me what I'd found? Still, I began to perspire—one of my first signs of anger. I tried to open my balcony door, which resisted my first few tugs, then a mighty whoosh blasted into the room. The horizon was blurred by the billowing crests. For the first time in several months, I yearned to be safely home. Crossing my arms to keep myself warm, I realized that I'd been spinning my wheels chatting up all of Tatiana's contacts. I even had assumed that Rolf—or someone under his orders—had breached my computer. What were they hoping to find? Maybe they thought I was feeding information to police contacts—or more worrisome for them—the media. So far, I had learned one essential fact: everyone loved her. Not a single person had uttered an ill word about her, which led me to believe she had died at the hands of a stranger—one who could strike again.

I checked the time. It was just after eight in the evening—prime dinnertime when the pathetic

Internet connection wouldn't be under siege. I logged onto Chrome, gave my password for my now-free minutes and typed in my first query. I felt a stomach-churning bout of paranoia, as if someone were looking over my shoulder. Relax, I told myself. In a few days, you'll be in your own bed, your book will get finished, you'll see darling Bodhi, and your life will go on—unlike that of the radiant light that had kindled Tatiana, which had so cruelly been snuffed out.

Bodhi! I turned on my email and found six from him, via his grandmother. I loved the way she faithfully transmitted his messages, which were hardly like any traditional correspondence. "Hey, dude," he wrote. "Mrs. Wiggins got a paper cut and she said some bad words and I told her to calm down 'cause she would grow a new skin!'"

"Hey Mommy!" began the next one. "Do you think the president is going to deport Dora the Explorer?"

Oh my! How many kids his age worried about immigration policies. I guess there were enough Hispanic kids in his school who talked about it. My chest burned with the desire to gather him into my arms and tell him all would be well with Dora and everything else.

The rest of the message involved needing a new box of crayons, his grandmother's stinky farts (she must have loved transcribing that one!), and his fact-of-the-day about the discovery of Antarctic crabs that were eaten by elephant seals. My heart swelled with the knowledge I'd see him in a few short days and could go back to our sweet life together.

The Internet speed was blissfully constant—not fast, it was never fast—but adequate with no freezes. There were so many unanswered questions: suffocation, asphyxiation, Ehlers-Danlos syndrome, SIDS, cardiac problems, corpses and refrigeration. I followed a meandering trail of related topics. Like a traveler dazzled by the scenery, I trekked deeper into uncharted territory until I was overwhelmed with the surfeit of information. I fished around in my tote for my flash drive, plugged it in, opened my spreadsheet, and began typing the stream-of-conscious connections that I'd made throughout the day.

I stood and stretched. I had forgotten about dinner, which is tantamount to mutiny on a cruise ship. Not wanting to lose inertia, I dialed room service. "A steak salad, medium rare with croutons, black olives, sun-dried tomatoes, bleu cheese, bacon crumbles and balsamic vinaigrette dressing on the side."

"Would you care for some bread, Mrs. Lany-air" came an unfamiliar voice that was reading my name off a screen. "Tonight, we have cheese breadsticks, sesame seed flatbread, Irish soda muffins, popovers, gluten-free pumpernickel, pretzel buns, and assorted hard rolls."

"Popovers!"

"We have some nice soups." The woman replied in an accent somewhere between Hungarian and Lithuanian. "Greek lemon-chicken, mulligatawny, ham-and-green pea, broccoli-cheese, Chinese hot-and-sour, and..."

I remembered the soothing orzo-infused chicken soup in Santorini. "A bowl of the lemon-chicken."

"Any beverages?"

"Ginger ale, San Pellegrino, and peppermint tea."

"For dessert?"

"Nothing, thanks."

"What about some freshly-made sorbet?" She didn't wait for my response before adding, "Kiwi, passion fruit, tangerine, coconut, and wild raspberry, served with freshly-baked ginger cookies."

"Surprise me," I said, thinking how I was not looking forward to cooking for fussy Bodhi who would beg for ice cream even if he had barely touched his food. I always...always gave in. There was much in life to regret and I wasn't going to be chintzy with my child.

Back to my computer, I Googled _La Biennale di Venizia_ to cross-match the art festival's dates with when we were in Venice to see if Vance's story held up. It did! I jumped to injectable steroids, human grown hormones, and their side effects...

The knock on the door startled me out of my trance. Cozmin, his face wreathed in a smile, wheeled a trolley that converted into a table into the room. "I set this up myself," he said. "Only I know how you like it—small plates, the rest covered to keep warm, right?"

"You are amazing, Coz. I shall miss you the most!"

"Oh no, madam, I am coming with you. I love Florida very much."

"Well, that settles that!" I clapped my hands like a happy child.

"The soup first? It's perfect now—not too hot."

"Sure."

He moved the rolling table so it faced the television and locked the legs. Then poured the velvety liquid into a porcelain bowl from a large gravy boat.

"Busy night?" I asked.

"Yes, indeed! Lots of soup and sandwiches. The dining room is half empty."

He showed me that the steak slices were wrapped in foil to keep them moist before tossing them on the crisp salad greens. "No onions," he said, remembering my preference. "Don't forget the sorbet." He pointed to a domed plate over a dish of crushed ice. Beside it was a pretty arrangement of cookies and fresh berries covered with plastic film. He held up the can of ginger ale, guessing I'd want it first, and poured it into a glass pre-filled with ice.

"Lots of ginger ale too!" he said. "I bring it even if they didn't ask, especially to the ones I know get sick."

"Thank you so much, Coz," I said with heartfelt warmth.

"Now don't work too hard, promise me?" he said, and backed away without waiting for a response.

I took some long gulps of the soda, something I rarely drink, but ginger ale does quiet a queasy tummy.

I hadn't been bothered by the ship's movement until I picked up my soup spoon, which didn't make the center of my mouth on the first try. The soup sloshed in the bowl in a similar manner to the swimming pool water, baring the bottom on one side as the ship swayed. David had been an avid surfer before I met him but had cut way back due to an ACL injury. He still watched the Surf Channel and one time explained that "wavelength is the horizontal distance between two successive crests or troughs." I wondered if you could measure wavelength in something as small as a soup bowl. The ship gave a peculiar shudder.

The combination of the lemony soup and ginger ale left a bitter aftertaste, which prompted me to go back to the computer and query: "Most common poisons for murder." Over 400,000 results populated, beginning with Socrates' hemlock and including toxic reptiles, none of which were likely to be on board. Most experienced travelers carried a variety of current and emergency meds. My own arsenal included sleeping pills for jet lag, both over-the-counter and prescription pain relievers, and several antibiotics. Given the age of the average cruiser, I presumed that their Dopp kits were overflowing with antidepressants, blood thinners, cardiac regulators, even transplant anti-rejection drugs. Considering the number of "supersized" folks like Harriet, there also had to be a high percentage of diabetics. I searched for "how much insulin does it take to kill someone?" and discovered that it is rather uncommon to die from an overdose of insulin, even though I remembered the sensational murder trial of Claus von Bülow who allegedly tried to murder his socialite wife with an overdose of insulin.

The scent of warm popovers lured me back to the tray. I buttered one and bit into the crispy crust that collapsed as the steam was released, marveling at its reverse crenulations that were reminiscent of the inside of the Statue of Liberty. My mother likes to tell the story of when she took me there when I was about ten. When I read the Emma Lazarus poem at the base, I cried, "They all drowned!" and burst into sobs. I'd thought that "the wretched refuse of your teeming shore" were bodies that had washed up on Liberty Island because they had been "tempest-tost" in a storm.

Smiling, I turned back to the computer, switched between the tabs for SIDs, genetic heart conditions, and medications for stage fright.

Tatiana's body was pristine, although if she had ingested—or was injected—with something toxic there wouldn't be external marks. The doctor, nurses, and Grisha all had syringes and needles—as did passengers carrying insulin. Overdoses of opioids were at epidemic levels in the US and rarely sparked a murder investigation. Then there was Grisha's bizarre stockpile of vials and needles and bottles, most with Russian labels. I searched for what constituted a fatal dose for everything from Tylenol to digitalis.

Tatiana—at the end—did she know what was happening? Was it painful? Did she suffer? She did not end up overboard—dead or alive. Why not? If she had wanted to kill herself she would have jumped; if someone wanted her to die, they would have found a way to dump her body where it would never be recovered. Anything else...was either accidental or a dreadful mistake.

A bite of popover stuck in my throat and a gulp of fizzy water didn't dislodge it. I bent over and coughed. A clump of food rose in my gorge. I stood up and spit it into the wastebasket just as the ship listed. Reaching for the trolley to steady myself, my foot tripped the cart's brake and it hurtled toward the balcony door. My outstretched arm flailed just as my right side crashed to the floor. A piercing pain zigzagged from my hip to my knee. As soon as it passed, I rose gingerly to my feet, and with cautious handholds, made it to the couch. My computer wobbled close to the edge of the desk.

"Don't you dare!" I said aloud. As the ship heaved to the other side, it slid back. I stayed focused on it as if I had telekinetic powers.

Dreadful mistake reverberated in my head. A searing sciatic pain bolted from my hip to my heel as I fell back on the sofa with my limbs askew. The repulsive memory of Tatiana's legs in the air reminded me that I couldn't give in to my injury. Time was running out. Someone traveling on this same ship at this very moment might get away with murder.

Four

*I cannot know what tomorrow will bring forth. I can
know only what the truth is for me today. That is what
I am called upon to serve, and I serve it in all lucidity.*
—Igor Stravinsky

Monday, November 23
At Sea: Position: 350 Nautical Miles South of
Bermuda

By the time I'd made it to the bed, I had managed to
swallow two ibuprofens and placed a bottle of
stronger pills prescribed by my dentist after extracting
the last of my wisdom teeth in the bedside drawer.
One miserable hour later, I succumbed and took one
of the painkillers.

Every roll of the ship triggered more pain until I
used pillows as wedges. Then the meds kicked in
enough to turn sharp stabs to a dull ache. Still I
couldn't sleep.

My thoughts drifted from a violent man attacking
Tatiana to a crazed woman. Years ago, David was on
a panel discussing gender and crime. "Women don't
go after strangers," one of the other experts had
lectured, "they usually kill for revenge." They also
prefer poison to guns. Maybe Callista was jealous of
Tatiana's many admirers, although I just couldn't
bring myself to believe she had a dark side. Joy
Barbarosa, the nurse with the incongruously dyed
hair, came to mind. In a novel, I might characterize

216

her as aloof, chilly, withholding, tense and...unknowable—and she had easy access to the pharmacy. I tried to conjure a motive and soon discarded her as a suspect. There were the shop and spa ladies representing more than a dozen nationalities who could have run away to sea because they were sociopathic—although the same could be said for an insane female passenger.

My doorbell sounded, followed by a knock. I pushed myself up with my hands, managed a wobbly stand, and stumbled to the door.

"Early grey time!" Cozmin said before he saw the cart from the stormy night wedged behind a chair. "Oh! You had a rough time. No worries and not so bad as some!" He poured a cup of tea and handed it to me, then he removed the dishes from the night before, and artfully arranged breakfast on the coffee table. He backed away with the sideways wave that I found endearing.

The hot water eased my scratchy throat, but a spasm zipped from my butt to the back of my knee. I slowed my breathing until the spiky feeling abated. My hair appointment was in less than an hour. Maybe they could squeeze in a massage, which might relieve the butt cramp that was holding the longest nerve in my body hostage.

□ □ □

I had the forward elevator all to myself. When the doors opened, a splash of sun from the starboard side illuminated the crystal and glass fountain that trickled and tinkled with a sound meant to trigger blissful

217

meditation. If I pivoted right, I'd enter The Panorama, the lofty name for the gym, which boasted floor-to-ceiling windows that offered splendid views of the approaching horizon from the stationary bikes, stair-climbing and jogging machines. Callista once convinced me to try one of the new "effortless" bikes. "Isn't this marvelous?" she had cooed. "I feel like I'm propelling the ship because every time the wheel spins the ship plunges forward."

"All I feel are my thighs burning," I retorted. "I'll let everyone else be the hamsters on the wheel." To me, that sort of exercise seemed to be a form of mass psychosis.

As I approached the spa doors, someone called, *Dobroye utro!*" I cupped my hand over my eyes to figure out who was approaching me in the glare.

"Good morning to you," I said to Jerzy Skala, one of the personal trainers—the man who first introduced me to Tatiana.

"Do you have a moment?" He beckoned me inside the gym. From this height, the ocean stretched like a shimmering quilt of blues and whites. The waves from the night's tantrum of a storm had flattened, although there was enough spume to indicate a strong tailwind.

"Usually the gym is full by now," he said, "so I'm guessing they worked out by gripping the bedrails last night."

"I can't remember when it's been that rough."

Jerzy held up his hand, which clenched a wrench. I followed his glance to several bikes in pieces in the middle of the floor. "We're starting flywheel classes on the Canal cruises—it's all the rage, you know," he said in a snooty British accent, which reminded me that Olek once labeled him the "great pretender." He gave a wry smile. "Tania told me, 'Those machines make a bad salad.'"

"What do you mean?"

"You know, oil and vinegar that will never mix no matter how much you try."

"Bad salad" was the sort of fresh metaphor worth remembering to use in a character description and reminded myself to make note of it.

"What's the advantage over those?" I pointed to the exercise bikes by the window.

"Supposedly, they're the best workout in the shortest time. Want to try one?"

"Right now, I need body work, not a workout. I'd give anything for one of Agata's massages."

"Funny how things work out," he said. "At least they can't blame her for what happened to Tania."

"I don't understand..."

"Her father..." He flexed his arms forward in a cat-like maneuver. "He didn't like Agata giving her massages that were not a part of 'his program.' In fact, he objected to her using the gym when he or Olek couldn't supervise!" He made a spitting sound and rambled on. "He was so predictable, so Russian."

"Her father or Olek?"

"The old man. As long as he had his firewater he was fine. He'd tell me, 'You are my friend; you make me happy'—meaning I provided him with bottles."

"Couldn't he get a drink anywhere on the ship?"

"He's too cheap to pay for vodka by the glass. We're not permitted to bring our own bottles on board. That's why I always carry water bottles in my backpack." He gave a mischievous grin. "Some men have a girl in every port, I have a shop girl in every duty-free store."

I forced a laugh.

"We traded."

"Vodka for what?"

"The other kind of shot." Jerzy pointed his trigger finger at his shoulder. "The pain from an old rotator cuff injury is always with me, but every few weeks I needed a—how do you say?—booster."

"Like the steroid injections he gave Tania?" He raised his hands in a so-what gesture. "Did you ever give anything to her?" I said, fishing.

"Only my heart—so very long ago."

"You also loved her."

"What do you mean, also?" Anger flickered across his narrowed brow. "Also, besides taking something from her? I never took anything she didn't want to give!"

"Sorry, I didn't mean—"

"*Nichego*! Nothing is left. I wish there was"—now he pointed his trigger finger at his forehead—"something to take away the tortures in my head. Why? I was angry with her because she has been avoiding me since…" He shivered. "I had leave to see my mother in hospital and when I came back—" He rubbed his temples with his thumbs. "I made the mistake of telling her that I'd seen an old girlfriend, who I bumped into accidentally. I mentioned that she's married with a little baby." He threw his head back as if looking for divine intervention. "It took me awhile to realize Tania was blaming me so I wouldn't be suspicious of her." He paced to the windows and back. "You know what I think? I think she ended up with a very bad salad—a very, very bad boyfriend." Jerzy's shoulders heaved.

"I'm so very sorry."

"You are a detective, yes?"

"Not exactly."

"Not KGB?" He gave the sly, polished smile that had probably felled any female he set out to get.

"I helped troubled children."

He raised eyebrows in an unspoken question. "The people who are...who have Tania..." He lowered his voice. "They need to know something. She was always hungry, like starving herself. She said that if she was even a half a kilo over, her balance was off." He pinched his skin underneath a tattoo of a turtle on his forearm. You couldn't get this much skin from her." He sucked in his chest, revealing his six pack beneath his tight gym uniform. "She said, 'Only mother helps.' You know what she meant?" He continued without waiting for an answer. "More than a thousand years ago there was this Russian prince named Vladimir. He had to choose a religion for the people of Kievan Rus and he picked orthodox Christianity over Islam, why? Because they permitted vodka—mother vodka."

"So, duty free for her too?"

"How could I not do anything she asked? She was so simple in her love. She'd meet me late in the outdoor movie theater. I'd push some lounge chairs together and we covered ourselves with blankets. She called it 'naughty time.'"

"When was the last time you...watched a movie?"

"Not since I left to see my mother."

If that were true, I could cross him off the baby daddy list. "You still gave her vodka."

"I would do whatever she asked."

"When was the last time you bought her a bottle?"

"After Ponta Delgada, but never a whole bottle. I filled an Empress coffee thermos every other day so her father wouldn't know."

"How could she drink without impacting her performance?" I asked, while thinking: she didn't care about it affecting the baby because she never planned to keep it.

Jerzy blinked in the sharp slant of blinding light that bounced from the sea. "Tania wasn't anything like her father. She only took a few sips to take the edge off. It dulled her hunger and gave her courage." To counter my dubious expression, his voice changed from conciliatory to strident. "She lived a horrible life!"

"Because of the pain?"

"That...and the way she prostituted herself—turning her body into a freak show. What's more dehumanizing than stuffing yourself into that *chertov* box to amuse rich perverts?"

He made a spitting sound and balled his fists. "Have you ever been to a place where children are maimed to make them better beggars? What's so different about folding yourself into a cage? They both suffer in agony!" He wiped tears from his eyes. "You know what she liked best? Aerial silks!"

"Here you are!" A platinum blonde with bouncy breasts rushed toward Jerzy with the enthusiasm of a child seeing her gifts on Christmas morning. "Sorry I'm late! I was up half the night on that trampoline of a bed." The woman oozed "cougar" and wasn't shy about it.

"Mrs. Petrone, no worries. I was just setting up a new spinner for you to try." He pivoted to me. "Have you met Mrs. Lanier?"

"No, delighted," she said extending a freshly-manicured hand. "I hope Jerzy doesn't work you as hard as he does me."

She had no interest in my reply so I gestured that I was headed out. Jerzy opened the plate glass door and slid in front of me and whispered, "At least now Tania can fly as far as she wants, free from gravity— and suffering, s*lava bogu*, thanks to God."

□ □ □

"Good morning, Mrs. Lanier." Hilde bowed her head deferentially. "Haircut with Fernanda?"

"I know I should have called ahead, but is a massage possible?"

"Today, no problem. We had many cancellations this morning. Always happens after a rough night." She glanced at her computer and exhaled. "I know you must be missing Agata. We all are."

"What about Iska?"

"She's on the later shift, however I'm free— Agata taught me some of her techniques."

"That would be lovely."

She showed me to a private room and left me to undress and place myself face down with my nose protruding through the hole in the massage table.

"Is there anything in particular you'd like me to work on?" Hilde asked.

"I tripped and fell last night and I have sciatica on my left side."

Hilde gently approached the knot in my buttocks. The slightest pressure made me wince. She walked around to my left side. "Did you know you have a large bruise here?" She pointed to my hip. "And here." She lightly touched my calf. I hadn't taken time to look in a mirror because my back pain had overshadowed the milder throbbing in my leg. "I'll get some ice for the swelling."

"Isn't it too late for that?"

"Not if it's been less than twenty-four hours." She left the room for a few minutes and then returned with plastic bags filled with crushed ice, which she wrapped in towels. She arranged one under my left shinbone and the other by my hipbone. Hilde used her fingers to gently trace a line from my spine across my left buttocks, and down my leg to my knee. "Is this the path of your pain?"

"Yes, exactly."

Hilde centered her fingers on a spot just to the left of my spine and pressed slowly. "Your knot is here." Two fingers began a combination of rotation and increasing pressure.

"Oh! Argh!" I groaned as she recreated the pain for a millisecond and then it seemed to abate. "Your touch does remind me of Agata's."

"She was like a sister to me and—" Hilde cleared her throat. "Would you like some other music?"

The tinkly-bubble-spacey background wasn't too annoying, although her urgent tone prompted me to agree. "What do you have?"

She handed me an iPad. I scooted up on my elbows and read from a playlist. I pushed Brahms, then the *Academic Festival Overture.* Soft violins started to play. Hilde turned the volume annoying high, pointed to a light fixture, then put the tablet as close to it as possible.

"Thanks." I said, more loudly than necessary because she had made it obvious that someone could be listening in. I knew there were cameras throughout the ship but not necessarily microphones, especially in a place like this where one assumed there was complete privacy.

Hilde began working on my neck. "That feels wonderful." I said. The music amplified into the well-known theme that became the basis for a popular song.

"You knew the Russian girl?" she whispered.

"Yes," I said into the hole in the table. Ship gossip was faster than the internet.

"A terrible business." Hilde pressed both hands into the thigh on my uninjured side. "Did she ever say anything about Agata?"

"She recommended her massages."

"Did you know that Agata has seven sisters and brothers to put through school?" Hilde concentrated on my feet. "That's why she would sometimes agree to do a man." She paused until the music built to a crescendo. "Clients are quite generous if they are...satisfied." She kneaded my left instep with both hands aggressively. "What got her into trouble was *not* doing it!"

Hilde started on my shoulder blades as one of Brahms' Hungarian dance sweetened the air. "Only one person dared to speak up for her."

"I hope you didn't suffer because of it."

She handed me a towel to cover my chest. "No, not me! I had not the courage." Tears filled her pale blue eyes.

"Tania?"

Hilde stroked my arm affirmatively. "She hasn't been to the spa since then. I was hoping to see her because Agata left something for her."

"What?"

She opened a cabinet and handed me a pouch marked with the spa's palm-tree logo. I loosened the cinch and pulled out a bottle of Pepcid. Hilde pointed to her chest. "We both had burning hearts—for me after citrus or tomatoes."

"For me it's coffee," I said.

"Agata had a problem with her favorite food: pepperoni pizza."

"What bothered Tania?"

"She said it was the greatest tragedy of her life!" Hilde smiled, revealing teeth so pearly she could be an ad for the spa's dental whitening treatments. "Chocolate! One of the dancers gave her a box from Belgium and she brought it to share with us. We ate a few together and when she said her heart burned, Agata gave her one of those pills and she felt better in a few minutes. So Agata left her bottle for Tania."

"I'll give it to the doctor."

Hilde didn't seem to be listening. "I never got to say goodbye to Agata. She got the 'Oh-six-hundred knock.' You know what that is?" I shook my head.

"The socos—they wake you at six in the morning on a port day and say you have to leave the vessel immediately. They supervise while you pack, take you to get your last pay envelope and pay your bills at the purser's office, and then you're escorted down the gangway."

"Just like that?"

"Sometimes there isn't even an explanation. "This company wants happy! happy! happy! all the time, and no problems—or we're sent home." Hilde had busied herself putting together a bag of sample beauty products. "Tania told a few people that she wasn't going to let them get away with it but that's just what you say when you're upset." She positioned several silvery bottles on the counter. "We recommend Combi-Three for your face and hands at bedtime," she said loudly, hoping this time to be overheard.

"Do you get a commission?"

"A little one."

"Give me three," I said, since my shipboard account was going to be comped. It was my tiny salute to Agata, who had been damned if she did what her customers demanded and fired when she didn't. "I'll use them as holiday gifts."

A loud whirring sound drowned out the music. I glanced toward the window in time to see a flash of red in the sky. The helicopter from Bermuda! I had to hurry to dress if I wanted to pay my respects as Tatiana left the ship.

"I have something else to say." For a moment, I thought Hilde was going to blurt that she too loved the performer. "She was found naked, right?" I nodded. "Why don't they look for her clothes?"

227

□ □ □

Helicopters don't attempt a landing on the crowded deck of a moving ocean liner because a sudden burst of wind or unexpected wave motion could be catastrophic. The one other time I'd seen a medical evacuation we had been headed to Galveston. The ship diverted north to be within range of New Orleans. From my balcony, I watched someone lying in a rescue basket being winched up to the hovering chopper with remarkable precision.

"Fernanda is ready to do your hair," Hilde said.

"Does she have any time later?"

"She's booked up for formal night portraits."

"I apologize, but I'm not going to be able to fit it in."

"No worries. Tomorrow is wide open."

"Please add a haircut to the bill." Hilde gestured that it was not necessary. "Just paying in advance for tomorrow." I signed my receipt and put a significant tip to cover the hairdresser and Hilde.

In the corridor, the loudspeaker announced: "This is to inform all crew and passengers that a medical evacuation in underway. All open decks are closed. Please remain indoors until you are given the all-clear. Due to the risk of flying debris, this includes balconies and outdoor eating areas. No photography is permitted during hazardous maneuvers. Thank you in advance for your complete cooperation."

"I snova zdravstvuyte!" Jerzy waved to me like a long-lost friend.

"Hello again to you. Where's the best place to watch the evacuation?"

"From the Arctic Deck above the Lido pool."

"We're not supposed to be outside."

"I have a secret spot where nobody will see us." After noting my limp, Jerzy took my arm and helped me up two flights of interior steps. We turned a corner and he opened a door that led to the indoor/outdoor miniature golf green. He pulled me up onto a hilly surface and over a low fence that led to the outside area of the course. The helicopter swooped fifty feet above us but remained about the same distance off the port side. "Watch how the helicopter synchronizes its pace with the ship's," Jerzy said like an excited child.

"Wouldn't it be easier if the ship stopped?"

"No. The ship is more maneuverable when it's under power."

The chopper broke rank with the ship and turned south. "Is something wrong?" I asked.

"They always try some practice runs." He opened the gate and headed out on deck. "Watch! It's coming back toward the bow."

I followed cautiously behind Jerzy. "Look, you can see the crew deck from here." A few decks down from the bridge there was a large open area leading to the bow, where an "X" marked the center of a large circle.

"I thought they didn't land on the ship."

"That's only a reference target for hovering." He pointed to a sign that read: Winch Only. "We should be able to see them lowering the basket stretcher to that—" A deafening whirring drowned Jerzy's voice as the helicopter lined up the ship's bow. For a scary second, it seemed on a collision course with the bridge, then it plunged lower, managing to hover while flying forward in sync with the vessel.

I stumbled slightly and a pain shot from my hip to my toes. Jerzy caught my wobble. "Took a fall last night," I said. "Still sore." He stood behind me and supported my back in the wind as we watched a wire snake out from the helicopter's open bay. I leaned into the warm curve of his shoulder and inhaled a whiff of ginger. How long had it been since I'd trusted someone's supportive touch? His muscular arm curved protectively around my shoulders, momentarily offering me safety and a closeness I had not realized I craved. I closed my eyes for a second.

Jerzy snuggled me a tad closer. I could feel his heart beat faster, or was it my own? When I didn't resist, he pressed his chin into my neck. His breath ruffled the hair on my nape and I felt the electrifying rush that had been dormant for so long.

"I adore a woman who has no idea of how beautiful she is," he murmured.

For that second I did not care that the trainer had a reputation for courting wealthy passengers and seemed immune to the non-fraternization rule. I laughed easily, if shyly.

"No really." His free hand slid down my side and rested on my hip. His long fingers touched my rear and patted me. "Your body is perfection."

I pulled away from him to see whether his expression was mocking. He grinned sweetly. "I see them all, yes! But the ones who look best in clothes are the most disappointing without. Real women have curves." He squeezed appreciatively.

I was wondering whether he was referring to Tatiana's skeletal frame or just was trying to butter me up for a tip when he relaxed his grip and pointed. "Look!"

I blinked in the stinging air as someone in an orange jumpsuit with metallic stripes oscillated over the circle like a pendulum before the deck crew pulled him to safety. The cable was hoisted back up before the aircraft dipped away from the ship and flew back to the stern. On the next pass, it dropped a metal basket that carried another rescuer in a black jumpsuit in a seated position.

"That's odd," Jerzy said. "They usually only send one guy down."

"Maybe that's how Bermuda does it."

"It's your US Coast Guard. You Americans think you should police the whole world."

I pulled away from him. "Hey, right now we're the good guys."

"Look!" Jerzy pointed to a small twin-engine plane that crossed the ship's wake. "That's the spotter plane."

Peering down the railing, I saw that a temporary windsock had been affixed to a forward railing—and also that most of the balconies were dotted with passengers taking photos. So much for heeding the captain's instructions.

As the chopper approached, Jerzy pivoted me under the overhang to avoid the vortex of the hovering propellers. Several crew carried out a heavyset person bundled into the rescue basket. The man in the orange jumpsuit snagged the swinging rope and fastened it to the basket. I held my hand to my mouth because it rocked wildly in the wind as it was winched up. Two crewmembers on the chopper caught and steadied it on a small platform outside its sliding door. The prone passenger managed a wave before disappearing inside. Once again, the aircraft flew away from the ship and continued to match its pace.

"Looks like the husband went first," I said. After a long delay, the basket was lowered again. "Hopefully his wife will get the treatment she needs in Bermuda."

"Yah," Jerzy replied.

I stared at the trainer's muscular neck, understanding why he might have appealed to Tatiana. I closed my eyes to try to work out a thought. Tatiana drank vodka to quell hunger pangs and she dieted to the extreme. Every performance caused her anxiety, which is why she took Olek's proffered beta-blockers. "Jerzy, did Tania ever complain about heartburn?" I asked, tapping the area on my chest that sometimes bothered me.

"She moaned about everything hurting everywhere all the time."

"Nothing specific about her digestion?"

He shook his head. "I don't recall."

"Did she ever ask you for medicine?"

"I would never give anyone painkillers!"

"No, not that. Her father had everything she needed in that department."

"I'm telling you, Grisha's hand is somewhere in this." Jerzy spit on the deck, then his tone softened. "Actually, I did give her something to make her feel better. I was her candy man. Isn't there a song about that?" He grinned. "Not what you think—she liked my Swiss candies. You know Ricola? She wanted to hide her breath from her father."

One of those lozenges was just what I needed for the rawness in my throat. I was about to ask if he had any more when the chopper shifted back into the parallel position. The lowered basket was caught by a crewmember before it slammed into the bucking deck. Ten minutes later they carried out someone that I assumed was Mrs. Greenberg. She was wearing an oxygen mask and various tubes poked out between the basket straps. The crew clipped the basket to the winch wire and up she went before being swallowed into the chopper's maw.

"It's getting windier," Jerzy said, tightening his arms around my shoulders. "Let's go in."

"No, wait!"

"It's over."

"I want to see Tania leave."

"Tania? Why?"

"Rolf said they were sending her to Bermuda."

"Sounds like something the Castle would do as an end run around US officials." He pointed to the chopper. "Looks like you were right. It's getting in position again."

The hook swayed above the heaving deck until it was snared by crew. The medic in the orange-and-metallic jumpsuit grabbed the cable from the other crewmembers. In one fluent move, he signaled he was ready and was hoisted skyward. As he neared the chopper, he saluted the audience on the balconies and they cheered him until the bay door slid closed. The chopper banked and turned northeast, gathered speed, and became a diminishing red dot on the horizon.

"Looks like Tania missed her ride," he said. I turned to go back through the miniature golf course. "Not necessary," Jerzy said, guiding me to another entrance.

I hesitated and looked out to sea. "Something's wrong," I muttered. "Two went down..." I said. I counted on my fingers. "One in black, one in orange. Then three went up: the husband, the patient, and the medic."

"But not Tania," Jerzy said impatiently, and steered me through the door.

I stopped. "You saw it; there were two guys in jumpsuits. Two people went up in the basket and one guy was winched up last. Maybe it was Tania instead of the husband."

"I doubt she was the one waving," he said.

"Something doesn't add up," I said, then counted to myself again. "The other one was too bulky to be Tania but..." Jerzy shrugged. "Didn't you notice that two men came down and only one of them went up?"

☐ ☐ ☐

I wandered through The Terraces although the odor of clashing ethnic dishes nauseated me and turned to the sandwich section, settling on grilled eggplant, mushrooms, and tomatoes on a baguette with a side of brie. At the beverage station, they were out of Earl Grey, so I substituted a green tea, which supposedly helps prevent colds. Since it wasn't a traditional meal time, I was able to find an empty table by the window. The sea state was mellow compared to the night before, but there were serious white caps indicating a surface wind.

I pulled out a notebook to jot down my mental ramblings. At the top of the page, I wrote Jerzy in one column and Hilde in the next and drew a line down the center. Under Jerzy, I scribbled: lover, prior girlfriend, jealousy (by her and/or him), hunger/pain, vodka-Grisha, vodka-Tatiana. I debated with myself for a moment, then scratched out "Hilde" and wrote in Agata, who couldn't be a suspect, yet might be a link. My word associations came tumbling out: masseuse, fired, and Pepcid. What was I forgetting? My pen hovered over Jerzy's list. What the hell, I thought, as I scribbled "Ricola."

The sandwich tasted drier than it looked and the tepid tea left a sour aftertaste. The catchy theme from the Brahms overture playing in the spa clouded my thinking. David, who had played the oboe in both high school and college, used to say, "I don't know why it's called overture because nothing comes next." Like being all set up to wave Tatiana off in the helicopter... Still, I was relieved that she was still onboard.

Even the most complex situations could be distilled into a simple syrup, if you could figure out the formula. In child protection, violent caregivers often are set off by some combination of jealousy and drug-or-booze fueled rage. Being on a ship narrowed the suspects down to two categories of perp: passenger or crew. These could be divided further into acquaintances or strangers of Tatiana. Either could have had deranged fantasies of a relationship

235

with her and been rudely rebuffed. Or—since she seemed far more generous with her body than anyone knew, she could have been willing—but what if an inability to perform triggered rage? With her blonde braids and fairytale smile, Tatiana radiated innocence, yet her act was unabashedly sensual with her skimpy outfits revealing every cleft. I cringed remembering the crude guys who snickered about her crotch; yet if one of them had snapped, wouldn't there have been more physical evidence? I started coughing, and a waiter handed me a glass of water without being summoned. I hoped I wasn't about to join the cruise-cough clique.

I turned the page and headed two more columns: <u>Loved Her</u> and <u>Her Lover?</u> Under those who loved her one way or the other I wrote Grisha, Jerzy, Vance, Olek and—Callista, checking the name again as a possible lover for all of them, except her father. My pen pointed to Callista's name. How had I missed those clues entirely? What about Agata? I penciled her in. Mutual admiration or something more? I put a question mark in the second column. Who else? The doctor in the first column and another question mark. And how many others?

The outmoded word "nymphomaniac" rose to the surface. These days, "sexual addiction" or "hypersexuality" were the preferred terms, although I thought both were sexist because men would be congratulated for the same behavior that labeled a woman with a diagnosis. The child-welfare system considered a child was at risk if the mother was promiscuous. "Baby Daddy" was an honorable title in the same communities, yet a woman who didn't raise her own child is considered an abandoner, who could lose parental rights.

"Context is everything," David said. Some psychologists believed that hypersexuality was a form of addiction to the neurochemical highs produced in the early stages of a romantic relationship rather than by the sex act itself, which really doesn't last very long. I would have thought that Tatiana's intense practice sessions and daring performances would have given her enough of an endorphin high, but maybe she also craved the adrenalin surge that came with a fresh conquest. Or perhaps she was just a healthy woman with a normal libido. Her whole life—from infancy to a few days ago—had been about using her body to perform and delight others. She'd had only a minimal education; and although she had traveled with Cirque and now the ship, her forays into the world were circumscribed by her father, who slept in the same cabin most of the time. Any young woman with blood in her veins would have looked for a clandestine outlet. Since Tatiana wasn't permitted to have candid relationships, the subterfuge made deep attachments impossible, while encouraging intoxicating, if illicit, hookups. Besides, friendships required time to nurture; covert sex didn't. Everyone had access to a locked bedroom only a few minutes from any point on the ship. She just as easily could have slipped in and out of a guest stateroom as that of crew. Hopefully, her movements had been caught by security cameras, although by the time all the footage was scrutinized, the cabin would have been scrubbed and the guilty party could be anywhere in the world.

I felt like I was drowning in a soup of suspicion and sorrow and pressed the cold glass to my forehead to quell the painful pulsations. A few more days, then it will be over—at least as far as I was concerned. Until then, I couldn't help trying to untie the knots and follow where the threads led.

"Sometimes the simplest answer is the only one" was another way David had encouraged his staff to look at the obvious first. I finished the last bite of cheese and tried to figure out what was worming in my brain. I checked the time. The medical center was technically closed, but maybe somebody could clarify what happened during the evacuation.

I rang the off-hours bell. Joyce opened the door. "Hello, Mrs. Lanier. How may I assist you?"

"Is the doctor here? I had—" I was going to say I wanted to ask him a question, still I hedged. "I fell last night during the storm and—"

The nurse held the door open. "He's with someone. I'll sign you in."

"Is that necessary?"

"We're required to document accidents." Joyce waved for me to take a seat. "I'll tell him you are here."

Dr. Kotze came right out. "Another casualty?"

"Mostly to my pride."

"We had two broken collarbones last night, several sprains and one fractured finger." He stuck up his middle finger. "The guest said, 'I hope immigration has a sense of humor!'" He chuckled. "Come on back."

As soon as he closed the door to the exam room, I changed the subject. "Have you heard how Mrs.

Greenberg—the woman who was evacuated is doing?"

"In stable condition." He made an exaggerated sigh. "Her blood pressure plummeted while we were getting her ready." He fluttered his hand by his heart. "I couldn't wait to be relieved of her case."

"Did her husband go with?"

"At first they didn't want to accept him due to weight and balance in the chopper; and then when they strapped him into the basket, he had a panic attack. Ended up giving him something for anxiety."

"In other words, a basket case."

The doctor's grin could not hide his exhaustion. "Have a seat on the table and tell me what happened last night." I described my skirmish with the food trolley. "Which side?" I pulled down my slacks and showed him the spreading discoloration on my hip.

"And your leg?" I cuffed the leg on my slacks and slid down my sock. He pressed my shinbone. "Does this hurt?"

"Yes, with pressure. The worst has been the sciatica."

"Do you have any compression hosiery?"

"You sound like my mother-in-law. She loaned me hers, but I didn't wear them on the flight to Rome."

"I'd like you to wear them around the clock until you can get an ultrasound at home because the most common place for a blood clot to occur is in the lower leg. Once an hour you must sit down and stretch your toes upward. If the pain is worse anywhere—your leg, your chest—anywhere—please contact me immediately." The doctor pulled a pen out of the pocket of his lab coat and marked dashes around the swelling on my shin. "That demarcates what you have now. Notice that it's the size of a scone, or about five millimeters. Call me if it gets past here." He made a second mark about two centimeters farther up. He looked at me sternly. "Promise you'll call."

"Okay."

"Good, because you're the type who thinks of everyone else first."

"You've got my number," I said with a pained smile, then blurted, "Is Tania still on board?"

"Yes. They couldn't take the extra weight." He made a whistling exhale. "Best that way. There would have been no way to hide the fact that there was a body on board and those people have been through enough."

"So now you'll have to deal with the American authorities."

He helped me down. "We already are," he said as he opened the door.

"What brings *you* here?" Rolf's voice boomed from the next exam room.

I glanced through the open doorway. "Let's just say the score is food trolley one, me zero."

"Join the walking wounded," Rolf said, sounding more upbeat than usual. I peeked in and noticed that he was holding a rubber glove filled with ice on one side of his nose."

"Did you fall too?"

"My sinuses are so inflamed I keep having nosebleeds."

The doctor said, "He has to take it easy until he gets a firm clot."

"And I'm supposed to avoid a clot. Shall we trade?"

We all laughed and I felt warmly toward both men. "I'm curious about something…" Rolf gestured for me to continue. "From where I was, I thought I saw two men come down from the chopper, but unless I missed something, only one went up."

"Very astute, isn't she?" Rolf said to the doctor, then to me, "You're still bound by our confidentiality agreement so I can tell you that an FBI officer was winched onboard."

Two down…three up. Now it made sense. "Is he taking over the investigation?"

"We're…cooperating but they won't be of much help."

"More of a nuisance?"

His military stance stiffened. "It's nothing to me besides more paperwork. Nobody's going to run the data any faster because the satellite link is democratic: it annoys everybody. No matter her questions, we'll all arrive in Florida at the same moment."

"Yes, the time limitation and losing most of the suspects—"

"Sometimes people have to satisfy their own curiosity, to see something first hand…her cabin, the crime scene…"

Rolf moved the ice to above the bridge of his nose. Dried blood crusted in his five o'clock shadow. "They're running the names of every soul on board through Interpol, the FBI, and other international databases."

"Does Grisha know that the body's still on board?"

"I was on my way to see him when my nose exploded."

"Would you like me to tell him for you?"

"You must be still for another thirty minutes at least," the doctor said to Rolf and then turned to me. "I was going to check on Mr. Zlatogrivov anyway and it would be helpful for you to translate. Then, *you* should lie down with your leg higher than your heart and rest for several hours."

◻ ◻ ◻

Marius had been right. As soon as I left Grisha's room, I broke out into an icy sweat and began to shiver. Right foot, left foot, hold the handrail…a few more steps…I told myself. Key in slot. Press shoulder to door to keep it from slamming into my throbbing shin. Bathroom. Take two tablets—the good stuff, meant for emergencies only. Grab two towels. Remove ice in plastic bag from the bucket on the shelf above mini-fridge. Pour half the ice back into the bucket. Tie knot in bag. Wrap in towel. Get San Pellegrino and twist open. Pull back bedspread. Take one pillow and stand it horizontally against the headboard. Take a second pillow and place it vertically on top of the other in a cross shape. Roll second towel like a sausage. Get in bed and place that towel behind head and ice-wrapped towel on throbbing shin. Take another pillow and prop up the knee of the sore leg. Sigh. Close eyes. *Breathe. Pain…leg.* Knot…opposite thigh and buttock,

242

probably from compensating. Right temple still pulsing. Long breaths in and out. Take a deep breath. Another. Cough. Pain. Cough. What was that about a clot getting to my lungs? Too soon...soon...

Soon the meds whisked me from the jaws of the present into a shimmering room where a current of faces drifted around me like flakes in a snow globe. *Pain turned inside out was imagination...which birthed new paths...which led to... The particles colonized...and came to rest in a pattern I almost recognized.*

The door chimed. Ping-a-pong. I turned slightly and a snake of pain uncoiled down my leg, nipping at my ankle. Using hand-holds from bedside table to room divider to hallway, I wobbled across the room and peered through the peephole. Callista's face blurred; she looked like she was drowning. I unlatched the door.

"'Scuse me for a minute." I waved her in and stumbled to the bathroom where I splashed water on my face and snagged a comb through my hair. Even without a fresh cut, my bob rebounded so I didn't look as deranged as I felt.

Callista was mopping a spot where the ice must have leaked. I staggered to the bed. "What the hell happened to you, mate?"

"I lost a fight with the dinner trolley," I said, gingerly getting into bed and landing on another puddle.

"Did you call the doctor?"

"Been to the clinic...following orders."

She held up the dripping ice roll. "Be right back."

I replaced the pillow under my foot and slipped partway back into my otherworldly swoon.

A towel was placed over the wet bedspread. Two cold packs covered with several layers of linen napkins were tucked around my shin. "Where else hurts?"

I pointed to my hip and buttocks. The door opened, closed, opened again. Callista rolled me on my better side, wedged a large pool towel under my back, and without asking permission pulled down my slacks. "You really came a guster, didn't you?" she said in her best down-under accent. "Your whole side is going sunny-side up. Did you get an x-ray?"

"Dr. Kotze didn't suggest it."

"When you get home, try to get that area in direct sunlight for about ten minutes a day. The UV rays will break down the bilirubin so it will heal faster."

"Where'd you learn that?" I slurred.

"Mum's a nurse," she said, "and if she were here, she'd give you a blistering reminder to stop trying to save the world and take care of yourself for a change."

"Mum's a nurse…lost her purse…in a—curse!"

"Aye?" she twanged. "You are acting like you've been away with the fairies."

"Meds…help…"

She shook the prescription bottle on the table. "Who's Dr. Tsien?"

"Dentist, gum surgery."

"How many?"

"Two."

"Be right back."

I closed my eyes and flew off to Waikiki. Callista disrupted the sound of waves pounding on the beach by plopping herself down on my bed. "Got some Greek yogurt and a cuppa." She handed me a spoon, which I clasped like a baby. She had to steer it to my mouth.

"You're a cheap drunk, you know that?" She handed me the tea cup. With concentration, I sipped without spilling. I grimaced. "Too sweet!" Then I giggled. "*Tout suite*! Ha ha! How's your French?"

"You've got to metabolize that as fast as possible."

"Doc said to rest."

"I came to tell you about the FBI—someone came aboard off the chopper."

"I know."

"She wants to meet with you?"

"Who?"

"The FBI agent, Bernie." She saw I was still flustered and encouraged me to eat more.

I did, and then fell back on my pillow. "FBI? A woman!"

"Her name is Bernice…Fledermaus…or something like that. She's already talked to me and Ellwood—and you're next on the list."

"Why me?"

"She wants statements from everyone who found the body. Mae has you down as a witness."

"Makes sense."

"They're going through *all* the tapes."

"I know."

"Just because there's a shot of her coming or going with me doesn't prove anything, does it?"

I blinked until my eyes focused better. "Are you worried about something in particular?"

"We were together a lot."

"Unless the time and date stamps were around the time that they think she died, it won't matter."

"Even so, it could. Rolf said some horrid things."

"He's just doing his job. This happened on his watch and he has a lot riding on both containing it and solving it."

Callista sobbed, choked it back, and swallowed hard.

"It's okay to cry." I reached for her hand.

"He's going to ruin everything for me—"

"You were friends—one of many."

"Whatever you're thinking...it's worse." Her faced blanched chalk-white.

"Don't tell me there are cameras in cabins!"

"No, we were in a dressing room backstage. I was helping her out of her skintight costume and I couldn't help but notice—" She closed her eyes. "I—her belly—she's so thin—just a tiny pooch—but I asked. I how-you-say-it?—flipped out on her, and—" Her voice shattered. "My last words were unkind." Callista was wracked by heaving sobs.

Last words syndrome...I knew it well. It wasn't what I said to David, but what I didn't say...or do. It had been a busy morning and he'd gone off in one direction, me in another...no kisses or hugs or routine "love you." I punished myself over that slip, not that anything I might have said would have made me feel a micron better.

I waited a beat and started again. "You were angry about her pregnancy?"

"I hadn't had a chance to know what to feel before she said that she was getting rid of it in Florida." She swallowed, then blurted, "I told her that was the wrong way to go so I said we could raise it together in New Zealand."

"That was kind of you."

"She refused point blank and said something ridiculous about a family curse."

"Could you have misunderstood?"

"It was spelled out in my translation. She said both her mother and a baby brother died suddenly and she couldn't live with herself if something happened to another child." Callista's face glowed with a memory. "Tania said, 'My brother was called to be an angel.' Then she wept and said, 'I wish I could fly as easily.'"

"She did fly," I whispered. "On silks."

We both were quiet for a few long minutes. "I'm glad you're here," I said finally. "Those pills knocked me out. Tonight, I'll take only one."

"At least it looks like clear sailing the rest of the way."

"That's a relief." I closed my blurring eyes. "Cal, what do *you* believe happened?"

"I can barely stand to think about it." She tossed her head back to clear the hair clinging to her wet cheeks. "I go around in circles. Do you know what the average age of our guests is? Almost seventy! And Tania was stronger than most men."

"What about the crew?"

"Nice group. Not a single rotten apple."

"What about suicide in someone's cabin? That might have been reason enough for someone to want to move the body for self-protection."

"Impossible! She said that performing is her life."

"Maybe someone was jealous—maybe of her feelings for you."

"I didn't think of that."

"Many crimes are caused by a possessive rage."

"But who?"

"That's the question."

"I know it makes no sense," Callista said, "but I believe that she just fell asleep and didn't wake up."

□ □ □

My stateroom looked tossed. Wet cloths, thawing ice packs, cups, saucers, empty bottles, three pairs of shoes, and several layers of outfits cluttered the small space. No point in picking up when the next step was packing. Since I was going home, I could just toss laundry in one case, fold the better clothes, and stack my research material in my carry-on. Back in bed, I propped my legs and searched for that sweet spot that leads to sleep. The image of Tatiana flying on golden silks was comforting for a few seconds until questions started reverberating through my brain.

Of course, there was no such thing as a family curse although many diseases were inherited like the hemophilia that Queen Victoria passed to the last Tsar's only son, Alexei. Except for the baby brother, everyone else died in their prime—this was a family that maximized every fiber of their bodies—so there was no reason to believe the child succumbed to the same cause. In my child-welfare world, a parent was assumed guilty until an official diagnosis proved otherwise. However, regardless of whether a parent was culpable or not—sorrow, guilt, and a thousand "what ifs" left a permanent scar.

All I knew about Galina's death was that she'd been grocery shopping, hardly an exertion. The only reasons for sudden death that came to mind besides various kinds of heart attacks was a brain hemorrhage, pulmonary embolism, or ruptured aorta. The incidence of severe alcoholism in Russia was well known. I had investigated several cases of fetal alcohol syndrome in children adopted from Russia— an insidious condition without a cure. As far as I knew, most alcohol-related deaths involved progressive deterioration. Then what about Tatiana's uncle Yegor, also a gymnast—the one who had introduced Grisha and Galina? Wide awake and fulminating with questions, I stumbled out of bed, unplugged the laptop, and hoped I'd have enough battery life to satisfy my curiosity while still following doctor's orders.

I typed Galina and started listing what I knew:
Gymnast and coach
Top athletic condition
Lost infant son
Guilt?
Grieving?
Died suddenly
Grocery shopping
Kept secret from Tatiana until she finished a competition
Alcoholic?

I searched online for gymnast, athlete, sudden death, and alcoholic. The connection time on the Sea-Link connection was interminable by land standards. While waiting for URLs to populate, I limped to the mini-fridge, selected a ginger ale for an energy boost. Back in bed I clicked: <u>Sudden death in young people; Heart problems often blamed.</u> I brought up the Mayo Clinic site. "Long QT syndrome is an inherited heart rhythm disorder that can cause fast, chaotic heartbeats, which can be life-threatening."

I selected the highlighted <u>Long QT and Alcohol</u> and tabbed to one study's conclusion. "These results suggest that alcoholism causes dysfunction of the autonomic nerves as well as worsening QT prolongation, and this may predispose such patients to sudden cardiac death." I amended the search to include SIDS. "The studies strengthen the molecular evidence that some SIDS cases result from cardiac electrical diseases such as congenital LQTS."

My eyes watered and blurred. I stretched my arms over my head and extended my legs. A searing pain whizzed from my back to my toes. I reached for the soda to stem a wave of nausea, I swallowed hard, and then tried to distract myself reading: "Treatment of Long QT: Therapeutic measures include beta-blockers…like propranolol, nadolol, metoprolol, and atenolol." Peggy took atenolol for high blood pressure. I strained to connect some dots, yet my thoughts flitted, a side effect of the pain meds. Agitated by my fuzziness, I bumped the bedside table, causing the ginger ale can to flip and spill. I ripped out a handful of tissues, tossed them on the carpet, and used my better foot to blot moisture. When I turned back to the computer, the connection had timed out. Frustrated, I switched to my spreadsheet and scanned my notes and found that in the column headed "Olek," I had written "blood pressure." I blinked to focus on the tiny cell where I had written "stage fright." I tried to log in again, but the screen froze. The best way to get a fresh connection was to reboot. Fighting the urge to toss the laptop across the room, I resigned myself to the task.

My nerves sizzled with expectation. My tired fingers made several mistakes before a moving bar indicated that my laptop was attempting to connect me—some random woman in a stateroom on a ship in the middle of a vast ocean via an orbiting satellite to an infinite amount of information available to millions of people who simultaneously were also searching for answers. I moved the computer to the desk, plugged it back in, and left it to find an electronic embrace. Like the proverbial pot that doesn't boil under scrutiny, I decided that a hot shower might soothe my back. Next, I changed into a nightgown and robe, cleaned up the floor, and grabbed an apple from the never-ending fruit bowl— all before allowing myself to glance at the screen.

My mouse prowled around until it once again landed on Propranolol (Inderal) "May reduce peripheral symptoms of anxiety such as tachycardia and sweating...controls symptoms of stage fright."

"So, if she really had inherited Long QT..." I said aloud, "the pills Olek gave her could have unwittingly prolonged her life."

I reminded myself that even though I had found curious correlations, I couldn't assume that either the pills or the theoretical heart problem had anything do with her mysterious death.

"Googlitis" was what Margot called it when you just follow breadcrumbs of information into the weeds. "It's a form of writer's block—or in your case—procrastination." I'd argued that research helps define a character or adds vividness to a location. However, Tatiana was not one of my creations, and if I was honest with myself, we probably had spent less than five hours together in total, most of that time with me translating for her. She was too wrapped up in her own career and the complication of her pregnancy to have asked me anything about my life. It had been a one-way street, and a narrow lane at that.

I hovered before logging off because it was so exasperating to reconnect. Did I need to know anything else? Bodhi! I'd forgotten to email him since…how many days had it been? I hurried to write something.

There once was a boy name Bodhi
Whose ~~face~~ fingers were ~~quite~~ grody.
He picked up a can
Poured Coke on his hand
And soon he was covered in sody!

Silly—but it might elicit a giggle. Ugh, not good at all, even though he'd jump and giggle at the idea. I centered it and would have looked for a picture on the internet but could lose the connection. I added an emoji with a kiss and pressed SEND. I signed off with my usual sigh and never-ending refrain: If only David could have watched his beautiful boy grow.

Where David had been methodical about facts and the process of elimination, I relied on intuitive guesses. We solved several difficult cases by combining our perceptions. Even after I was writing fulltime, I still read his files and offered my two-cents.

I blinked at my lists, which seemed to contradict each other. "Never confuse correlation with causation," David had often reminded me when I tried to make dubious connections. My supposition that Long QT might have caused the death of Tatiana's mother, brother, and uncle could never be proven even if indications of the syndrome were discovered during the autopsy.

"You can have pneumonia and fall off a cliff," he'd once said, "although the disease isn't the actual cause of death," David said when he disagreed with one of my conclusions.

"What if the victim had a coughing fit and that's why she didn't see where she was going?" I'd retorted. "Cough or Cliff" had become our shorthand in this sort of cause-and-effect argument. The fact was that Tania didn't fall into the hamper as a result of a heart attack.

There were few mysteries in child-protection cases. Most adult deaths involved overdoses; most of the child deaths and severe maltreatment cases also were related to parental substance abuse. Once we had the toxicology reports, we rarely investigated further even though there was a remote possibility that something other than an overdose actually caused the death, but unless there were stab or bullet wounds, we took the easy way out. Dead was dead when it came to a parent. The children—well that was a different story—but malnutrition or bruises or body scans usually revealed a brutal history. "The dead kids are the tip of the iceberg," I used to tell new hires. "For every one who died, there are a hundred suffering. Those are the ones we need to find and protect."

The links on the right side of the computer screen claimed my attention. I selected: <u>Drugs to be avoided in LTQS</u>. "Oh no!" I said aloud. I had missed something that should have been there. Sweat from my brow stung into my eyes. I knew I needed help, but there was nobody I could trust—and everybody to fear.

Control…shift…numeral three. The screen was saved. My heart raced as I tried to remember how to delete my browsing data. First, I did it in Safari and then went to my web history page on Google. The page took forever to populate. I pressed the setting gear, pressed DELETE ALL, then did it once more for good measure. Now only a forensic IT specialist with special equipment would be able to resurrect the data. For good measure, I made certain that none of my notes remained on the hard drive, although if the person who had violated my computer earlier had installed a key logger, it still could be transmitting everything I had been doing. "Good luck on that," I said aloud because whoever was tracking my cyber movements also was held hostage to the same dreadful satellite connection.

Now pain was my friend. My muscle aches and nerve zaps would keep me alert. No more analgesics. Sleep was no longer the answer; I had to make a plan.

Five

In all chaos there is a cosmos, in all disorder a secret order.
—Carl Jung

Tuesday, November 24
At Sea: Position: 397 Nautical Miles East-Northeast
of Ft. Lauderdale, Florida

The phone jarred me awake. I opened one eyes. My travel clock read: 9:00 sharp, but I hadn't synced it with the ship's time. After a few rings, the phone was quiet. What time was it really? We were headed west and gained almost an hour a day, so if it wasn't nine, it was later—maybe ten or even eleven, giving me some leeway. Long ago I had learned not to take ships to Europe because when we lost an hour a day, I was always trying to catch up with myself.

I sat up tentatively. The jagged pain arched through my hip and leg. My head felt heavy, my tongue thick. I glanced around the room pleased that I had used my last surge of adrenalin to start packing. All the soiled clothing was stuffed into my extra duffel. I'd placed all the dirty dishes and glassware in the corridor for the middle-of-the-night room service fairy to ferry somewhere. I grinned, punchy with my pun. Just before I allowed myself to lie down, I'd made three digital copies of my book: one for my rollaboard, one for my purse, one in the security pouch clipped to my bra. That one also contained all my notes and files about Tatiana. If anything happened to me, I expected one of them would make it back to my publisher.

Again, the phone. "Hello." My untested voice sounded husky.

"Officer Ocampo here."

I felt limp with relief. "Yes?" She seemed to be the right person at the right time.

"Sorry to disturb, but we wondered if you would be kind enough to join us at eleven in the Colonnade."

Although I knew an official summons when I heard one, I asked, "Why?"

"We would appreciate your help in explaining the plans to repatriate Ms. Zlatogrivova to her father."

"May I ask what time it is now?" Not a stupid question since there were few official clocks on board.

"A few minutes after eight. We wanted you to have plenty of notice." She didn't give me to time to respond. "For security, please bring your passport and ship ID."

I decided on a room-service breakfast, if only to reassure the staff I was alive. While Cozmin poured my first cup of "Early Grey" tea, the phone rang again. He handed it to me.

"Dr. Kotze here. Just checking on your injuries."

"A little better, thank you."

"Any additional pain, swelling?"

"I don't think so."

"Warm sensation anywhere?"

"No."

"Please point the toes on your sore leg. Do you notice any new pains in your calf?"

"Just the same nerve pain, although it's not too bad when I'm sitting."

"Good, just keep checking for anything new, especially bluish discolorations."

"Thanks doctor."

"It would be no trouble to stop by and check you at any time."

"Not necessary, really," I said, feeling more uneasy the longer he stayed on the line.

"Very good," he said with reluctance. "Just remember I'm not going anywhere you aren't."

Coz had let himself out and I was left alone with my thoughts pinging and ponging like pinball machinery. I had started to crack the puzzle about Tatiana's death, but every time I fixed on a scenario, it would bounce off the flippers triggering my neurotransmitters to produce overdoses of cortisol, insulin, and dopamine and creating waves of anxiety. Too many people, too many variables filled my head with flashing lights of conflicting theories.

David had been developing interrogation techniques that were not abusive. "It's very difficult to keep a secret," he said. "If you tell a child about a big surprise for a parent or sibling, he's immediately filled with an overwhelming urge to blab to *someone*."

"Is that why it is so much easier to get kids to tell the truth?"

"Some, yet not all. It takes an incredible amount of energy to suppress a confidence; so, what happens is the more you try to repress the thought, the more you think about it—which keeps it on the proverbial 'tip of the tongue.'"

I whetted my tongue, which seemed chokingly thick, wishing there was someone I could trust with my revelation—someone who could help untwist the scrambled skein and find the loose ends.

☐ ☐ ☐

I had only been to the Colonnade, a rectangular room set sideways on the Arctic Deck behind the basketball court, once to give a talk at the Empress Book Club as a favor to Callista. A long line of columns made out of Styrofoam marched along the inside walls. There was a door on the port side and another starboard and each was flanked by windows with heavy cream curtains, guaranteeing privacy. The columns were festooned with silk floral garlands for weddings and vow renewals. Other times the room was the right size for Jewish Sabbath services and daily bible study. Affinity groups like a university archeology tour, birders, or astronomers could book the room for lectures. At cocktail hour, the Friends of Bill W. (named for the founder of Alcoholics Anonymous) met there as did the Friends of Dorothy (code for LBGTQ+). Callista told me that small companies held annual meetings there, making the trip tax deductible.

Only two elevators went to the top deck. When I arrived at the forward bank, the central elevator, which was the "local" for every deck, was out of service—probably the same one that had trapped the passengers briefly. Warning cones threaded with yellow tape blocked the area right in front of it and the brass doors were propped open. Loud banging reverberated through the shaft. I pressed the UP button and simultaneously heard a groaning sound and worried that I had summoned the faulty elevator until I realized that it was merely the rush of wind when someone in a cabin with their balcony door open also unlocked their corridor door. The sudden roar was followed by a colossal bang as suction slammed the door shut. Passengers who startled at that din at the beginning of the trip now took it as just another resonance from the ship's percussion section.

I turned back to the elevator and startled. A slight man in an emerald-green jumpsuit appeared in the open doorway of the center elevator, seemingly hovering in mid-air. He was so slender and short that at first I thought he was a child. One foot was balanced on a niche that held the control panel while the other dangled freely. He wore a white harness and was tethered to the underside of the car above him. A testing meter hung from his work belt. His fingers made the okay sign and I nodded back.

According to my watch, it was almost eleven o'clock. I wheeled around to the staircase, grabbed the railing, and walked up three steps before a bolt from my butt to my calf stopped me cold. The elevator door opened behind me. "Hold that please!" I called. A man inside blocked the door with his arm. The woman with him was doubled over coughing. It was going down. I tried not to inhale until the couple inside got off on the Pacific Deck, heading to the clinic no doubt. Now I had the car all to myself as it skipped all the stops and landed on the top deck.

Officer Ocampo was standing at the other end of the corridor, obviously waiting for me. "There's someone who wants to meet you," she said, ushering me into the Colonnade. Several tables had been placed together and covered with a long cloth printed with nautical signal flags. The sideboard had glass jugs with spigots filled with ice water, iced tea, and a third marked pineapple juice. A tray held a wheel of crustless tea sandwiches and another had fresh-baked chocolate chip cookies. Each place at the table was set with sharpened pencils and notepad sporting the ship's logo. It looked like the setup for a corporate meeting.

A formidable woman who had been sitting at the head of the table rose before I crossed the sill. With her short heels, she must have been close to six feet tall. Her smile was that of someone running for election. "Bernice Flederman," she said. As I shook her hand, which was twice the width of mine, she flipped her other wrist to reveal an FBI badge. "Do you mind if we sit?" Ms. Flederman asked. "I don't have my sea legs yet."

Officer Ocampo stood at attention near the doorway. She caught the agent's eye. "Anything else, ma'am?"

"No thank you," the officer said.

"Mae—Officer Ocampo," I said before taking my seat. She raised her eyebrows. "Would you be able to check the medical registry for me, please. I need to consult with a cardiologist."

"Are you having a heart problem?"

"It's only a medication question."

"Surely the doctor..." she slipped before realizing she couldn't question me further about my health. "I'll be happy to check," she said before leaving the room.

"Are you sure you are okay, Mrs. Lanier?" the FBI agent said, appraising me from head-to-toe.

"Dale, please," I replied.

"Of course. I'm Bernie." She smiled, revealing extraordinarily large teeth.

"It's been a rough couple of days on all fronts, but so far I don't have a heart condition." I looked her straight in the eye. "The medical registry is a list of passengers who are specialist doctors who might be willing to consult with the ship's physician, if needed. The ship's doctor is a generalist with extra qualifications in emergency medicine who sometimes needs to confer with an obstetrician or eye surgeon or cardiologist."

"Sounds like a good system. I wonder how often they're called."

"I once met a nephrologist—a kidney doc—who helped out when a passenger's portable dialysis machine malfunctioned. Also, I heard about a pediatrician who assisted when a child having an allergic reaction had to be intubated."

"This Dr. Curtsey—is he the one who did the rape kit?"

"It's pronounced Coat-see," I said and waited for her to fill in the beat.

"I understand you were present."

"Yes."

"As was Officer Brandt?"

"No. He was supposed to be, but he was occupied with the plans for the evacuation."

"So, who did witness the rape kit?"

I indicated the door Mae had just used. "Officer Ocampo and one of the nurses joined us for the collection of the specimens."

"You were the only non-crewmember?"

"Yes."

"Can you tell me why you agreed to put yourself through that?"

"I didn't exactly volunteer."

She gave me a thank-you nod. "Were you satisfied with the manner in which the rape kit was conducted?"

"Yes. It was very professional."

"We think the company used excellent judgment in having someone there who was unrelated to the shipping line."

"Which is the main reason why I agreed. I felt an obligation to Tania—Ms. Zlatogrivova."

"Who asked you to be a witness?"

"The cruise director."

The FBI officer checked her notes. "That's Callista Standard."

"Standish."

"You were with her when the body was discovered." I nodded. "I understand that you knew her before this cruise. Did you select this cruise so you could be together?"

I had not seen this coming. I didn't want her to think I shared Callista's preferences because that could lead to several false conclusions. "It was one consideration, otherwise I wouldn't have known anyone on the ship. However, my choice was made based on the dates that suited my schedule."

"Does she open her heart to you?"

"We're not that sort of friends."

"You also had a relationship with the victim."

Her line of questioning with hot words like "heart" and "relationship" was making me feel defensive, but I answered smoothly. "Our only commonality was the Russian language."

"Did she also see you as a girlfriend in whom she could confide?"

I sidestepped that question. "You've been briefed on the victim's health status, right?"

"She was pregnant and had an infection."

"Both private issues. I translated what the doctor said to her, so in a sense I was the first one who told her about the baby, not the other way around. She made me swear to secrecy."

"Did she tell you anything about the father of the baby?" Bernie asked, all business.

"No."

"But you have an idea?"

"Actually, I don't." I wasn't going to reveal my list of lovers, even if asked, because it put Tatiana in an unfair light.

Bernice stood up and went to the water jug. "Want some?"

"Yes, I'm parched." I waved my hand to cool my face. "They're going to have to turn on the air today for the first time."

"Hard to believe it's only two days before Thanksgiving!"

"Where are you from?"

"Portland—Maine, not Oregon."

She poured two glasses, both too full for the rolling conditions. One sloshed close to the brim as she moved toward the table. Concentrating, she managed to hand me mine without spilling it, but had to sip from hers to contain the mess. She laughed at herself. "Boats are not my thing."

"What is?"

"Fair question. I'm second in command in New York City, which turns out to be the closest office to Bermuda. Empire invited me so we could get a head start before the ship docks."

"May I ask whether you have jurisdiction?"

"That's the million-dollar question." She held her hands palm up. "We might if the ship, regardless of flag of convenience, is American owned—in whole or part."

I shook my head. "I thought Empire was incorporated in Bermuda and chartered out of Malta."

"You're right."

"So even though it has corporate offices in Florida and headquarters in London, it doesn't matter."

She took a long swig of water. "However, if the victim was a US citizen *and* the crime was committed outside of the jurisdiction of *any* nation—for instance, at sea—we would be in charge. Likewise, if the crime took place within twelve miles of our coastline—which means inside our territorial waters."

"She was Russian and we were in the middle of the Atlantic."

She hesitated a few seconds. "There's one other loophole. If either the victim or perpetrator is an American citizen on a vessel that either departed from or will arrive in the United States, we have full authority."

"Since we're arriving in Florida and we know the victim is foreign, you would have to have an American perp, right?" I swallowed a lump in my throat. "There must be a thousand Americans on board."

"Nine hundred and forty-seven, but who's counting?" Bernie pulled out the chair two down from mine and angled it to face me. "You and I have more in common than you think." She folded her hands and held them under her chin like a brace.

My mind raced to whether she too was going to spill out her guts about being widowed by violence. I clutched the sides of my chair so hard my knuckles blanched. "When I was in the DC office, my assignment was missing children." She waited a few beats. "I once heard your husband lecture in Miami. He had unique perspective on family trauma." She stared at me with her brown eyes flecked with gold. "I'm so sorry for your tragic loss."

I knew she was playing for my trust and I desperately needed someone to confide in, although I was not yet sure it was her. Yet where else could I go? Mae was impossible to read, so I had no idea of her philosophy or loyalties. Even though I had turned sympathetic to Rolf, I was now working from an entirely different perspective and just his name set off the buzzers and blinding lights of my inner pinball machine.

"You understand the problem we are facing?" the FBI officer asked rhetorically. "This ship docks tomorrow with several thousand passengers and crew—and the body of a homicide victim who's a Russian national."

"Have you narrowed it down to any persons of interest?"

"The technological advances since nine-eleven have been astonishing, so we've accumulated quite a lot of info from international databases and have everyone's security files already. The Florida task force will decide who will be allowed to disembark."

"Miami's involved already?"

"Yes, and so is headquarters. We're trying to prevent an international incident."

"I don't understand—"

The agent drummed her fingers on the table. "With Russia. There's an unexpected link with Putin." She looked at me expectantly.

I strained to make a connection. "One of the Russian president's girlfriends was an Olympic gymnast. I know her father ran in those circles, but Tania's been out of the country ever since she joined Cirque."

"She's returned to visit relatives."

"And she met Putin?"

"Yes, at least once…that we know of."

"Isn't that a stretch?"

"We have reason to believe that when we repatriate her, there's a chance the information will go to the top."

I rolled my eyes. "Hey, I'm a novelist and the idea of a political reason for the death is farfetched, even for one of my plots."

"I agree, although you can imagine the memos that zipped around when someone found a connection between her and Putin." She looked bemused. "What kind of a woman was Ms. Zlatogrivova?"

"Everyone liked her," I said protectively. "Nobody has said an unkind word about her. She was sweet, gentle…ah….generous with her friends, and went all out for her audience."

"So, I hear, which is why we think it was probably someone she hardly knew, someone with a fantasy, a fetish, maybe someone who came on to her and she rebuffed him."

"I was thinking along the same lines." My wariness was waning. Unlike Mae and Rolf, Bernie had no reason to place corporate interests before public safety.

"What's your opinion of her father?"

"He was a demanding coach but also loved her deeply." She waited for me to continue. "I know many people thought he was a harsh taskmaster, still he was devoted to her. Also, why would he want to kill his golden goose?"

Her head did a little bobble and I realized she had been doing the same after each of my responses as a sort of Skinner-like reward. "There seems to be some coolness between Officers Brandt and Ocampo. Why would that be?"

"Isn't that always the way it is when the big guy from headquarters shows up? Everybody thinks of Rolf as the Big Bad Wolf, even though he is usually funny and charming."

"Did you know he was brought up in a communist country?"

"Yes, and I just found out that he speaks Russian."

"Do you sense that he's one of those 'absolute power corrupts absolutely' types?"

"Anyone who's charged with retraining and cleaning house will never win a popularity contest."

"I know all about being unpopular...and I expect that you do too." She folded her arms across her chest. "I guess they did turn on the air conditioning— full blast." She stood and walked back to the sideboard to refill her glass. Mine was still half-full. "Is there anything you want to add that might point me in the right direction? I've seen the doctor's reports, the photographs taken at the scene and afterward, but we won't have the basic toxicology reports until tomorrow. Some can take more than a week. Empire is cooperating fully because they want us to facilitate their twelve-hour turnaround in Florida. They have more leverage in terms of detaining crew, although none with the paid guests. And, if the ship is delayed, it will be all over the press. As you see, I'm under pressure from both sides."

I shifted in my seat to lessen the ache in my hip. "Agent Flederman, let's suppose it wasn't a homicide for a minute."

The FBI officer's expression was somewhere between incredulity and suspicion. "Weren't you there when the body was found?"

"Which is why everyone's ruled out suicide or natural causes. But what if somebody found her already dead and decided it would be prudent to dispose of the body?"

"Okay...explain...please."

"I'm not saying she took her own life. How she died is one question; the other is who moved her body—and why."

"This isn't a fictional plot," she said sourly.

"Right, but indulge me for a minute." She sniffed but didn't interrupt. "What if there were compromising circumstances and the person thought he or she could get away with disposing of the body." I paused. "Think about it for a minute. We're in the middle of an ocean. How hard would it be?"

"Are you saying it was suicide because of the pregnancy?" I didn't respond. "Girls in their twenties don't just keel over—"

I cut her off. "My guess is it was accidental. She drank vodka, took a lot of pills—some her father gave her without much of an explanation. For this minute, let's assume that even though we don't know exactly why she died, we do know where she was found."

"I've been shown the scene."

"It's on what they call I-95." I described the proximity to several crew elevators and the clinic. "I'm sure you know that many people go missing on ships every year, which is why there are cameras constantly recording all sides of the vessel from stem to stern. When someone can't be located, the first tapes they check are those."

"So far the recordings are unremarkable."

"That's because she didn't go overboard, did she?" I clenched my fists. "What if a crewmember found her body in, say, his cabin—or some other place that somehow implicated him and his first thought was chucking her overboard."

"He would know about the cameras," Bernie said with a new light in her eyes. "Have you thought about the other ways to dispose of an 'inconvenient' body?"

Bernie was rigid with expectation as I explained the location of the handicapped elevator on the Pacific Deck. "It leads to a lower deck where there's a door that's used by the harbor pilots who come aboard to steer the ship in or out of a mooring. Also, people in wheelchairs can be rolled down a ramp from there. Are you following me?" She gave another head bob. "Someone could have wheeled the laundry cart onto that special elevator, taken it down one level, opened the hull door, and tossed out both the cart and its contents."

"Aren't there cameras in that area?"

"Most of them are higher up. This spot is so close to the water that a camera might miss it, or so someone may have believed. Anyway, it's a moot point because that elevator was out of service."

"Are you certain?"

"It wasn't working in the Azores—our last European port—and that was less than a week ago. Also, I've seen a maintenance man repairing it."

Bernie closed her eyes for a few seconds. "You are suggesting that this woman either committed suicide or died of natural causes, then her body was found by someone who had a good reason not to want to be associated with her. And that it had to be a crewmember because only they know how to access this non-public area of the vessel." I nodded with every conclusion. "Although it didn't work out because of a malfunctioning elevator, so the body was abandoned in the basket."

"Exactly."

"It's one hypothesis," she said in a noncommittal tone. She scribbled something on her notepad and turned the page. "You were with her when she learned she was pregnant."

I paused. It was as if Bernie had rejected my hypothesis and moved on. "Yes."

"How did she react?"

"She freaked."

"Can you break that down for me? Did she cry? Seem angry? Mention any names? Have any questions?"

"She didn't believe it. Said it was impossible. Then she tried to put it together for herself, asking if that was why her breasts were sore or was that why she'd been dizzy. The doctor confirmed that these were normal symptoms and asked about nausea and weight gain, which she denied." I closed my eyes at the memory of her lovely hands fluttering over her flat chest and belly. "Then she cried for a minute or so and went to the clinic restroom for quite a while—long enough for the doctor to ask me to check on her. I stood up just as she walked back into the exam room." I waited a beat. "She'd fixed her makeup."

Bernie tilted her head. "I didn't expect that."

"She was the consummate performer. On the ship, she was always on stage."

"Is that when she asked about abortions in Florida?"

"Yes."

"What was her demeanor? Did she seem forlorn or confused or—"

"She was serious…almost businesslike, then she became annoyed when the doctor said he didn't know where to go or what it cost: although if that is what she wanted, it was safest now because it was early in the pregnancy. So, I spoke to her—in Russian—and said that I knew where to go and it was legal." If the agent had any qualms about a woman's choice, she didn't flinch. Tania pointed to Mari—Dr. Kotke—and spoke in English, saying, 'You tell him where to take me.' She assumed that he would do that for her."

"Wasn't that a bit presumptuous?"

"I thought so, at least her tone was…sort of imperious."

"And how did he react?"

"He didn't. It just seemed like a *fait accompli*, as if it was part of his regular duties."

"Baby daddy?"

"I wouldn't cross him off the list, even so I wouldn't place him on top either." I winced at the double meaning. "You might as well know she was very likely promiscuous, which leads me to worry about a Mr. Goodbar, if you know what I mean."

"The Diane Keaton movie, right? It was based on a real New York case, which involved drugs." She stopped. "Do you think that's what happened here?"

"Absolutely…"

"I thought there was a zero-tolerance policy on ships and our ports use detection dogs, as do many around the world."

"Yes, to drugs, but not recreational, and not on purpose."

The agent gave me a crooked grin. "You've lost me."

"If I was in your seat, I'd think that I was deluded by too many weeks at sea. The pregnancy, her plans…don't get sidelined by them. One thing I know for sure is that Tania was loved by everyone who knew her—and I mean *everyone*. I have not spoken to a single person who harbored any resentment or would have wished her harm. What's even more surprising is that she inspired more than just likeability—or sexual attraction. Everyone—friend, crew, partner—and of course her father—express not only a deep affection but also a desire to guide, protect, teach, and assist her. Perhaps some of them—like her father—were misguided in what they thought was best for her, and several others probably placed their self-interests first. Nor should you discount someone with a perverted interest—if you had seen her act you would realize how she might provoke a twisted person—"

She interrupted me. "I've watched videos of her Cirque performances. I get it." She smoothed back her hair. "I gather you believe it was a sick stranger."

"It's complicated and I need—"

The side door to the Colonnade opened and Rolf barged in. "Did you get her list?" His question was directed to the agent.

"Not yet."

He came around to the opposite side of the table from me and placed his hands on the back of a chair—slightly touching my neck—as a reminder of our private conversation. "I assured Agent Flederman that you would share your insights."

"Mrs. Lanier has been exceedingly helpful."

Rolf shifted his feet. No matter how intimate he felt he was with me, I never stopped believing that even if he wasn't the one who hacked my computer, he surely had access to the files—but only the earliest ones—by now. And while he actually might have liked me, he had no loyalty to anyone besides himself.

"Perhaps I should explain about the list," Bernie said in a dry tone. "My office, coordinating with Empire security in London and Ft. Lauderdale, is trying to minimize the delay in Florida. To that end, we are working on a master list of people that may need to be detained for further questioning. At the conclusion of our interview, I was going to ask you to suggest names." She looked up at Rolf. "We've been productive, although it's taken longer than expected."

I turned in my chair and saw Rolf trying to compose his expression, but he couldn't stop his eyelids from twitching. He started to speak then realized he was going to sneeze. "Ah...ah...ahcoo!" He pulled out his handkerchief just in time.

"I hope you're getting hazard pay," I said to Bernie. "You're on the plague ship. Seriously, though, wash your hands like Lady Macbeth."

"Excuse me," Rolf said. "I do have to confer with Agent Flederman for a few minutes."

"I need to get back to my packing." I slowly stood and balanced myself with one hand firmly on the conference table. "Officer Brandt knows everyone I've talked to. Tania was extremely friendly with the art auctioneer, the Russian trainer, her partner, and her father, of course." I purposefully left out Marius and Callista because we'd already discussed them.

"Your perspective was most helpful," she said as I backed toward the door.

"One more moment," Rolf said. "You were asking for a cardiologist."

"Yes, something for my book."

"There are four, actually. We were able to reach one of them and mentioned your request." Rolf handed over a card: Dr. Isaac Zohar, Pembroke Pines, Florida. Cabin: G-443. "He said to try him any time today."

I nodded thanks. "Is the elevator back in service?"

"Not yet. A replacement part will be loaded in Florida. Hopefully you won't have a long wait for the other one. Most everyone's at lunch." He made a slight bow. "Thanks again for your valuable assistance." I half expected he would click his heels.

□ □ □

My usually sturdy sea legs had failed me and I was no longer in sync with the swells. I slammed into the walls twice, bouncing off the bruised hip. After I'd made an awkward entrance into my stateroom, I took my own advice, scrubbing my hands using the hottest possible water. I used antimicrobial soap and a nailbrush and then lathered past my wrists, rinsed in one direction only, and dried with a fresh towel. I hoped I wouldn't be stricken with some contagious cruise crud and give it to Bodhi.

The fruit bowl on the coffee table had been freshened and two perfectly ripened bananas caught my eye. This ship had a locker reserved for bananas so they could plot out the ripening schedule. I unpeeled one halfway and took several bites before pulling out the cardiologist's number. "G" meant he was on Gulf Deck, so I add a seven before his cabin number.

A woman answered with a sing-song, "Hel-low!"

"Is this Dr. Zohar's stateroom?"

"Yes, are you the woman who needed help?" she said with an accent I couldn't quite place.

"Yes."

"Sorry my husband is not in, but he said if this is emergent, please dial the clinic. They will contact him if necessary."

"There's no emergency," I replied. "I just need some technical information for…for a presentation. I'm a writer."

"I see," she said, something people say when they really don't.

"Could you tell me when he might be back in the room?"

"I'm not sure, although right now you'll find him in the Pirate Cove for the Trivia play-offs."

"I'd better not disturb him."

"No worries, his team was eliminated yesterday. He's just playing along for fun."

"How will I know who he is?"

"His team calls themselves 'The Beach Boys' and they're all wearing Hawaiian shirts. His is blue with pink flamingos. As they say, you can't miss him!"

"You're sure it is okay to bother him there?"

"I'm certain he'll be quite interested in your question. I've pushed his patience with this long cruise so he's ready to talk shop."

"I'm ready to get home myself."

"We'll make it for Thanksgiving, but someone else will have to do the preparation this year."

"Aren't we the lucky ones?" I thanked her again and hung up.

It was standing room only for the trivia championship. On longer voyages, the passengers formed teams and there were both daily winners and an accumulation of points for the overall champs, which was usually a bottle of mediocre champagne for each team member. The real prize was the bragging rights.

"Question number nineteen." Callista's Kiwi twang was broadcast to those outside the venue. "What was Eleanor Roosevelt's maiden name?"

"Oh, that's tricky," a lady blocking the aisle in front of me whispered to her friend. "It's Roosevelt too. They were cousins!"

"Number twenty," Callista said while I was still searching for the doctor's team. "This is a multi-part question. There will be one point for each correct answer. How many of Henry the Eighth's wives were named Catherine and how many were named Anne? There's a two-point bonus for each correct surname."

Anne Boleyn, Catherine of Aragon…I said to myself just before I spied the Hawaiian shirts. I slid sideways through the dense crowd. "Dr. Zohar?" I asked to the flamingo on his back.

"Oh! Well done, you found me." The doctor had a cap of thick, snowy hair and a physique so slender he probably was on one of those starvation diets that were supposed to increase longevity.

"No, I'm not going to tell you the total number points you could get for this last question," Callista was saying, "because that would be a clue to the number of wives, wouldn't it?"

"Does spelling count?" someone called out.

"No, and no more hints!" The cruise director wagged her finger like a schoolmarm.

The doctor directed me to the side exit.

"Sorry to take you away from the grand finale."

"The winners will be rubbing it in all evening." He pointed to two barrel-shaped chairs by a large window.

"Thanks for this," I said.

"How can I be of assistance?"

"I'm a writer and I have a medical question that is essential to the plot."

His eyebrows arched. "Are you published yet?"

"My pen name is Dale Lane."

He made the I'm-not-worthy flutter with his hands. "You wrote those books that usually have stars and planets in the titles, right?" I nodded. "I think my wife read 'How You Spend your Lights,' or something like that."

"*How My Light is Spent*," I said, "it's a quote from Milton."

"I knew it sounded familiar." He grinned. "Wait till I tell her. She'll want to meet you."

"That would be lovely," I said, preferring that it would never happen.

"I do hope I can help you sort this out."

"Okay, so in my story there's this young woman in her early twenties and she dies suddenly and mysteriously. The authorities suspect she's been murdered by a jealous boyfriend. I'd like it to be a natural death, if possible. I thought it might be a cardiac event because her mother also died young from some sort of heart condition and her infant brother was considered a crib death."

The doctor rubbed his cheek with his thumb. "Was she in good health?"

"Extremely. She was an accomplished athlete."

"A runner?"

"No, she was a—" I hadn't thought this out but went with my first thought. "A figure skater with Olympic ambitions."

"Does she die during a competition?"

"No."

"Was she with a boyfriend?"

"Yes, that's why he's blamed."

"Totally unexpected?"

"Yes, so I was wondering if Long QT syndrome would fit my scenario."

"That's often the post-mortem conclusion when young runners die during a marathon; and because it's genetic, having a mother and a baby as a precedent would support that diagnosis. About ten percent of SIDS cases are due to heritable cardiac arrhythmia."

"What proof would someone need to exonerate the boyfriend?"

"Sometimes an autopsy is inconclusive until frozen tissue samples undergo DNA testing."

"Just examining the body wouldn't prove anything?"

"Most coroners would put it down as a SUD—a sudden unexplained death."

"Would there have been any early warning signs?"

"Unfortunately, most cases are first seen in the morgue, not in clinical settings. I'm sure you've heard about collegiate athletes in top form collapsing and dying during a game." He pursed his lips. "In retrospect, we hear about episodes of syncope—fainting—which is caused by an irregular heartbeat. Usually they've blamed it on over-excitement, a girl's time of the month, hot weather, skipping a meal, dehydration."

"What about pregnancy?"

The doctor stroked his chin. "While it seems paradoxical because pregnancy puts an additional burden on the heart, some patients improve when they are carrying a baby."

"Could sex trigger a fatal episode?"

"Would that help your plot?" He grinned. "Not in most cases, although the exercise load is a bit longer and more sustained—again like running a race or in a competitive sport like basketball, so it wouldn't be out of the question."

"Not impossible?"

"Fairly remote in someone that young."

"If someone was lucky enough to be diagnosed early, what would you prescribe?"

"Beta-blockers may diminish the risk of arrhythmias and reduce the QT interval."

"Are there drugs that could make it worse?"

"Many rather ordinary medications have been known to trigger a fatal incident—even some common antibiotics."

"For example?"

"Cipro and Levaquin come to mind." He cleared his throat. "Any chance that your story is located in a tropical area?"

"No, why?"

"I guess not with figure skating!" He chuckled. "Still, some anti-malarial drugs have been implicated in fatal episodes." He knitted his hands together. "Healthy athletes don't take many meds, but—" He pulled his fingers apart. "Although...if she suffered an injury, she might be taking an opioid."

"Yes...that's part of her story. She performs even when she's in pain."

"Would she do party drugs?"

"She's very health conscious."

"Many a granola-eater does a line now and then. For someone with an undiagnosed arrhythmia, even a small amount of coke could be lethal."

A bitter taste rose in my throat causing me to cough.

"Ike!" A man wearing a dolphin-patterned shirt pounded the doctor's back. "You won't believe it! The Skinny Dippers won! One of their gals is an Anne Boleyn groupie. Their twelve-points bonus pushed them over the top."

A woman wearing a lei said, "Hey guys, they've opened the Crow's Nest and we're all meeting for one last chance to catch a green flash at sunset."

The doctor glanced at me as if for permission. "You okay?"

He must have noted my face was aflame. My chest had knotted. I swallowed to clear it. "G-getting the bug, I guess. Thought I'd dodged it..."

"I'll join you shortly," he said to his friends, then to me, "And here I thought I'd gotten you all hot and bothered!" He winked in a flirtatious way.

Trying to compose myself, I said, "Can somebody die after a few lines of—what do they call it?—blow?"

"If they also had a cardiac arrhythmia."

"That might work." My own heart skipped a few beats. "The guy she's with could have had access."

"Happy I could help. Any other questions?"

"Just how common is the link between Long QT and cocaine?"

"There's a recent Spanish study in people from age fifteen to fifty, I believe, who were affected by sudden cardiac death and found they were almost sixty times more likely to have used cocaine than their peers."

"So, it's not rare."

"The drug or the condition?"

"Long QT alone is responsible for about four thousand deaths of adults and children in the US each year. I don't have the worldwide numbers. Coke is fairly ubiquitous."

I stared out the window trying to order my swirling thoughts. "Well, if that's all…" He stood to go, bent toward me, lightly touching my shoulder. "May I ask the title of your new book?"

There was no ice skater in my book and I couldn't think of any way to dissemble, so I gave the name of the real book I was writing onboard. "*The Comet's Tale*…although the heart issue is more back story."

"T-A-I-L or T-A-L-E?" he asked.

"The latter."

Another Hawaiian shirt waved. "Coming with?"

"Yes, be right there," the doctor said. Then to me, "Pun intended?"

"That's for the reader to decide." There was something more I wanted to ask, one last question to be resolved, yet he did not hold the answer. "Thank you so much for taking the time…"

"Really, my honor." He patted my shoulder collegially. "Wait till I tell Noreen!"

□ □ □

The room seemed to be revolving. I needed fresh air, which on a ship is never far away. To avoid the long delay from the trivia crowd, I avoided the area where one of the elevators was out of service and walked a bit farther to the glass atrium elevators. Out on the promenade I leaned in to the rail and filled my lungs with long draughts of the sultry air that was a premonition of Florida.

"Heavy evidence…" was what David demanded from his staff before taking a case to a judge. He wanted everything in writing, including contradictory data. "We're not looking to match a court's burden of proof and we're not trying for 'beyond the shadow of a doubt' here; although if we're right, we may save a child's life. If we're wrong, we may have traumatized a family with long-term consequences."

In measuring evidence where there are conflicting opinions, experts weigh one group of findings over the others. What else should I be considering? There wouldn't be a scintilla of proof until the forensic studies were complete, so did I dare present it without any factual basis? Bernie had hinted that the global search may have yielded a few passengers or crew with suspect backgrounds, so they would know if anyone had been caught with drugs. Plus, they did random urine checks of crew and anyone testing positive would have been put off at the last port.

Still, there was something I had to find, something I once had but misplaced like a coin lodged in the corner of a jumbled purse. Mentally I reviewed the rape kit. Tatiana's body had been free from a single mark of violence except something that had seemed of no consequence: a smudge of blood on the sheet in the laundry hamper. My first assumption was that it was post-coital discharge. I'd spotted in the earliest weeks of one of my pregnancies, fearing a miscarriage that never came, so that was another possibility. Now, though, I was almost certain of the blood's origin.

"Blood is the voice of the victim" was one of David's weirder maxims.

"It worked for Shakespeare," I'd said and quoted one of my favorite lines while staring at my palm: "'Here's the smell of the blood still: all the perfumes of Arabia will not sweeten this little hand.'" Blood and guilt. From Lady Macbeth to now.

How many people have I known—clients, co-workers, one of my publicists—even my dental hygienist—who had said, "It's nothing." Happens when I get a cold or when I rush around too much or when I skip lunch or during allergy season or when I'm overexcited or when I get a migraine." I'd heard every excuse; and I nailed them every time, if only to

284

myself. Validation! I laughed into the wind. It was as plain as the nose on her face!

I moved so fast I was able to ignore the jagged pulses of pain from my hipbone to my big toe. My first stop was my cabin. I placed the most up-to-date flash drive in my computer and pulled up my saved copy of "Drugs to be Avoided by Congenital Long QT Syndrome Patients." Just scanning it brought up red flag after red flag. Vance had given her Xanax, which was on the contraindicated list as trazodone, yet how would he have known? Even the Pepcid that Agata had left for her could have had a negative effect. I organized my notes alphabetically by medication, which also listed who had supplied it. While technically illegal to give prescription meds to someone else, there wasn't a handy drug store on the ship and so crew probably shared what they had with friends. My initial solution had been far too simple. Maybe it was part of the cause, but while the doctor's Cipro or her father's pain meds might be factored in, they were hardly the final straw. Wishing I had a portable printer, I copied the new file onto a fresh stick.

The computer center was two decks up. More than a dozen people were crowded by the elevator bank and I assumed it was time for jackpot bingo or the karaoke finals. Adrenaline spurred me up the midship staircase, using the brass banister as a fulcrum. A line of people waiting to print boarding passes snaked around the atrium. I turned around and went back down the curving atrium staircase to the passenger service desk. Fortunately, going downstairs hurt less.

"There must be some mistake!" a woman in a sundress was showing her bill to her neighbor in the queue. "I think they doubled the prices of the wine."

"I see duplicate charges too," said her companion wearing too-short shorts.

"You might be misinterpreting the 'two-for-one' beverages," said the man in front of them.

Only two people were standing in the velvet roped area for the "Loyal Royal" passengers, those that were either in suites or had been on board an Empire ship for a total of 100 days.

"Sorry," I said, "Do you mind if I just lean on the counter while I wait? I've injured my leg and I can't put any weight on it."

"Why don't you just go next?" said the man in front with a gracious nod. The woman behind him scowled, even though she grudgingly waved me forward.

"I owe you both a drink!" I said, "but I'll do better than that."

"How may I be of assistance, Mrs. Lanier?" the assistant purser asked.

I handed her my computer stick. "I need to print out a few documents," I said, then lowered my voice, "although the computer center is slammed and Officer Brandt is waiting for them."

"Certainly," she said. "Why don't you take a seat by the coffee bar and I'll bring them to you when they're finished."

"Thanks so much," I said, "and if these kind people will give you their stateroom numbers, I'll send over a token of appreciation." I winked at her and limped away.

I heard the purser say, "Well, good deeds are sometimes rewarded. You two are in for a pleasant surprise!"

The lady grumbled, "Really?"

"Do you know who that is?" was the last I heard before I landed in a plush chair.

Kester, who usually served beverages in the buffet, came over in a flash. "Your usual Prosecco?" She grinned with expectation. "Or a cup of Earl Grey?"

"Oh, I will so miss you!" I said to him, "How about a Courvoisier instead?"

"No tea?"

"Why not both?" My shoulders sagged because I needed both the caffeine and the fortification—not to mention the painkiller—and I hoped it would not only go on my comped tab, but that somehow Rolf would end up paying for it himself.

▢ ▢ ▢

The next quarter hour passed by like a quick blow across the bow that was almost over by the time the stern passed through. I still felt the fruity burn of the brandy when the purser handed me my papers in a manila envelope with a note taped to the front. "The staff captain has asked you to meet him in the library."

"When?"

"Now."

Although I must have seen the staff captain around, I'd never been introduced to him. He managed the affairs of the crew and had little contact with guests. I limped across the atrium to a chart of the ship's officers along with their photographs. Right under Captain Giambalvo was Staff Captain Antonio Castanga. Now I remembered asking Callista who the man with a thick mop of black curls was.

"Captain Tony?" She looked at me as if I had turned predatory. "Don't bother. I think he has something like seven children."

"Then being on board must seem like a vacation."

"Actually, I think he has the worst job on the ship. He's our sheriff, priest, and judge."

"I thought the captain was in charge."

"He has the final say, but Captain Tony handles conflict resolution personally in crew matters; although he also solves disagreements between a crewmember and a guest—or even between the passengers themselves."

"Isn't that the job of the socos?"

"They're more like the constabulary and he's the magistrate."

"Con—stab—ulary!" I had said mocking her accent. "Anyway, those dimples would settle me right down."

Under his photo was one of Mae Ocampo labeled "Chief Security Officer." Rolf, who was only on temporary assignment, was not considered crew.

I felt a wave of relief course through me. I was unsure of how Mae or Rolf would take my report. My documents would be safer in Captain Tony's hands. I exhaled and reminded myself that by this time tomorrow, I would be unlocking the door of my home. Bodhi would rush into my arms and cover me with peanut-butter-breath kisses—the best medicine of all.

The Venetian blinds were drawn on the library's closed glass doors. A sign on the stanchion read: PRIVATE PARTY. I hesitated long enough to see Vance enter first. He gazed in my direction but avoided eye contact. Something was going down. My sense of liberation dissolved. This felt like a summons to the principal's office to account for my behavior.

Three game tables had been moved together to create a long rectangle. At first glance it seemed like almost everybody on my list was already seated.

"If you please." Staff Captain Castanga pointed Vance to a chair next to Callista. Captain Tony's drawn face looked more devastated than devastating.

Tatiana's father, even more gaunt and ashen, sat beside Jerzy, whose eyes were closed, as if in prayer. Across from them, Olek's gaze was fixed at a faraway point. Rolf's back was to me, rigid as ever.

Dr. Kotze, who was standing by the door, came to my side. "Your leg, is it worse?" I made a so-so gesture. "You must see your doctor on Thursday."

"It's Thanksgiving—nobody works."

"Then the day after that."

Captain Castanga waved me over to the librarian's desk. "Your passport and cruise card please."

He moved out the way to reveal a woman with three stripes on her epaulet, indicating she ranked just under him. Her name tag read: Annemarie Sorenson. I hadn't seen her before, so I assumed she was a bridge officer. There already was a stack of multicolored passports on the desk in front of her. A maroon one was open. She finished copying some information from it to a form before acknowledging me. I opened my child-decorated tote bag, which seemed nonsensical in this setting, and foraged for the passport that I had tossed in this morning.

"Thank you." The woman took my navy-blue passport without looking up. "Crew card?" She glanced at me. "Sorry, *cruise* card."

I fumbled for it in the outside pocket where it was easier to find when I needed to unlock my door. Officer Sorenson scanned it into a handheld reader. She glanced from my face to the photo ID on the device's screen to confirm my identity. The only other time I'd seen scanners used for something other than embarkation and debarkation was during the lifeboat drills to ensure everyone was at their assigned muster station.

"Thank you," she said. I reached for my documents, but she covered them with her hand. The message was clear: I was no longer a free agent.

Dr. Kotze, who still hadn't taken a seat, guided me by the elbow to a chair next to Callista and directly opposite Olek and Jerzy.

A few minutes passed. Rolf Brandt and Mae Ocampo sat at attention. There was an empty seat opposite them flanked by the doctor and Grisha. The only sounds were from Captain Castanga's pen scratches and many coughs, either due to the virus that had gripped so many on the ship, or nervous tension. I riffled through my tote for a pen and the envelope with my printouts. I almost could hear Callista Standish and Vance Sharkey, Oleksander

Lopatkino and Jerzy Skala all trying to remember what they said to me that could implicate them. Even Dr. Kotze and Grisha Zlatogrivov appeared equally edgy.

Every twitch and throat clearing echoed in the small space. There were no clocks in the room, as usual, and I hardly ever wore a watch because there had been so many time changes in the last few weeks as we zigged east, zagged west and had lost daylight savings time somewhere in the journey. My eyes flickered toward Grisha, whose heavy lids were half-closed in what might have been taken for a prayerful repose if I hadn't noticed the knots bulging in his still-muscular neck. Marius seemed the most at ease. He had many of David's qualities, both intellectually and physically. I felt a familiar flutter in my loins and wished we had met under different circumstances. He hadn't mentioned a child nor a marriage—not that it would have been appropriate—even though he wore no ring. Ship's doctor was probably a role for a single man and his skills would be welcomed anywhere he chose to settle. Florida wasn't all that different in climate to South Africa... I halted my absurd line of thinking, which had been just a ploy to quell my apprehension. At least the doctor was above reproach, although David believed that nobody was ever beyond suspicion.

There were still a few empty seats. At least one was for the FBI agent. What had she said? There were more than nine hundred Americans on board including Vance Sharkey—and me. I supposed the FBI was double checking every one of us.

A few long minutes later, Captain Castanga stood and opened the now-locked door for the agent. Bernie was wearing a black-and-white tweed pantsuit that flattered her mature, yet fit, figure. She strode to her chair at the table, placed her hands on its back, and spoke without sitting.

"Good afternoon. I'm United States FBI agent Bernice Flederman of the New York office. As some of you know, I boarded from the helicopter offshore of Hamilton. The Empire Cruise Line has requested our agency's assistance prior to our arrival in Florida in order to avoid inconvenience for arriving and departing passengers and crew. Be assured our legal attaché has received the full cooperation and consent of Bermuda, this ship's flagship country. The principal law under which the United States of America exercises its Special Maritime and Territorial Jurisdiction is set forth in Section Seven of Title Eighteen of the US Code, a full description will be available for you or your counsel by verbal or written request."

At the word "counsel," the tension in the room peaked. Rolf remained statue-still. To my right, Callista was visibly trembling. Bernie backed toward where I was sitting. She touched my shoulder. "Mrs. Lanier, would you please step outside for a moment." Gingerly, I stood and tested my weak leg. I started to walk back the way I had entered, but the agent caught my elbow and steered me to a door that led from the game area to the reading room, which was lined with floor to ceiling books in locked glass cases. Normally the comfy armchairs and sofas were staked out by inside-room passengers who considered this their daytime territory, even though it had been emptied for obvious reasons.

"Who's in charge of this?" I asked, waving my arm toward the group assembled on the other side of the door.

"I requested the meeting."

"Okay," I said, "but before you do whatever it is you are planning, might I say a few words about Tania? We've all been alone with our sorrow."

"That's very thoughtful," she said without a direct answer. She handed me a folded piece of paper. My spreadsheet! Passenger services must have given her a copy. She indicated for me to sit on a sofa. "Would you be kind enough to interpret this for me?"

"The bottom line is that I don't believe Tania was murdered."

"Really?" the agent's voice was accusatory. "She just jumped into the laundry cart and died."

"Someone who didn't want her body to be found in his—or her—cabin foolishly tried to dispose of the body but failed. I think I have an explanation for that too."

"Why didn't you show me this earlier?"

"There were missing pieces…it didn't make sense until—" Bernie's eyes were riveted on my data. "First you need to understand that there's a good chance Tania's heart failed—a genetic disease—same as her mother and brother…" I blurted in staccato.

"Which the medical examiner may or may not be able to confirm." The agent pointed to my list of names. "Why is there a medication in every row?"

As rapidly as possible, I tried to walk the agent through my discovery process.

"Toxicology might not be able to prove your notion."

The word "notion" was belittling. "I know how long the tests can take so you won't have any results by tomorrow except—" I used my finger to circle one of the items. "You could get confirmation on this in a few minutes."

"Can they do that test on this ship?" Bernie asked.

"Apparently, it's done routinely."

"Would it still be detectable?" Bernie wondered aloud.

"Possibly, but definitely in the samples sent via the helicopter."

"I meant testing someone who is still—alive," the agent said, "because if I remember correctly, it doesn't remain in urine for very long."

"I know, although benzoylecgonine—the byproduct after it degrades—can show up for several days."

Bernie nodded. "You're right, but if it's still being used, we'd see a clear positive."

"My idea is to test a sample from Tania and compare it with one in the lab in Bermuda."

"That won't help find the perp!"

"What if there isn't one?" My words came out shakier than I had intended.

She stood and walked to one of the floor-to-ceiling windows and stared at the endless ocean—the blank slate that often helped me order my thoughts. I pulled another sheet from my envelope. "Did they give you copies of all of my documents?" I walked over to the window with the contraindicated medicine list that I had printed along with my notes. "Like this one?"

She waved at the paper without really looking. "Frankly, I couldn't make sense of it." Her voice was dismissive.

"Hey, this is not my circus, but I was asked to help," I said, feeling my face flush. "Now you've taken my passport and cruise card as if this has anything to do with me. If they want to subpoena me in Florida, fine." I turned on my heel and headed for the exit at the far end of the room that led directly to the starboard corridor. I heard a shuffle as she caught up to me in one long stride, yet I kept going. My hand on the brass door panel, I turned. "I assume I am free to leave."

"Please...Mrs. Lanier—" I pushed on the door, which was locked. "I can let you out through the card room if you insist, but I've been up all night talking to Florida, London, Bermuda, even some odd-ball in Malta." She spoke in a rushed, clipped voice. "Most were dubious that she died accidentally as well as your notion that someone who didn't want to be associated with her death tried to dispose of her body but was foiled by the broken handicapped exit. And now all these people, all these drugs...how does it help solve this case? There's no blood, no dagger, and no railroad track, so I don't think we're on the Orient Express."

I couldn't help but smile at her literary reference. I relinquished my grip on the door. "No, everybody didn't do it and nobody wanted to see her vanish— and Agatha Christie I'm not! Still, I believe all Tania's friends believed they were helping her. In fact, one of them may have prolonged her life by mistake."

"The answer to that riddle is what?" The agent sounded exasperated.

"The beta blocker for stage fright. That's one of the medications that is supposed to help people with the syndrome."

"Maybe so, although her partner is still a suspect." Bernie turned to me, her imposing body silhouetted by the sun pouring in. I had to squint to face her. "Please spell this out for me because I'm exhausted and none of this is making any sense."

"Based on my research, I suspect that Tatiana had a congenital condition called 'Long QT Syndrome.' If someone has it, many factors—especially a long list of medications—can trigger a heart arrhythmia that can cause sudden death." I placed the chart on a table close to the window so the tiny lettering could be read more easily. "This indicates which prescription and over-the-counter medications might be hazardous to someone with that condition." I pointed to the box at the bottom of the page that read: 'We recommend that patients with Congenital Long QT Syndrome avoid use of these medicines or only take them under close medical observation.'"

"I can't believe that you went around asking everyone who knew her what dope they peddled."

"I didn't. For some reason each one felt compelled to mention it. I think they were worried that they could have harmed her when their intentions were pure."

"Why would someone give her Xanax and another Cipro and yet another an opioid?"

"I didn't notice there were so many at first—it seemed inconsequential. Vance knew she had trouble sleeping. The masseuse offered her Pepcid for heartburn and her father gave her something to cope with the pain so she could perform her backbreaking routines."

"That's illegal."

"In the US…not necessarily worldwide. In some countries, you can get many of these pills merely by talking to the pharmacist—and anyway, some of these *were* prescribed for her." I pointed to Cipro in the row next to Dr. Kotze's name. "She had a urinary infection and he put her on this broad-spectrum antibiotic. Besides, it's not like she could run to a pharmacy and buy what she needed."

The agent's posture stiffened. "That's not the point—"

"Not everything was harmful," I said in a rush. "I found out that Tania suffered from crippling stage fright, especially for some of her more dangerous routines on the ship's unstable landing pad. Olek had been told that his blood-pressure pills had the secondary advantage of relieving performance anxiety. The most astonishing part is that it's one of the drugs that actually benefit someone with that condition."

The agent stared at the list and taped her finger on Cipro. "If she did have this Long QT problem, are you suggesting that Cipro might have been the cause of death?"

"If she did have the problem, it's unlikely that she took enough of a dose of any of them to have been fatal. Yet perhaps some combo of meds triggered heart failure the way—I searched for a metaphor—bleach and ammonia are both good disinfectants; together they produce a lethal gas." The ship lurched a bit and I leaned against an arm chair for stability.

"Let's sit," Bernie said, "although we can't keep them waiting much longer." She took the chair opposite me.

I slipped into the chair gratefully. "I realize that there might very well be a far simpler explanation, although the cardiologist I spoke with thought that Long QT could be a likely diagnosis."

"You talked about the victim with a passenger!"

"I told him it was for a novel I was writing."

Bernie's right hand stroked the left arm of her jacket as if it would yield an answer. "Even if she had a heart problem, even if she took some drug—or combination—that could have exacerbated the problem, some depraved or crazy person on board could still have—"

"Could have what?" I asked seething. "You know better than I do how hard it is to kill someone especially without a weapon. Did you see her? Did you watch someone prodding every orifice, searching her skin for the slightest blemish? She's more pristine than—"

"She has bruises."

"Many are quite old and all are consistent with the various falls and errors she makes—made—during her routines." Tears flushed my eyes. "She was always in pain."

The agent stood up and took long, purposeful strides to the other side of the room, cracked open one of the glass doors, and bent over to whisper something to Dr. Kotze. He followed her over to where I was seated. The door opened again and the staff captain came into the room and stood slightly behind Dr. Kotze, who leaned against a bookcase.

"Is there any chance the cause of death was sudden death from heart failure?" Bernie asked the doctor.

He scratched his neck. "I don't understand…"

"Long QT syndrome," I explained. "Death by sudden arrhythmia."

"*Torsades des pointes*?" I had seen that term online but wasn't sure what it meant. He continued, almost talking to himself. "Torsades is a specific form of polymorphic VT in patients with a Long QT interval characterized by rapid, irregular QRS complexes, which appear to be twisting around the ECG baseline. This arrhythmia may cease spontaneously or degenerate into ventricular fibrillation."

"I don't follow…" Bernie said.

"Yes…well…it's rather complicated." He looked at me, then out toward the ocean. "Basically, QRS is the combination of three of the graphical deflections seen on an electrocardiogram. Why are you asking such a technical question?"

"Our *novelist* has come up with an unusual *plot*," the agent said in a peer-to-peer tone meant to isolate me. "She thinks that the victim may have suffered from this condition."

"Ms. Zlatogrivova never revealed any cardiac history to me." Dr. Kotze shook his head as if trying to clear the idea that was beginning to bloom.

"You remember that Tania's mother died young from a sudden heart attack and Long QT is usually congenital, right?"

"Her mother was an alcoholic," the doctor responded.

"And her infant brother died suddenly too." I gulped for air and blurted, "Also her uncle."

"There are many causes for SIDS. I think you may have jumped to some"—he gave me an apologetic glance—"amateurish conclusions." Then to the FBI agent, "With the internet, everyone becomes a medical savant."

"That's true, but Mrs. Lanier doesn't have—as we say—any skin in the game. Also, you asked a civilian to cooperate, so she deserves to be heard."

Captain Castanga shifted weight between his feet and leaned in. "I'm not following this very well."

The doctor swiveled in his direction. "Tony, I'm not sure what this means either." Then he nodded to me. "Mrs. Lanier, please make your meaning clear."

"I don't believe anyone meant Tania harm. Her death was most likely from something that wouldn't have bothered most people but triggered a congenital weakness that she didn't know she had."

"Even so, she was a fantastic athlete!" the staff captain interjected. "I've watched her run, workout, perform... She was a most remarkable—" His voice choked.

Was he just another admirer who fantasized about her...or one of her myriad of lovers? I thought unkindly.

"She also was having...some physical...problems lately," I said haltingly. "She'd been dizzy, even

300

fainted a few times. She was worried about having an episode during her act—and she was pregnant. Doesn't that put a further strain on the heart?" I asked the doctor.

Marius spoke slowly, forming his thoughts aloud. "...And she had had a fever...was taking antibiotics—not to mention all that other shit her father shot her up with!" His normally gentle eyes radiated anger.

Captain Castanga gestured to the other room. "Agent Flederman, we can't keep everyone much longer."

"Wait," I said. "There's something else you need to know." I handed the doctor my spreadsheet and tapped a line. "My guess is that everything else might have been contributing factors, but this was the final straw."

"*God in die hemel*!" he said, lapsing into an Afrikaans. Marius looked from Bernie to the staff captain. "I should have known! I should have seen it!"

"Both of them, right?" I touched the side of my nose. "Also, it might explain the blood on the sheet."

The doctor pressed his trembling hands to his temples. "How did I miss it?" Dr. Kotze groaned. "Not a one-time event...how much? ...How long?" He shook himself back to the present. "Tony...please...." he said as if he needed rescue. "We need to test..."

"For what?" the officer, who had lost the thread, asked.

Bernie looked up at the ceiling, which was painted with cherubs entwined with ribbons floating on poufy clouds, and then back down at us mortals. "Would you ask your communications officer to send an encrypted message to my office to request a stat drug panel?"

"Certainly, madam," the staff captain replied.

The door to the other section of the library opened a crack. Bridge Captain Sorenson peeked in. Captain Castanga waved her off. "We'll be there shortly," he said. He glanced at Bernie, who turned toward Marius, who was too distraught to take the cue.

"We will cooperate with anything you want," the officer said, "but…" He paced toward the windows and then wheeled back to face us. He shook his head back and forth. "*Impossibile, è stata trovata nuda nel carrello della lavanderia,*" he said, lapsing into Italian.

I knew that he was referring to the laundry hamper and was trying to reconcile how her body was found with the new information.

"Captain," Bernie began, "if I am right, this is who was with her when she died." She tapped a name on my list.

Captain Castanga bit his lower lip, then cleared his throat. "I'd rather wait on the test until after the meeting. After all, nobody's going anywhere the rest of us aren't." He turned and was across the room in three military strides. When he opened the door, everyone at the table turned like a multi-headed creature. Each face was etched with disciplined panic.

□ □ □

Ellwood Hawthorne arrived late due to essential duties in preparation for debarkation. He squeezed in at the corner, between the doctor and me. His forehead was shiny and his aftershave couldn't mask his excess perspiration.

"Could we have some bottled water delivered?" the staff captain asked the bridge captain. Officer Sorenson picked up the wall phone and made the request.

Staff Captain Castanga squared his shoulders and addressed the assembled group. "I must apologize for the long delay. You are aware, of course, that the company and your officers are under immense pressure because of this tragic situation." He managed a polite smile, which did nothing to lighten the mood in the room. "Homeland Security is requiring us to retain your passports as well as those of others they have flagged from both our crew and passenger manifests. Further, each person present right now will be required to remain in their cabin between the hours of midnight and nine tomorrow morning. A deck officer accompanied by local law enforcement will escort each of you to meet with officials from Empire and the US government—most likely in the officer's mess. At that time, you will either be asked to return to your cabin or will be cleared to conduct your duties on the ship—but not disembark—without further clearance." He inhaled deeply and nodded toward the FBI agent.

Agent Flederman walked over to where the bridge staff stood at ease—and blocked the exit. "The reason we have called you together is that you have been identified as Ms. Zlatogrivova's family and friends.

We need your assistance to clarify the movements of the deceased in the days and hours prior to her death, which will be added to the photographic and clinical evidence that Florida law enforcement requires before they will clear this vessel."

Despite the agent's calm, almost maternal tone, I felt the tension rev up a notch. "Any questions so far?"

"Are we—or is anyone—here considered what you call 'a person of interest'?" Vance asked in his silkiest sales voice, the one that could promote a Picasso and a Peter Max in the same sentence.

"I understand your concern," the agent replied, but did not respond. Instead she turned to me. "Mrs. Lanier would like to say a few words next."

I stood up and steadied myself with one hand on the back of my chair. My temples pounded as I tried to gather my thoughts. "Most of you knew Ms. Zlatogrivova—Tatiana…Tania—" My voice caught. "…Knew her far better than I did but—" I felt the undertow of grief that had always been in the room yet had been subsumed by waves of anxiety. Sorrow was an ocean. At first a survivor floated with the currents. It ebbed and peaked yet was always there. Stormy waves could rise without warning and blast you with stinging tears; other times it was deceptively placid, gently bobbing beneath you—but always, always there. I glanced at the few rough notes I'd made while waiting.

"In the short time I translated for her, she touched my heart." My right hand patted my chest. "Talking to so many of you I found we have something in common, something that can never be taken from us.

304

We all loved Tania. We each loved her in our own way from Grisha, her father, who has now lost his entire family; to Olek, who must go on without his artistic partner. Tania showed us all the brilliant versatility and beauty of the human body as well as the breadth and width of the human spirit. Her smile—so luminous, so bright, so honest, was without guile or malice. She was a glorious butterfly who dazzled with her sheer exquisiteness and astounded with her agility. And like that wondrous creature, her time on this earth was short, even so the memory of her radiance will resonate in our memories forever."

Tears as large as chandelier crystals coursed down Callista's flushed cheeks. Vance heaved painful, dry sobs. Marius blotted his face with his folded handkerchief. Mae's delicate hands shielded her eyes as she turned to face a wall. Rolf's head was bowed with his chin pressed to his chest. Olek knelt by Grisha's chair and the older man ruffled his hair like a father comforting a small child. Jerzy sat ramrod straight, yet his arms vibrated from his fingers to his shoulder, shaking his end of the table.

I struggled to steady my quavering voice. "I know we all want to extend our deepest condolences to Grisha Zlatogrivov and Oleksander Lopatkino and thank our security and deck officers for handling a most difficult problem with admirable discretion. Thankfully, rumors have been contained as to the cause of death, especially because—despite everyone's worst fears—homicide may be dismissed as a possibility."

"Mrs. Lanier!" the agent barked.

The collective exhale was interrupted by Olek rapidly translating for Tatiana's father.

"H-How is that possible?" Vance stammered.

"I knew it!" Jerzy rose to his feet. "I knew something was wrong with her!"

Bernie came to where I was standing, pulled out my chair, and pushed on my shoulders until I took my seat. "That is a premature supposition," she said loudly to drown out the flurry of exclamations.

Grisha looking at me pleadingly. "*Kakiye? Kakiye!*"

"*Problemy s serdtsem,*" I answered softy. To the rest, "A heart problem."

"Let me clarify what Mrs. Lanier—who is *not* a medical professional—believes may have contributed to this complicated case. She has a theory; however, it doesn't begin to answer some of the fundamental findings in the case." Bernie stretched her hand out to Marius. "Could you explain it, doctor?"

"So far there is no clinical data that either proves or disproves that Ms. Z—Tania—had this problem. I am not sure it is proper to discuss this publicly."

"Perhaps her father will waive privacy concerns," Bernie said.

Dr. Kotze rose to his feet and walked over to Grisha. Olek was patting Grisha's hand. "May I ask you a few questions about your family's medical history?" Olek, who was angled next to him, translated.

"*Da,*" Grisha said.

"I was told that your wife's mother also died suddenly. Do you know the cause?"

Grisha tapped his heart with his fist. Olek frowned and mimed drinking from a bottle. Grisha shook his head. "Always problems," Olek translated. His hand fluttered in front of his chest.

"Did anyone else in your wife's family complain about an irregular heartbeat?"

"Yes," came Grisha's reply through Olek. "One brother, her grandfather, cousins—that whole family—strong bodies, broken hearts."

"Did many of them die in the prime of life?"

"Either they were gone by forty or they lived till eighty," Olek said, working hard to translate Grisha's rapid responses. "I was sure Galina was one of the tough ones. She was a superb athlete, a tireless trainer and then—" He gestured like he was popping a balloon and mouthed, "Poof!" Grisha rubbed his forehead. "Not possible...not my little girl," Olek said, then jumped to his feet. "Of course not! Somebody threw her in that basket, someone who had something to hide!"

Grisha kept muttering.

"What's he saying?" the staff captain asked.

Olek didn't respond so I translated. "He is saying he gave her medicines to keep her strong." I tilted my head toward Grisha. "I know that you wanted the best for your daughter, but if she had a heart condition some of the pills you gave her could have been dangerous."

"What *chertov* condition?" Olek demanded crudely.

All eyes were on the doctor. "It's possible that Tania inherited a potentially fatal condition called

Long QT syndrome from her mother's side of the family."

Officer Ocampo spoke up for the first time. "I don't understand."

"It's a congenital heart condition that alters the heart's rhythm," Marius said. "Sudden rapid, irregular heartbeats can be triggered by strenuous exercise, an illness, or…a reaction to a drug."

"Her whole life involved strenuous exercise!" Vance shouted. "How could she just die without…warning?" He folded his arms across his chest.

"Again, may I remind you that no diagnosis has been made. However, she may have exhibited some symptoms that were mistaken for more benign issues."

"Like what?" Vance said, leaning in.

"Sometimes the person faints or has seizures," Dr. Kotze responded. "Other signs can be dizziness or nausea. Not that unusual when you are at sea…" He glanced around the room and saw a few heads nodding, so he added, "…or pregnant."

Olek ran his fingers through his lush, black hair. "All summer she's been complaining that certain routines made her shaky—even before—"

"I told her she needed to drink more water and to stop her constant dieting!" Jerzy added.

"Did she ever faint?" the doctor asked no one in particular.

"One time she blacked out in the gym but blamed it on something she ate," Jerzy muttered.

"More likely something she drank," Olek, who must have known about the vodka, muttered.

308

"Last week in the gym she dropped a weight," Jerzy said. "She said she felt 'weak in the knees.' She felt better after she drank some juice." He glanced at Grisha. "He thought she was manipulating me; he wanted me to be harder on her. Yet how could I?" he bellowed. "I loved her and—"

Olek interrupted. "When she was tired, did she ever stare off in space."

Jerzy nodded. "Yes, like I wasn't there." He touched the side of his mouth. "She drooled and didn't try to wipe away."

"Is that one of the signs?" Olek asked.

"Possibly," the doctor replied. "Don't beat yourself up; there's nothing anybody could have done. Even I was fooled. She mentioned syncope. I made clear that it was normal in her…condition."

"She told me she was pregnant," Vance said, "but swore me to secrecy." He looked around the room. "I guess a lot of you knew." He stared at Olek, who was translating for Grisha, who looked more despondent than shocked, so I supposed he had been informed about the baby already.

"What if somebody had diagnosed the Long Q— or whatever?" Vance asked. "Could she have had surgery or…?"

"There are medications that help prevent a chaotic heart rhythm," Marius replied. "When possible, a pacemaker may be implanted. After that, patients are cautioned against vigorous exercise."

As Olek translated, Grisha covered his head with his arms as if to block the flow of painful information.

"Olek," I said speaking in Russian first. "Remember when you told me that you gave Tania some of your pills to help her with stage fright?" He froze. "No, it's not what you think! They may have *helped* her—maybe even prevented an earlier episode." His mouth gaped while I explained in English. "He gave her some beta blockers for performance anxiety, which is the same drug that modulates heart rate. Right, doctor?"

"Yes, the medicine might have reduced the likelihood of a life-threatening arrhythmia, especially in times of heavy exertion."

"Are you saying that I may have given her the correct pills by accident?" Olek asked incredulously.

Marius nodded. "There are many more drugs that make it worse." He gestured to me. "Mrs. Lanier—she has a list."

I ran my finger down the "medications" column. "The ones I think she may have taken that are not recommended include Sudafed for colds, Pepcid for stomach acid, Benadryl, which is an antihistamine, some cough suppressants."

"I gave her something once for a cold," Callista blurted, then hushed herself with her hand over her mouth.

"Not your fault." The doctor stood and moved behind her chair. He placed his hands on her bowed shoulders. "Even if something you shared is on the contraindicated list, a few doses wouldn't have harmed her. I gave her a powerful antibiotic for an infection and it is one of the worst things she could have taken. If anyone's at fault, it's me. I missed the diagnosis."

"Is there any equipment we could have on board that could have saved her?" Captain Castanga asked.

"No. These are usually sudden, unexpected deaths."

"*A malen'kaya devochka*! What did I do to my little girl?" Grisha asked some questions.

Olek said, "He wants to know if he poisoned her."

The doctor could have berated him for his unorthodox treatments, although Marius was nothing if not kind. "Just tell him that he also may have prevented the problem for a while."

"What about booze?" Jerzy asked with a childlike grin that belied the fact that he had been her vodka supplier.

"Her mother—heavy, *heavy* right from the bottle!" Olek said using his water bottle as a prop.

For the first time, Ellwood spoke up. "Could...just a Ricola made her heart stop?"

"That's extremely doubtful, but we will never know what was—what do you call it?—the tipping point," the doctor said, slipping back into his chair. His jawline was mottling with four-o'clock shadow.

Agent Flederman stood and pushed her chair under the desk. "While this medical discussion offers one option for how the victim may have died, it does not begin to solve the case. Nor is it the only possibility. While we do our work, each of you need to be vigilant. Report anything suspicious: If you remember anything, overhear a conversation, or whatever you see that might warrant additional scrutiny. Many a crime is cracked by an alert person. Do not delay in communicating with the nearest security officer or by contacting your staff captain.

We will be in continual contact with each other. Somebody was trying to dispose of or hide your friend's body and it is likely that person either had a hand in her death or knows how she died." The agent's eyes darted around the room, landing on each person and leaving an invisible stain.

Captain Castanga glanced toward Bernie. She nodded as a handoff. "Please everybody, we realize that this has been a nightmare." His face lit with a shy, dimpled grin. "Now you are free to..." He smiled insouciantly. "...Go back to work!" He pointed to the stack of passports. "Please remember the instructions for tomorrow morning. There are no exceptions and they are captain's orders."

People stood slowly, almost reluctantly. Olek put his arm around Grisha, who was tired and bent, and steered the childless father toward the exit.

Jerzy walked around to where I remained sitting. "*Vy sdelali khoroshuyu veshch,*" he murmured. "You've done a good thing." Then, in English, "Your words were like a bit of sun in a dark room. *Spasibo.*"

Callista dabbed her face with the edge of her navy shrug. I pointed to my own eye as a signal to check her makeup. "Someone might want to know what the other guy—" I began, then I caught a glimpse of Rolf, who was still seated. He had been silent throughout the whole ordeal, which was out of character for someone who was usually in charge.

Mae stood impassively just outside the door to the reading room. Her thin, but always pleasant half-smile, was still in evidence, concealing her thoughts. Vance mumbled a few words to the doctor before turning toward the door that opened to the corridor.

Captain Castanga stepped sideways to let him pass by, then planted his feet behind Rolf's chair.

"We need a few more minutes of your time, Officer Brandt," Agent Flederman said.

Rolf gripped the edge of the table so hard his knuckles whitened. His brow formed deep fissures and a muscle that extended from his ear to his collarbone bulged obscenely.

"Just a technical matter." The staff captain's Italian accent was less concierge and more mafia henchman.

Rolf rose to his feet, using every scintilla of his Prussian reserve to hold himself in check. He snapped his shoulders back and straightened his spine. He took a long sip of air like someone trying to suck helium out of a party balloon. An eerie whistling noise accompanied his long exhale. And then—

Rolf sneezed. He clamped his nostrils with his right thumb and forefinger just before a second paroxysm ricocheted his head backward and then forward. The third expulsion rose from a chasm within his core and burst from his nose and mouth. His right hand flew forward revealing a burgundy clot in his palm. Blood trickled from his spoiled septum. He pinched his nose with his other hand, slipped by the staff captain, then darted sideways like a soccer player, knocking over what had been Callista's chair. He shoved Mae out of the way and lunged for the reading room door handle.

Mae was the first on his tail with Bernie close behind. It took a few extra seconds for the staff captain to negotiate the table and race after them. I stood too quickly and my bad leg buckled. The doctor supported me by the elbow and steered me into the foyer.

Rolf ran past the glassed-in atrium elevators, around the balcony overlooking the raised stage that held the grand piano, past the interior windows of the smoking area, and bumped into a display of duty-free watches, toppling it over. Without hesitating, he sprinted forward toward the theater. Bernie was on his heels, followed by Mae. Both women stepped into the forward elevator bank. I waved the doctor to go ahead of me, while I loped along, favoring my sore leg.

As I hobbled around the corner, Rolf's back was to me. Bernie and Captain Castanga faced him. Behind them, Dr. Kotze was punching numbers into a mobile phone that only worked on the officers' dedicated frequency. Two passengers approached the doctor. His hand shot up in a "halt" signal and they backed off. My heart pounded crazily as my mind substituted this scenario for the one in which David lost his life. I started to panic until I realized that nobody was carrying a gun. An elevator to my far right opened and a woman pushing a man in a wheelchair saw the blood flowing down Rolf's chin and screamed.

"Not serious." The doctor grasped one of the wheelchair handles and propelled him out of the way. "Just keep moving."

Two traffic cones were guarding the middle elevator's partially opened doors, which were propped open by another cone. Orange safety tape repetitively marked PLEASE DO NOT ENTER made a large "X" across the doorway. At first glance, the

314

shaft looked exposed, although the top of the elevator was only a few feet lower than our deck.

The elevator door closest to me opened next. I waved them away. "Stay on!"

Hearing my voice, Rolf whipped around. "You meddling bitch!" His gunmetal-blue eyes darkened like a fuming tornado.

Captain Castanga lunged toward him, but Rolf was more jacked up. He wheeled behind me and pressed his right arm against my throat. Both feet went out from under me. Only his chokehold kept me from falling. His sweat-soaked shirt was as cold as ice crystals.

"Don't be an idiot!" the staff captain shouted. "Let go of her!"

As Rolf's arm depressed my windpipe, I clawed at his arms to loosen his grip. "It's—it's—" I caught my breath. "It's not a crime." His arm slackened just enough for me to blurt: "Concealing a body—not even a felony—not if you didn't—didn't intend to harm her." His elbow sagged slightly. "Not your fault—you couldn't have known…"

"Everything, you ruined everything!" he grunted into my ear.

"Not if it was an accident!" The heavier chokehold returned. My pulse pounded in my temples as I teetered on losing consciousness.

He bent his mouth to my ear and spoke in Russian. "She was going to destroy my life!"

I tried to answer but couldn't even gasp.

"She said it was *my* baby—that *hure*!—how would she have known?"

I tried to shake my head.

315

Through a violet haze, I saw a figure—Marius?—dart out of view. In order to come up behind Rolf, he'd have to run down the long port corridor to the atrium and take the hallway that led to the elevator bank on starboard side. I needed to distract Rolf.

"*Pozhaluysta…*" I wheezed. "Please!" His grip relaxed when he realized nobody else could understand us. "She wasn't planning to keep it," I whispered in the tongue he supposedly despised.

"*Glupaya suka*! Stupid bitch! She was going to blackmail me for the rest of my life!"

His next words were blasted so close to my ear. "I made certain that she didn't suffer."

I tried to respond, but his grip tightened on my throat. "One shot, no marks." His guttural laugh verged on maniacal. "I mixed in some of her favorite potato juice. She smiled all the way home."

Staff Captain Castanga stood rigidly against the opposite wall. Out of the corner of my eye something was moving erratically. Either I was hallucinating due to the lack of oxygen or the FBI agent was dancing to the insipid elevator music. "By the sea…by the BEAUT-EE-ful sea…" crashed through my head like a rogue wave.

For some reason Bernie was repeating the same dance step over and over, kicking like a robotic Rockette. Knee up, kick right…knee up, kick left. "By the BEAUT-EE-ful…" She placed her left arm across her neck and used her right hand to tug at that elbow. At the same moment, she arched forward and did a partial squat like—like the line-dancing instructor. She made a follow-me gesture and suddenly I got the message and mirrored her and reached for his forearm.

Rolf's pressure yielded long enough for me to inhale. Captain Tony took a step closer. Rolf's neck craned to check his maneuver. Just then, Bernie lowered her right leg, curved it behind her, and used both hands to rip a phantom arm down and away, willing me to do the same.

"Officer Brandt," she called to divert his attention. "How about sharing your stash of confiscated coke."

Rolf's arm muscle sagged. Taking the cue, I inhaled deeply to lessen the pressure on my neck, crouched, pulled Rolf's uniformed arm while flinging my leg behind his. In what felt like slow-motion, his arm flew off my neck and the forward force flung me against the wall between the elevators. Rolf charged toward me with a vengeful ferocity. Officer Ocampo and the Captain Castanga approached him from opposite sides. Mae reached him first, but Rolf jerked sideways so fast that she only clutched his shirt momentarily. The staff captain tried to wrench Rolf's other arm but he was batted to the ground. As Rolf realized he was boxed in, I scooted out of lunge distance.

Bernie caught me by the collar, heaved me across the hall, and I landed on my feet between the opposing elevator doors. Shoulders hunched, knees bent like a stalking feline, Bernie hurtled toward the security chief, whose eyes darted like a cornered tiger. Captain Castanga's long arms blocked him like a basketball guard. Short and squarely built Officer Ocampo broadened her stance and held her arms

317

akimbo, giving her a more formidable presence. Dr. Kotze raised the champagne bottle he carried like a cudgel as Bernie lowered her head like a bull and charged Rolf.

Startled, Rolf backed up snapping the security tape. He tripped over one of the traffic cones just as Bernie rammed his crotch. He fell into the yawning elevator shaft and landed with his back on the top of the half-descended elevator car's ceiling.

"*Fick dich!*" he boomed in German.

Reflexively, I pressed my back against the wall, accidentally pressing the UP button. Rolf scrambled to his feet just as the car began to rise. When it was level with our deck, he lifted his leg to kick Bernie, who was reaching for his legs, aside. I sprang forward and reached to pull her to safety by her belt. She fell backward and collapsed on top of me just as Rolf vanished.

□ □ □

The world was crimson. Hot, wet. Ribbons of a warm, sticky, scarlet lava flowed around me. My mouth tasted iron; my heart seemed to be pumping outside my chest. I heard muted screams through my clogged ears. My voice was lost in a swirl of gurgles, bubbles, and gulps. Was I choking to death? Was this what it felt like when a last gasp of adrenaline attempted to oxygenate my failing brain? There was no bright, welcoming light; I heard no angelic choruses—just shouting, yelling, and—then— nothing.

Faraway…voices. And…PAIN! Not only running down my hip to my foot but pulsing like shockwaves from my right ankle. My eyelids fluttered open, then clamped shut against the purple light. Where was I? Someone was speaking with a British accent, no more German, no…Danish or Dutch—or… The doctor. He was reading aloud.

"Here's another reference from one of my emergency medicine journals. 'Cocaine use has been associated with many cardiac complications including ventricular arrhythmias and sudden death with idiopathic Long QT Syndrome. In a study of fifty-five patients admitted after cocaine use, the QT interval was increased in patients with and without chest pain and those with chest pain had greater QT prolongation. Cocaine and its metabolites, like many other substances have been shown to prolong the QT interval.'"

"How in the world did that passenger piece this together on her own?" asked Captain Tony, sounding like Marcello Mastoianni.

"Our dossier has her as a former child abuse investigator in the Miami area. Plenty of cocaine cases there," the FBI agent said, her slight Long Island twang identifying her.

"Brandt came in several times with epistaxis," Marius was saying. "I'm the one who should have figured out that his septum was perforated—and why."

"When we get his tox screen, I'm expecting the metabolites of a cokehead," the agent continued. "And with her small frame, the victim could have the

319

same numbers, only hers were fatal, probably due to that genetic defect you mentioned."

"No," I tried to tell them, although I could only mumble. I too had thought that Tania's heart had failed while snorting cocaine with Rolf. As much as I wanted my premise to win the day, Rolf had confessed to a deliberate murder—ironically in Russian. He hadn't worried about any evidence of an overdose because he planned to toss her overboard through the hidden handicapped doorway.

"What I can't believe"—Bernie's *sotto voce* carried to wherever the hell I was—"is that a video of the accident is already running on YouTube!" I saw the flicker of a computer screen reflected in her face.

"It's the most repulsive thing I've ever seen!" I recognized the nurse's Canadian accent. "The elevator—for some reason it just came up and…crushed him like…like a giant tomato."

"Can't your agency shut it down?" Captain Tony asked.

"Shut what?" I managed to mumble.

"She's awake!" the nurse announced.

"How are you feeling now?" Dr. Kotze asked.

"Pain. Leg."

"I'm sorry to say that this time it might really be broken." His words reverberated but didn't make sense. "Your doctor asked us to stabilize it until you can have an MRI tomorrow."

"My doctor?"

"Yes, Dr. Willoughby. You'll be transferred from the ship to Holy Cross as soon as we dock."

"But—"

"Don't worry," Captain Tony said, "Empire will cover the expense."

I tried to lift my arm and felt the sting of an IV needle. "What happened?"

"What do you remember?" Bernie asked.

"The curtain—the red curtain."

"Before that?"

I touched a bandage in the delta of my neck as my mind struggled to unravel the sequence. "Where's Rolf?"

"Behind the red curtain," Bernie answered bizarrely.

"What?"

"There was an unfortunate accident," Marius said.

"You saved my butt," the agent said, "although you injured your leg in the process."

"At its worst it's no more than a simple fracture, thankfully," Dr. Kotze explained. "I am more worried about your loss of consciousness."

"How long was I out?"

"We're not sure, although we also gave you a sedative and pain meds, so you've been sleeping for several hours."

"Is everyone else okay?"

Marius took my hand in his. "Officer Brandt tried to escape by jumping on the roof of the elevator car—the one that was being repaired." He let that sink in. "It was supposed to have been deactivated...but—for some reason—it started to move."

"He tried to hide in the electrical alcove," Captain Tony said.

I remembered the niche where I had seen the young electrician working. Rolf was twice that man's size. The elevator went up…and I fell…and everything went—behind the red curtain…

I felt the doctor slapping my hand. "Lane? Lane!"

"Is she having a seizure?" Bernie asked.

"*But…but who would have thought…*" I murmured. "*Hell is murky…no one can…lay the guilt…upon us.*"

"What's she saying?" The doctor bent closer.

"Macbeth," the nurse responded. "I was one of the witches in college."

"Why doesn't that surprise me?" Marius chuckled.

"I played Lady Macbeth," I responded, surprised at the clarity of my voice. I took a deep inhalation, which stung my raw throat. I tried to swallow the discomfort away. The clinic reeked like an abattoir. "What's that horrible smell?" I asked.

"Now that you're stable, I can clean you up," Joyce said.

I touched my clotted hair and brought my sticky hand to my face. "Oh my god! When can I wash it out?"

"We'll do the best we can without disturbing your leg," Joyce said apologetically.

"Is it what I think it is?"

"I'm so sorry…"

I shuddered. "'*But who would have thought the old man would have had so much blood in him?*'" I muttered,   mostly   to   myself.

322

Epilogue

Anything can happen...at any time...to anyone.
—Callista Standish and Barbara Joy

Position: Ft. Lauderdale, Florida

I was discharged from Holy Cross Hospital Thanksgiving morning diagnosed with a mild concussion. Fortunately, my leg was not broken, although I had—in medical terminology—an L-4-5 diffuse disc bulge indenting the anterior thecal sac with hypertophy of the facets producing moderate bilateral neural foramen. My fall during the rough night at sea had caused a disk—one of the shock absorbers between my lower back vertebrae—to put pressure on my sciatic nerve, which is what had sent agonizing pangs from my butt to my toes. Bernie—by way of Rolf—had done me a bizarre favor. When she fell on top of me, the pressure caused that disk to rupture, making it operable—and completely curable. Although my ankle was swollen almost double its size and sported a colorful bruise, it wasn't fractured. Dr. Willoughby injected an epidural anesthetic to keep me comfortable during the holiday, scheduling a lumbar microdiscectomy the following week.

After the surgery, I was prohibited against horseback riding, skydiving, or performing gymnastics. "Mommy, don't worry," Bodhi said, clutching my hand between both of his. "I'll do *all* those things for you." I wanted to discourage any activity besides Legos but knew better than to make something off limits and thus more desirable.

Bernice Flederman visited me after my neurosurgery to thank me for "padding her fall" and to apologize for adding to my injuries. I'm not sure she believed that by making my disk worse she had actually helped me.

"That little dance you did…it took me forever to figure out you were showing me how to break Rolf's grip."

"You caught on faster than you think. It's a classic defense against a rear chokehold, especially if you are smaller than the assailant."

"I go over and over it…"

"That's normal, but it will fade. At least you won't be part of any further investigations. Rolf's death is being classified as accidental."

"How can they do that?"

"The fact is that he fell into the shaft and…died."

"What about the cocaine—and hiding Tania's body?"

"There's no proof. And besides that, he's dead."

"Was the rape kit processed?"

"Yes."

"Do you know who the father is yet?"

"Frankly, I was surprised." She waited a few beats.

"Not Rolf!"

She nodded her head.

I was quiet for a minute as I mentally ran down the list of other putative fathers.

"I'm glad of that," I muttered—as if it mattered. I suspected he had intuited—or calculated—that it could have been him. "There's no way of matching with anyone else, is there?" I asked rhetorically.

"I don't see why she fell for him," Bernie said with a shudder. "Maybe it wasn't even consensual."

I didn't answer because there was a brief moment when he could have charmed me.

"You told me that Rolf believed that Tania was 'going to ruin him?' I'm thinking that she expected him to be the father," the agent continued. "Could she have been pressuring him to marry her?"

"No. She was clear about getting an abortion the moment the test was positive." I said. "What she wanted most was freedom—to make her own choices. Her father probably controlled her earnings. Not only would Rolf's career have been over if she told about the drugs, he could have been arrested in Florida, right? "

"For the murder, yes, but they could have argued jurisdiction. If it had just been drugs, there are many scenarios. He stole confiscated drugs and now there's evidence that certain crewmembers procured for him. Empire is trying to untangle his web of lies." Bernie wiped her hands symbolically. "I'm off the case."

"I assume he was positive for cocaine. What else?"

"Empire did its own investigation. We're not privy to that information."

"Did you really find his stash before—the elevator and...?"

She laughed. "Couldn't you tell I was bluffing?"

"No, but later I wondered how you could have gotten access so quickly."

"Were her clothes ever found?"

"No trace, although we didn't expect any—not with incinerators, garbage compactors, and what is illegally thrown overboard." There was a long silence. "I don't mean to stonewall you, it's just that we'll never know the full story." Bernie grinned. "Here's one tidbit for you to chew on: I was able to get one of the security technicians to give me a run down on which cameras were either out-of-service or turned off, and while we can't be certain if they were in the same condition the night Ms. Zlatogrivova died, there's no record of any repairs during the crossing but substantial maintenance was needed in port."

"You think Rolf fiddled with them?"

"I made a diagram for you." She handed over a deck map. "The Xs mark the cameras that were not on line when we reached Ft. Lauderdale."

"The corridor outside of Rolf's cabin and—" My fingers traced the quickest route to I-95.

"Not to mention the ones outside the clinic and those in the debarkation area." She paused. "They all can be deactivated in the security office—or even by someone who had the passwords on any computer."

"So theoretically, Rolf shut down the ones by the handicapped elevator before he moved the body." Bernie nodded. A wave of peace settled over me. "That helps, thank you."

"There's something else…" This was a longshot, but I needed to know. "Rolf told me how his wife died while crossing the street with their baby…" His story kept nagging me while I was recuperating at home. Had we shared a similar tragedy or could he have fabricated it to win me over to his side?

Bernie looked like she was debating how much to tell me. "You two...there was a bit of chemistry, right?"

How could she have known?

The agent anticipated my thoughts. "Basic body language. You probably know some tells that suggest someone is lying like blushing, blinking, flared nostrils, fake smiles." I nodded. "We stare at people we like and avoid the ones we don't because elevated oxytocin—the love neurochemical—increases pupil dilation."

My hand fluttered in front of my eyes. I felt exposed and was about to protest before she jumped in. "Don't concern yourself. He was manipulating you, playing you on your vulnerability to steer you away from suspecting him."

I felt sick over being played, then anger simmered. "There was no wife, no baby!"

"Actually, he had both. She committed suicide." Bernie watched me parse the information.

"With...drugs?"

Bernie nodded. "There's no evidence that she was using for a long time."

"Hair samples?"

"Yes."

"Could he have—?

"He was on a ship somewhere around Cape Horn."

"How then?"

"We have theories. I am sure you could come up with a few. At best Mr. Brandt was a charming sociopath."

I pressed my thumb to my temple to try to suppress the painful pulses.

Bernie ended the conversation with a flurry of gratitude from her and her agency, sidestepping my guilt for having inadvertently triggered the elevator and ending a man's life.

▢ ▢ ▢

"Closure" is an overused, overrated, and pathetic term. No matter the reports, the censures, the insurance settlement, or the passage of time, the loss of David would always remain raw. I would never heal. This time, though, I felt that Tatiana had received a form of backhanded justice.

Callista visited me on her first turnaround day after my back surgery. I was supposed to spend as little time as possible sitting, so I served Prosecco in fluted glasses standing on my balcony overlooking the channel at dusk.

I mentioned the FBI agent's visit. "I can't believe that Empire is declaring Rolf's death an accident."

"Public relations at its finest," she said. "That video has gone viral with more than a million hits, so they had to call it a tragedy. Have you seen it?"

"Once." I closed my eyes. "I…I needed to…my memory is just bits and pieces—" I shook my head to clear it. "Not that it helped." I shuddered. "It was just a river of blood cascading down the inside of the elevator doors and flooding the corridor in a scene as ghastly as a slaughterhouse. There were no people in the shot so it didn't make sense to me."

That's because it was shot by a passenger a deck below where you were."

"Which is why PR covered it with the story of a brave security officer losing his life to protect passengers. There's even a commemorative plaque on the wall near where it happened."

"So he's now the big hero?"

"This way his kid gets his benefits—so that's something positive." Her voice broke. "Obviously I can't stay on that ship. Empire's transferring me to the *Empress of the Pacific*. Lots of sushi and noodles."

"Sounds like a welcome change of pace."

"You'll have to write your next book on board." She sounded concerned. "You have one in mind, right?"

"Always."

"Hint?"

"In my world, everything gets used eventually. Nothing is wasted."

"Title?"

"I have a few in mind. Maybe: *The Red Flash*. It will take place in Russia...and be dedicated to Tania."

"Oh, I'm glad."

We said farewell. I was relieved she hadn't pressed me for more. Writers are supposed to write, not talk about their stories, even though I had sketched out the opening in my mind. The city: St. Petersburg. The location: the Church of Our Savior on Spilled Blood.

☐ ☐ ☐

Dr. Kotze visited me after his Christmas voyage. I had invited him for a family dinner because he said he wanted to meet Bodhi, who decided to wear a skeleton T-shirt that named the bones of the body. Since it was stone crab season, I thought Marius might enjoy a taste of the crustacean that Floridians think beats lobster.

"Better make mac-and-cheese just in case," Bodhi said, pretending it was not a self-serving idea.

He insisted on carrying out our family's special ice tea brew himself. "It's a family secret," he told Marius. "You want to know what's in it?" he whispered.

"I don't want you to get into trouble."

"We tell everyone! You add frozen lemonade. Do you like it"

The doctor took a long sip. "Better than the ship's Arnold Palmer," he said with a wink.

During dinner we kept the conversation purposefully light. After tucking Bodhi in, I served limoncello and key lime pie on the terrace.

"I brought a copy of the autopsy report," he said with an apologetic tilt of his head.

I waved my hand. "Just tell me the official cause of death."

"Overdose leading to cardiac arrest."

"Did they test her for the gene?"

"Yes, she had it."

"Wow! I almost can't believe it." I blanched.

"Are you okay?"

"It's…well, what my husband would have called a confluence of contradictions."

Marius looked puzzled, then added, "Everyone was very impressed—Dr. Lanier."

"Could the drugs have precipitated sudden onset Long QT Syndrome?"

"Yes."

"So… she could have died from cardiac arrest before the overdose took effect."

Marius twisted his hands in lap. "What difference does that make?"

I blinked back tears. "I'd rather believe that in some way—even if it's just a technicality—that her life wasn't taken from her…that it was inevitable."

He shrugged. "I can't disprove it so you might as well believe it if it helps."

"At least we know the baby wasn't Rolf's."

"None of that matters."

"It might…to someone."

"Not something most men would wish to know."

I observed him closely because he would have been on my baby-daddy short list; however he was either poker-faced—or innocent. Only Tatiana knew the likely prospects, which could have included a crewmenber or some random encounter with a passenger. There was no longer any reason for me to speculate on that doomed spark of life—or for that matter, trying to fathom its mother's psyche.

"What about that other problem—Elhers-Danlos?—did she have that too?"

"Nobody looked for that." He opened a folder and pointed to the toxicology report. "Point one two six milligrams per liter for cocaine."

"Wow, that's high."

"It wasn't from the autopsy." He pointed to the report's date. "This is from the samples that went to Bermuda." We sat in silence watching the variety of boats crisscrossing the Intercoastal Waterway.

"The FBI agent said that the medical examiner tested her hair."

"Yes, it revealed a long pattern of alcohol use and also cocaine intake over many weeks. Their estimates coincide with when Rolf came onboard in Istanbul."

"Then it wasn't the Ricola..." I said, but my attempt at a joke flopped. "I can't believe he mixed vodka with the powder to draw it into a syringe."

"He may have just said that."

Why would he, I thought, but didn't speak for a few minutes.

"She pushed her body to the limit—in more ways than one," the doctor said almost wistfully.

"What if Rolf had played it cool and hadn't run?"

"He still would have tested positive," the doctor said, "which would have cost him his job. He might even have convinced the authorities that hers was an accidental overdose, but he panicked.'

"Fight or flight—he picked flight," I said.

The doctor nodded. "We'll never know what her last moments were like. She may have had a seizure or just a massive heart attack. In any case, her death was triggered by a lethal dose of cocaine—at least one that was deadly for her."

"Supplied by Rolf—would have been proof of some degree of murder—unless they could have come up with some other supplier."

Marius's hand was trembling. He put down his limoncello glass before blurting, "Or someone else with a reason to dispose of her body."

"Not many others could have disabled the cameras along the route to the handicapped exit."

"Isn't just hiding a body a crime?"

"The FBI agent told me that in New York the concealment of a human corpse is only a class E felony."

"Which means?"

"The maximum punishment might be as much as four years in jail, but with a good lawyer probably just probation—or nothing, if there wasn't hard evidence."

The doctor winced. "So he could have gotten off!"

"It's complicated. Crime at sea. Jurisdiction. German citizen..." I shrugged. "Not long ago there was something in the news about a funeral home that hid bodies somewhere instead of cremating them. They were charged with a misdemeanor for concealment of a corpse and got away with only a fine."

"Did you ever consider becoming a lawyer?" He gave me a shy half-smile.

"In another life." I finished my cordial. "What was the toxicology about the other drugs—the steroids, human grown hormone, antacids, cold medicine, the sleeping pills?"

"Don't you think I've been over and over this?" Marius looked far in the distance. "She had a lethal dose of cocaine in her system." His neck muscles bulged. Everything she ingested contributed to making her more vulnerable—most especially the antibiotics I prescribed."

"You mean everyone who tried to help her could have inadvertently hurt her?"

"All of us supplied something that may have added to the toxicity, although as you suspected, the beta blocker may have protected her...for a while."

"Without Rolf she might still be alive!" I gripped the balcony railing. "That bastard!" I screamed into the wind. Pent up rage flamed from my fingers to my face. "He corrupted her and—and he got away with it!"

"Actually...he didn't," Marius said gently, then gulped the last of his drink. He moved closer to me and rubbed my shaking back. "Are you one of those people who blink their lights when a cruise ship departs after dark?"

"No, but some of my neighbors do. They even post the schedule in the elevator."

"Next time I'll wave in your direction."

"Then I'll flash my lights."

"Or..."

"Of course you are always welcome to visit us."

"Now you are also a mindreader?"

"Same wavelength, perhaps?"

We laughed simultaneously at my accidental pun. Marius grinned. Our eyes locked momentarily. He leaned forward and touched my cheek. Limoncello or oxytocin? I mused as he cupped my chin and kissed me lightly, then with just the right amount of pressure to be sensual yet not aggressive. I wanted more, but he steered me to my seat and took his. A bit shakily, I poured us each another drink in the cut-glass glasses

I'd bought last summer in Sorrento. Neither of us spoke for a long interval.

"I've been thinking…" Marius said. "While not precisely a medical term, I believe Tania was an 'adrenaline junkie.'"

The ghost in the room once more asserted herself. "She had to be otherwise she wouldn't even have attempted those stunts. Did you ever watch videos of her Cirque performances?"

"Yes," he said. "They're online. I enjoyed her shows onboard, although in Cirque she took it to a whole other level."

"In what way?"

"Far too hazardous. I can't believe what they expected her to risk night after night at Cirque."

"Cirque needs a higher level of excitement to sell tickets."

"It's not healthy for people to be entertained watching others risk their lives." He turned away from me, masking his sorrow.

"We haven't evolved that far from the days of gladiators, have we?" I said. "Now it's lion tamers…race cars…stunt pilots…tightrope walkers."

"Or your crazy politicians!"

We laughed again.

"I couldn't find a single mention of her death anywhere."

"I'm sure Empire pulled strings, but did you search in Russian?"

"I didn't think of that."

"Anyhow, Freud would blame it all on sex," Marius said with a chuckle.

"I don't get what you mean."

"Daredevils: They live on the edge to compensate for what they really crave."

"She seemed to have plenty of"—I struggled for the right word—"conquests."

"And she still wasn't satisfied, not even when she was with someone who adored her." His pause gave him away.

"Not that I know this firsthand but cocaine supposedly has phenomenal aphrodisiac qualities. Maybe once you've tried it, plain vanilla sex isn't satisfying any more."

"Yes, like any addict. They're never satisfied. She *was* a type of addict. Her father programmed her to seek high-sensation experiences. Adrenaline was her drug of choice. Cocaine brought the rush on faster."

I closed my eyes, thinking: she flew…on silks…and also in orgasmic ecstasy…away from the pain…away from her father's severe coaching…away from the confines of the ship…away and out…out of the box. "She *hated* the box."

"I know that," Marius said.

Then another thought: "What did happen to her body?"

"She was repatriated to Russia to be buried next to her mother and infant brother."

"In a box?"

"Yes, a box."

☐

Gay Courter's Novels

Raves for Gay Courter's Bestselling Sagas:

The Midwife:
"Why is *The Midwife* such an important book? Chances are slim that you have ever read a novel by a woman that also provides an impressive body of knowledge about a subject of special interest to us." — *Chicago Sun-Times*

"It kept me up until four in the morning...the author, to use a timeless phrase, knows how to tell a story."— *Washington Post*

The Midwife's Advice:
"The trials and tribulations of Hannah Sokolow, beautiful Russian immigrant and pioneer sex therapist, could be the stuff from which television miniseries are made."— *New York Times Book Review*

Code Ezra:
"Engrossing....fast-paced...timely...provides a historical background for today's headlines... Gay Courter is a gifted writer." — *Bookpage*

"Gay Courter's international bestseller is "as good as the best of Le Carré!" —*Milwaukee Journal*

"A superior, multilayered espionage and betrayal...Intense, ambitious...it never relaxes its grip on the reader!" —*John Barkham Reviews*

"Awesome...one of the year's best spy novels...intrigue, love, and revenge!" —*Cincinnati Inquirer*

"A deft spy thriller...zips along entertainingly." — *Kirkus Reviews* "A captivating thriller...timely and fast-paced." —*The Detroit News*

Flowers in the Blood:

"*Flowers in the Blood* brings to life a nineteenth-century India never before portrayed. Irresistible in its storytelling power, it is one of the finest novels set in India. Compelling, informative, absorbing." – *New York Times Book Review*

"Gripping...Creates a mesmerizing reality, subtly etched with historical detail."– *Booklist*

"Exhilarating...Suspenseful!" — *Kirkus Reviews*

River of Dreams:

You will float with fascination down River of Dreams...through the landscape she explores brilliantly."— *Washington Post*

"Readers are treated to much more than a storybook romance. Courter...has a wonderful way with detail...makes absorbing reading." — *Publishers Weekly*

"Intricate, colorful, and entertaining." – *New York Times Book Review*

"Steamy, exciting romance and high adventure...recommended!" Chattanooga Times Exhilarating...Suspenseful!" — Kirkus Reviews

Acknowledgments

For editorial help: Philip Courter, Wanda Shelley, Sarah Flynn, Jerome Giambalvo, Elise Roenigk, Judy Weisman, Pat Gaudette, and Karen Warren

For Russian assistance: Amber Simpson and Olga Savage, MD

Forensic advice: Dawna Kaufmann

For lightening my load: Michelle Delosh

For inspiration: Zlata, Cirque du Soleil and Barbara Joy

Cover design: Rachel Chevat

Made in the USA
Columbia, SC
18 January 2021